R

D0407588

Other books by Margaret Bingley

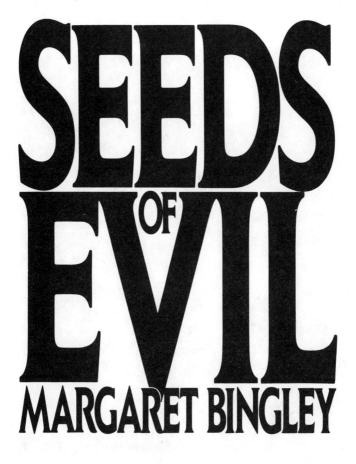

SEEDS OF EVIL

MARGARET BINGLEY

Carroll & Graf Publishers, Inc.
New York

First Carroll & Graf edition 1989
Second printing 1989

Carroll & Graf Publishers, Inc.
260 Fifth Avenue
New York, NY 10001

Library of Congress Cataloging-in-Publication Data

Bingley, Margaret.
    The seeds of evil / Margaret Bingley.—1st Carroll &
Graf ed.
        p.   cm.
        ISBN: 0-88184-471-3 : $15.95
        I. Title.
    PR6052.I7775S4   1989
823'.914—dc19   89-617
                                                          CIP

Manufactured in the United States of America

For my sister, Frances, who
had to listen to my horror
stories all through our childhood
and yet managed to stay sane!

Acknowledgements

I am once again extremely grateful to Dr Jill Baumber who found the time to help me make the right contacts. I am also indebted to those members of the medical profession who answered all my queries with great patience but who prefer to remain anonymous.

Prologue

The first thing that struck Dr Morris Tinsdale, Consultant Child Psychiatrist for the Croydon area, was the twins' appearance. They were tall, slender children with silver-blond hair and unusually mature facial features for four-year-olds. They would have been outstandingly attractive were it not for their eyes.

These were an incredibly light shade of blue, and the irises a strange milky-white with minute smokey-grey pupils. Their lashes were long but colourless, not even the silver-blond of their hair but instead soft, opaque strands like threads of a spider's web. He had never seen such eyes.

Smiling, he gestured for their parents to take a seat. He was pleased to see both parents; so often he saw only the mother and it was far easier to build up a picture of the family home if he talked to husband and wife.

'It's very good of you both to come,' he said pleasantly.

Charles Marshall nodded in acknowledgement. 'We both felt that it was necesary.'

'It certainly helps. I see from your G.P's letter that Olivia and Orlando have stopped talking.'

'That's right,' confirmed Charles. His wife, Meg, kept silent.

'Does this mean that they never say anything?'

'I'm sorry?'

'Well, quite often with twins they do talk to each other, even if the language they use is a distortion of our normal speech pattern. Have you noticed anything like that?'

'They don't talk at all,' said their mother quietly. 'They used

1

to chatter from morning to night; now they never say a word.'

'And you can't pinpoint any reason for their silence? Nothing that triggered if off?'

'We've thought about it of course . . .' began Charles, and after that there was no stopping him as he told the doctor how bright the twins had been, how exceptionally articulate and outgoing, how good-natured and amiable. He was like a clockwork toy who would keep talking until he ran down.

The twins looked round the room. It was large, light and relaxing. There were shelves of children's books, a doll's house, several stuffed animals and in one corner there was even a hamster in a cage.

As Dr Tinsdale listened to Charles he watched the children out of the corner of his ·eye. After surveying their surroundings they glanced at each other then walked in unison to the books. Orlando took out one on cars while Olivia chose one that explained all about a little boy who'd been adopted.

'. . . and they'd never been any trouble at all,' continued Charles. 'Considering their background, I felt we'd been exceptionally lucky, but now . . .'

The doctor had been waiting for some mention of their background. It wasn't unusual for a man in Charles Marshall's position to feel concealed resentment for children like these. Careful counselling couldn't alter human nature, but he didn't want to assume that such a situation was responsible for the twins' silence until he had explored all other avenues of possibility.

Orlando quickly tired of the cars and moved closer to his twin. Their eyes travelled over the pages. They saw pictures of a man and a woman gazing with rapt attention at a rosy-cheeked baby in a cot while the baby smiled back at them.

On the next page the adults were taking the baby back to their house, their faces wreathed in smiles. 'Mr and Mrs Black are taking Simon home with them,' informed the text. 'He is a very special baby. Mr and Mrs Black have waited a long time for a baby and now they have chosen Simon.'

Olivia took hold of the page with the picture of the smiling Blacks and their fictional bundle of bliss and ripped it out. Orlando reached out and took it from her, then she watched as

2

he carefully tore it into a dozen pieces which he scattered over the floor like confetti. This done they smiled at each other and began to examine the stuffed animals.

'No!' admonished Meg, horrified by such wanton destruction.

Dr Tinsdale raised a reassuring hand. 'Don't worry. Let them do as they like. I wonder, Mrs Marshall, if you could tell me when the twins' behaviour first started to worry you?'

'I suppose it all began about a year ago. They . . .'

Orlando picked up and discarded several species of bears, one koala with a face like a gremlin, and two green Kermits, before he came across a stuffed doll with black hair and enormous dark eyes. He examined this more carefully before handing it to Olivia. She looked at her twin, who gave the briefest of nods. Quietly and efficiently she tore off both arms and then began to pull out the stuffing until the rag doll was just a piece of patterned cloth with a disproportionately large head. It looked very strange and the twins both smiled.

Dr Tinsdale, who had missed this second act of destruction, was now planning his future sessions with the twins. 'I'd like to see them on their own next Thursday morning if possible,' he told Meg and Charles. 'I'm quite sure that this is just a passing phase. They're probably taking great pleasure in watching you both worry, but I'll know more after a couple of sessions. In the meantime, try not to show any concern and carry on as normal.'

'We wondered . . .' said Charles hesitantly.

'*You* wondered!' Meg's voice was sharp and accusing.

'Yes. *I* wondered whether it could be hereditary?'

'Donors for artificial insemination are *very* carefully checked out,' explained Dr Tinsdale. 'Their backgrounds and medical histories are thoroughly examined, and in most cases they are themselves medical students with a high sense of morality.'

'Most medical students that I've met waltz through their training half-cut!' snapped Charles.

Dr Tinsdale's laugh was rather strained. 'I think that's a somewhat sweeping statement, Mr Marshall. However, if — and I stress it is only *if* — I feel it necessary to look into their background more thoroughly then I will be able to see their father's medical history. If I'm still not satisfied, he can be recalled and the clinic will question him further. After all, we do know who their father is, which is more than can be said for quite a lot of children.'

'May I ask a question?' asked Meg hesitantly.

'Of course.'

'What is elective mutism?'

'It's a very rare condition where a person chooses not to talk although physically and mentally capable of doing so. However it is, as I said, very rare and in the case of twins there is scarcely a handful of cases on record.'

'But what else could it be? They used to talk.'

'I suspect they still do, Mrs Marshall. If they're as smart as your husband suggests they're probably merely being careful not to let you hear them.'

Olivia peered in to the doll's house and picked a tiny plastic baby out of a miniature bath. She held it up for her twin to inspect and then put it in her mouth. With a quick snap of her beautiful white teeth she severed the head before replacing the torso in the bath. The head she put in her skirt pocket. Orlando bent his head to hide his amusement.

'So you don't think there's anything seriously wrong with them?' persisted Meg.

'The less you worry the better they'll be. Naturally you're concerned; probably more than most mothers because you waited ten years to have them. Understandably you're terrified that even now things aren't going to proceed normally. Try to remember that over-protectiveness − however well-intentioned − can in itself cause serious problems with growing children.'

Orlando poked a finger through the hamster's cage. It scurried away from the wire and began to tread its wheel. Its feet went faster and faster until the wheel was just a blur. Olivia narrowed her strange eyes and stared hard at the furry creature. Orlando watched the animal with interest. Olivia concentrated even harder, her mouth a tight line and her naturally pale face now completely colourless. All at once the hamster stopped, squeaked in shock and ran off to its sleeping compartment. At the base of its tail was a small scorch mark.

'So you aren't too concerned?' asked Charles.

'Not at all. I'm interested, and I'm sure I can help, but I

4

don't imagine that there's very much the matter with the twins. I'm afraid that bringing up children isn't quite as easy as the books make out. These little problems crop up now and again. The important thing is not to let them get out of proportion.'

The twins saw their parents stand up and immediately ran to their side. Once again they stared blankly at the doctor, their eyes so lacking in expression that he realised it was rather like looking at androids. He winked at Olivia. She remained expressionless. Taking a large handkerchief from his pocket he deftly twisted and turned the material until within seconds he'd produced a very good likeness of a rabbit.

Orlando looked at the handkerchief, looked at the doctor, flicked his eyes to his twin and then reached up to the desk and grasped a pencil and a piece of paper. He ran over to the books, picked one up, rested it on his knees and appeared to write. Dr Tinsdale watched him carefully.

When he'd finished, Orlando folded the paper carefully in half and slid it across the desk to the doctor. He then followed the rest of the family out of the room. In the doorway both he and Olivia paused, glancing back to see what Dr Tinsdale was doing.

Aware of their scrutiny the doctor smiled to himself as he unfolded the paper. He glanced at the thick white sheet and his eyes widened in shock. There, beautifully printed in large capitals, was one solitary word. He looked up at the twins. Satisfied that he'd read the message, they walked quietly out of the door.

The doctor's mouth was dry as he studied the paper once more. The message was very well written for such a young child, and its meaning succinct. In the middle of the page Orlando had printed one word: 'FOOL'.

Chapter 1

It was a lovely sunny day and Meg was sitting in her back garden with her sister, Catriona. The twins and their cousin, David, were playing in the sandpit.

'They seem much better,' said Catriona cheerfully. 'They both said "hello" to us when we arrived, and I can hear them laughing now.'

Meg, who had always been slim for her height but had now become positively thin, pulled a face. 'They're certainly better than when they first went to Dr Tinsdale but they're not back to normal. However, he won't be seeing them any more.'

'Not at all?'

'No. I honestly get the feeling he's afraid of them, and I'm sure he doesn't take any notice of my opinions.'

'Surely Charles supports what you say?'

'Charles! He's washed his hands of them. As far as Charles is concerned *I* wanted the children, *I* conceived and gave birth to them, and if I don't like what I've got I can't blame him. He says that to him they're just a financial burden.'

'But you both wanted children! He was devastated when he found he couldn't give you any. Miles said he'd never seen Charles look as ill as he did when you found out why you weren't able to conceive.'

'It wasn't quite as simple as it seemed,' said Meg quietly.

'What do you mean?'

'I'm sorry, Catriona, I can't explain, but really and truly Charles is right. I was the one who pushed him into accepting artificial insemination.'

'You hardly had to twist his arm!'

6

Yes I did, thought Meg, he had no choice but to give in to me. Unfortunately this was something that she couldn't share with her sister. A secret that had to be kept in exchange for the twins.

'In what way aren't they back to normal?' Catriona knew when to change the subject.

'They won't talk to Charles.'

'Only Charles?'

'Yes, they completely ignore him. When he comes home they don't even look up. It must be horrible for him. They act as though he were invisible. They don't do anything he tells them to either. I have to repeat all his instructions. Family conversations are a complete farce. "Go and clean your teeth, Olivia," says Charles. Two minutes later I say, "Daddy said go and clean your teeth," and two minutes after that I have to say, "Olivia, *I'd* like you to clean your teeth now." And that fool of a psychiatrist says they're perfectly normal!'

'That's dreadful. Poor Charles.'

'I sometimes wonder if it's because they know he isn't really their father.'

'Don't be silly, how could they possibly know that? He's always been marvellous with them. When they were first talking he was as proud as could be. Miles used to laugh about the way he doted on them.'

'Miles laughs at most things: I'm afraid Charles is rarely amused.'

Catriona frowned. 'Are things all right between you?'

'As all right as they've ever been.'

'You *are* feeling down. We've always looked on you two as the perfect couple, yet right now you sound as though you've never known a day's happiness together. What you need is a holiday.'

'I'll get some more coffee,' said Meg quietly, and went into the large five-bedroomed house that was beginning to feel increasingly like a gilded cage.

'Look at my castle,' said Olivia, gently patting the perfect three-turret model that she'd carefully constructed out of the sand.

'This one's mine,' said Orlando, pointing to a heap of sand topped by an empty yoghurt pot with a lolly stick through the middle.

David eyed his cousins warily. They weren't like his other friends, and although he was a year older he always felt vaguely frightened in their presence.

'Where's yours?' Orlando asked him.

'I haven't made one.'

'Why not?'

'I like burying my feet.'

The twins glanced at one another and smiled. 'I'll bury your feet,' said Olivia. 'Here, I'll use my spade. It's bigger than yours.' She began industriously shovelling sand over David's feet and ankles. The sun was warm on his back and he felt quite sleepy as she gently patted the grains in place.

Behind him, Orlando stood thoughtfully, spade in hand, and wondered what it would feel like to hit David over the head. He tried to imagine what kind of a sound the spade would make as it made contact with the skull, but couldn't decide if it would be a dull thud or a sharp crack. Probably a dull thud, he thought, unless the bones of the skull were almost unprotected. It was difficult to tell just by looking for David had a mass of brown curls that completely hid his scalp.

Orlando realised that he'd never have a better opportunity of finding out because his cousin was quite off guard as Olivia played happily round his feet. Excitement stirred in him, causing his stomach to lurch and then glow with a strange, pleasurable warmth. All at once he knew he simply had to give it a try.

His excitement peaked to such a pitch that Olivia sensed it. For one brief moment she allowed her eyes to meet her twin's. The pupils seemed to vanish at the moment of contact. Then she quickly continued with her own game so that David wasn't alerted.

Orlando didn't bother to check that no one was watching him because he didn't think that he was doing anything wrong. He wanted to find something out and this was the only way it could be done. David was simply unfortunate in being there on that particular day. Raising his spade high in the air the little boy brought it down on his cousin's head with a mighty blow that split the skin, causing David to topple sideways. As he fell he hit his head against the side of the pit, and so it was never possible for Orlando to be sure if he'd managed to knock his cousin out or not. He rather regretted the intrusion of the concrete edge.

Catriona had seen it all. She had been so stunned by what she was witnessing that her tardy scream of warning had done David more harm than good for he instinctively tensed and half-turned towards her, which was why it was the side of his head that was split open rather than the top.

She ran over the lawn, nearly falling in her haste, and when she saw David lying in a spreading pool of blood she began to scream hysterically while shaking Orlando as though he were a small dog.

'You wicked, wicked boy! Look what you've done. David! David, can you hear Mummy?'

Olivia quickly stepped out of the pit and stared down at her aunt. 'You're crying!' she said in astonishment. 'Why are you crying?'

'David! Oh, God, please let him be all right. David! David!'

Meg, who had heard her sister from the house, took one look at all the blood and went to phone for an ambulance. Then she shepherded the twins away from the sandpit, telling them to go to their room and play until a doctor had mended David.

'Can a doctor mend him?' asked Orlando.

'Of course he can. He'll probably put in a stitch or two, that's all.'

'What a waste!' complained Olivia as they climbed the stairs. 'All that effort and they'll just stitch him up again. What did it feel like?'

Orlando's eyes were shining. 'Lovely! I went all hot and tingly from my head to my toes. It was just like when we . . . you know.'

'Was it?' This fascinated Olivia. 'What was the best bit?'

'Seeing the blood. It was nice when he crumpled up, but the blood was best.'

'I wonder why Auntie Catriona was crying?'

'Perhaps she didn't know about the stitches. Just before I hit him was almost as exciting as the blood.'

'Really?'

'I'd like to do it again, to see which bit was really the best.'

9

'We'd better wait until he's been sewn together,' said practical Olivia.

'I shan't do it to David next time. I'll try someone different.'

'How about Lee at playgroup?'

'O.K. Look, the ambulance is coming up our drive.'

They both hung out of the bedroom window, totally enthralled by the siren and uniformed men. They didn't take much notice of Catriona and David but the ambulance was really exciting.

Eventually a shattered Meg forced herself upstairs to the twins' bedroom. Catriona, while obviously hysterical, had been perfectly lucid about what had occurred and her final, screeching denunciation of the twins as maladjusted monsters had sounded an ominous warning note in Meg's mind.

'I want to talk seriously to you both,' she told them as they bounded blithely across the room towards her. 'What happened to David this afternoon?'

Orlando frowned. 'He got hit with a spade. Aunty Catriona saw that, she said so.'

'Was it an accident, Orlando?'

He shook his head.

'You've saying that you meant to hurt him?' She tried to keep her voice non-accusing.

'I wanted to see what would happen, that's all.'

'You mean it was an experiment?'

'A what?'

'A sort of test.'

He smiled briefly. 'That's right, a test.'

'And how do you feel now that the test is over?'

'*I'm* all right.'

'But David isn't, is he?'

Orlando shrugged. 'You said he'd be sewn up.'

'That's right, but he's going to have a terrible pain in his head for a long time.'

Orlando continued to smile cheerfully at her.

'Don't you realise what you've done? You could have killed him! What's the matter with you two? Why did you want to know what would happen? Couldn't you just play quietly in the sand like other children?'

'It got a bit boring,' said Olivia politely. 'Orlando wanted to make it more interesting.'

10

'I've a good mind to tell Dr Tinsdale. I'd like to know what he'd make of this.'

'He'd call it acceptable experimental behaviour.'

'Three months ago you couldn't say a word!' exclaimed Meg. 'Now you talk like a walking dictionary. I hope you realise that you've both behaved appallingly.'

'I didn't!' objected Olivia.

'Yes, you did. I saw you waving to the driver while your poor cousin was being carried into the back of the ambulance.'

'I didn't wave to David because he had his eyes closed.'

'Stop it!' shouted Meg. 'I'm telling your father all about this. Until he gets in you're both to stay here and start thinking up a suitable apology for David.'

Until that moment the twins had been good-humoured. They'd listened politely to Meg and even tried to look slightly confused, but at the mention of Charles their eyes became bleak and they moved closer together.

'He isn't our father,' they said in unison.

'Of course he is.'

'He isn't,' repeated Olivia coldly. 'He's nothing to do with us. He's just part of another experiment.'

'What do you mean?' asked Meg, wishing that they wouldn't stare so directly at her.

'When Orlando wanted to find out about hitting people you said he was doing an experiment. We're part of an experiment too, aren't we?'

'No!' exclaimed a horrified Meg. 'I don't know what you've heard but it isn't true. You're two perfectly normal children. How could you be an experiment?'

'He isn't our father,' repeated the twins. In the face of such an indisputable truth all that their mother could do was turn and run from the room.

'She was crying too,' remarked Olivia sitting on her bed. 'I wonder why people cry so much?'

'It's all to do with feelings,' explained Orlando.

'Like our tingly ones?'

'Not really. Feelings for other people.'

'I've never had any of them.' Olivia sounded quite regretful; she hated missing anything.

'Neither have I, but most people do. I'm glad I don't. I think

11

they'd get in the way of interesting things.'

'How funny!' laughed Olivia, staring unblinkingly in to space. 'I can see David sitting all bunched up in a wheelchair and his head's lolling around like a baby's.'

Orlando widened his eyes and began to stare as well. 'Oh yes, I wonder why he's doing that?'

'We'll have to wait and see,' replied his twin as she picked up pencil and paper. 'I'm going to draw David's head with all the blood coming out and see if *I* go tingly too.'

'I'm going to have a sleep,' responded Orlando. 'I always feel tired after the tingles.'

They stayed peacefully in their room for the rest of the day.

Charles felt very tired when he arrived home. Quite apart from a busy day in court — he was the junior partner in a thriving solicitor's practice — there had been a highly embarrassing meeting with Brian Heath, the senior partner and founder of the firm. He thought that he'd managed to allay the man's suspicions but all the same it was worrying. At times like this he was extremely grateful for the existence of the twins.

His gratitude didn't last long. As soon as he was in the front door, Meg — who usually had more sense and waited until he'd unwound — started regaling him with the tale of David's accident in the sandpit.

'... Catriona's absolutely furious!' she concluded.

'These things happen. All children fall down and bang their heads now and again.'

'David didn't fall down, Orlando knocked him over.'

'David is nearly five and built like a tank. I fail to comprehend how Orlando could have felled him with a plastic spade.'

'It was the metal one with the wooden handle; you bought it last summer because you couldn't cut a proper moat with the plastic ones.'

'In that case Catriona should blame me! Really, Meg, I think you're making a terrible fuss. Your sister's always flying off the handle. She'll get over it.'

'David won't,' said Meg quietly, following her husband in to the dining-room where he poured himself an exceptionally large scotch.

'Why on earth not?'

'They're operating to remove a small blood clot at this very moment. It's causing pressure on the brain.'

Charles sank in to his chair. 'What a ghastly day!'

'It's certainly been traumatic.'

'I meant mine,' he said irritably.

'Look, Charles, I'm sorry if you've had a bad day at work but you must speak to the twins. They seem to think that because they didn't intend to hurt David that makes everything all right.'

'And so it does. I know it's ghastly, and of course your sister's got every right to feel resentful, but the twins are only just four and they're used to *plastic* spades. They couldn't have realised . . .'

'Orlando wanted to know what it felt like.'

'Know how what felt?'

'Hitting David over the head.'

There was a brief silence. 'All right, I'll speak to them. Mind you, it's a waste of time. They'll pretend I'm not even in the room. Which reminds me, when do they see Tinsdale again?'

Meg stared at her tall, boyish-looking husband with his light brown hair and fresh complexion, and as he gazed questioningly back at her she hated him. Hated him for the way he'd deceived her and for the perpetual charade that was their marriage.

'I told you,' she said wearily, 'he's finished with them. There's nothing wrong any more. Well, he doesn't think there ever was, but even he agrees that their refusal to speak was a trifle anti-social.'

'They still don't speak to me.'

'You and I know that, but you wouldn't come along and tell him for yourself and he didn't believe me.'

Charles rubbed his hand over his face. 'I should have gone,' he admitted, 'but I've had a lot on my mind and . . .'

'And?'

'Nothing. I'll go and speak to them.'

The twins were sitting on the end of Olivia's bed when Charles entered their room. They looked up for a moment and then Orlando continued reading his book while Olivia went back to her drawing.

13

'Your mother has been telling me about David,' said Charles.

'Look, Orlando, do you think that's good?' asked Olivia.

Her twin gazed at the sheet of paper. 'Very good, but the blood came out in thick blobs, not a thin stream.'

'Bother! I'll have to do it again.' She tore up the paper and fetched a fresh sheet from beside the bed.

'Did you hear me?' Charles raised his voice as they continued to ignore him.

'Livvy, it says in this book that when you start school you play in sandpits and draw pictures with crayons.'

'We can do that now. I want to learn new things.'

'*Be quiet*!' thundered Charles. 'Do you realise that your cousin is having an operation on his head because of your stupidity today? What on earth possessed you to do such a daft thing?'

'Use my red biro, Livvy. If you press hard on it the blobs come out easily.'

Rage swept over Charles and he stopped forward to lift Orlando off the bed. Before he could reach him the twins looked up, their strange milky eyes fixing him to the spot, and he felt the hairs on the back of his neck prickle with fright.

'I wish he'd go away,' remarked Olivia. 'He's not very nice and he's making me angry.'

Charles wanted to shout that they were making him angry as well. He wanted to pick them both up and bang their heads together, do anything at all to disrupt their terrifying denial of his existence, but he found that he couldn't. The longer they stared at him the weaker he felt, until the room began to swim around him and he swayed on his feet.

'I'll talk to you later,' he threatened feebly. Olivia shrugged and turned away. 'As for David,' he continued from the relative safety of the doorway, 'I don't suppose that he'll ever want to play with you again.'

The twins turned to each other as though he wasn't there. 'Poor David,' remarked Olivia. 'He'll never play with us again.'

'He won't miss us,' Orlando assured her. 'He's forgotten everything he ever knew. He's just like a baby again.'

'Then we don't want him,' laughed Olivia. 'We never play with babies.'

They hadn't been looking at him but Charles knew that this conversation was entirely for his benefit. He closed their bedroom door and wondered what he should do about them. Meg was right, they weren't normal children, but if he supported his wife's observations the twins' background would be placed under a microscope and right now, with the memory of Brian Heath's accusations fresh in his mind, he didn't think that was a very good idea. Just the same he felt uneasy and spent the rest of the evening finishing off the bottle of whisky. It didn't alter anything, but it did help him to forget.

The next morning he asked Meg to let him know how David was as soon as she heard any news. He had never encouraged private calls to his office before and she wondered why this sudden concern for his nephew.

Unable to make contact with her sister, Meg telephoned the hospital for news. The staff nurse said that David had spent a comfortable night and was still sleeping, which told her precisely nothing. She was wandering the house, absent-mindedly straightening ornaments and wondering what to do next, when the twins came running up to her.

'Can we go to the park, Mummy?' begged Olivia.

'Please, Mummy,' added Orlando. 'It's a nice day for the park.'

It was probably the best thing possible, thought Meg to herself. Staying at home wasn't going to help anyone. 'All right. Do you want to take a ball?'

'We'll take Orlando's boat,' said Olivia firmly. 'We want to sail it on the pond.'

'I thought you were bored with sailing boats?'

'Not now. Today we're unbored.'

Smiling to herself, Meg watched them rush off to get ready. They were such strange children that it was difficult to remember they were her own flesh and blood. They were as much hers as if Charles had fathered them, but it never seemed like that. The social worker who had provided ante-natal counselling hadn't mentioned that this might happen, yet from the moment they opened their peculiar eyes and began to look at the world around them she had felt that they were strangers. In her heart of hearts she considered them adopted. The

15

Caesarean had added to this illusion since she didn't have any memory of their birth.

'Ready!' shouted a breathless Olivia, interrupting her mother's reminiscences.

'Good. We'll walk as it's such a lovely morning.'

Normally the twins strongly objected to walking anywhere but today, amazingly, they set off without a murmur. The schools hadn't yet broken up and they had the park to themselves. The few other pre-school children who were there were gathered round the swings and sandpit, none of them near the boating lake.

Meg sat on one of the wooden benches and watched Orlando launch his boat. It was a toy yacht that Charles' mother had given him for his last birthday and it was really too old for him, but today he was managing it quite well with the aid of a long stick left behind by another child.

The twins began murmuring to each other and as the sun continued to beat down, Meg closed her eyes. She'd scarcely slept during the night, all her thoughts with David at the hospital, but now it was difficult to stay awake. She allowed herself to drift into a light doze, opening her eyes now and again to check that the twins were still safe. It wasn't too much of a worry, they were unlikely to go off with anyone since they regarded most of the human race with either mild contempt or active dislike. No, the twins were safe enough.

By the water's edge they watched their mother carefully. They saw how her chin sank to her chest once or twice and then jerked upright again as she checked on them. Eventually, as they'd known she would, she fell deeply asleep. They looked carefully round the park.

'He isn't here,' whispered Olivia.

'He'll come.'

Five minutes later a man stepped on to the small bridge on the opposite side of the water. He glanced at the children, taking in their snow-white hair and the transparent blue eyes with the light irises. For a moment or two he studied them, then he put his hands in his jacket pockets and waited.

The twins moved towards him, hesitantly at first but then more confidently until they were running. Their eyes were wide with delight and they held their arms out in front of them ready to embrace this unknown man.

Not until they were standing within six inches of him did he acknowledge their presence. They waited for him to speak, anxious for recognition. 'Hello,' he said at last. 'And what are your names?'

They were so excited and keyed up that to their horror they found themselves unable to answer. The man crouched down in front of them. 'Don't worry,' he said softly. 'I know them. You're Olivia and Orlando.'

The children nodded.

'Do you know who I am?'

It was Orlando who managed to speak first. 'Daddy!' he whispered, and with one small fine-boned hand gently touched the stranger's face.

'That's right. I'm your father.'

The two silver-haired children and the stern-faced, grey-haired man remained together on the bridge as though locked in an invisible capsule that excluded the rest of the world.

On the park bench Meg suddenly jerked awake and realised that the twins had left the lake. She felt a brief moment of fear before spotting them on the bridge talking to a strange man. Quickly she hurried across the sun-baked grass to collect them.

As she approached the man's eyes flicked over her in quick appraisal. He saw a tall, thin, dark-haired woman in her mid-thirties with intelligent eyes and a mouth that hinted at a deeply sensual nature. Before she reached them he bent down and whispered in Orlando's ear. The boy nodded, then stood up and faced his mother.

'Time to go home,' called Meg. She gave a half-smile to the man whilst privately feeling that he ought to know better than to engage little children in conversation.

'They're quite safe,' he assured her in a beautifully modulated, slightly hypnotic voice.

'I'm sure they are but they know they shouldn't speak to strangers.'

The children stared sullenly at her. She was spoiling something very special and they were cross.

'Come on!' she repeated. Olivia backed in to the man's legs and stood there defiantly. Orlando reached up and took hold of the man's cuff. 'No!' he told her. 'We won't come.'

Her heart sank. The twins were plainly going to be difficult, and for some reason she already felt uncomfortable in front of this man. The last thing she wanted was for him to witness one of their temper tantrums.

She held out a hand. 'It's lunch-time, Olivia. We've got cold chicken and salad, your favourite.'

'I don't like chicken any more.'

'Of course you do.'

'She doesn't,' said Orlando, 'and nor do I.'

'Then you'll have to go hungry but we must get home now.'

'No!' they shouted in unison, and the man watched with interest as Meg became more and more hot and flustered. Realising that she could talk to them for the rest of the day and they wouldn't co-operate she stepped forward and reached for Olivia. Her daughter immediately kicked out and her sandal buckle grazed the front of Meg's shin, laddering her tights at the same time.

All at once the man moved. He gently propelled both children to their mother's side and bent down until his face was on a level with theirs. 'Off you go,' he told them crisply. 'I don't like to see children behaving badly. It shows a high degree of ignorance.'

I'm sure they'll respond to that! thought Meg with amusement, but they did. With one last glance at the stranger they obediently trotted back to the pond, collected their boat and began walking to the park gates.

'Thank you,' said Meg awkwardly.

'My pleasure. They're lovely children.'

Which just showed how little he knew, thought Meg as she hurried them back home. But she was baffled by their behaviour towards the stranger, and would certainly have told Charles about it if it hadn't been for the news that Miles, her brother-in-law, brought that afternoon. She was so relieved to see him that at first she didn't take in his pallor and trembling hands, but when he haltingly began to speak she knew that something was drastically wrong.

'David's still in a coma,' he told her, his normally laughing eyes clouded with disbelief. 'The doctors say that even if he

18

regains consciousness there's a strong possibility he'll be brain-damaged.'

'No!'

'Apparently the damage was done before they opened him up. I can't understand why they took so long to operate but they just blind me with science when I ask questions.'

'That means that Orlando . . .'

Miles shook his head. 'No, Meg, don't ever think that. It was the blow on the edge of the sandpit that caused the damage. Orlando's spade only made a little cut in the skin.'

'It's still Orlando's fault. If he hadn't hit David then . . .'

'He's only a child, there's no way anyone could have anticipated this. You mustn't blame him. It was an accident.'

'Catriona?'

'She's taking it badly. Naturally she can't be logical yet and she's saying stupid things, but she'll get over that, Meg. You'll just have to be patient with her.'

'I could kill Orlando!' Meg's eyes sparked with fury.

Miles put a hand on her arm. 'Please, don't talk like that. He's only four years old. Do you know, when I look at David and remember how he was when I left him yesterday I can't believe . . .' And finally Miles broke down and sobbed. He sat at Meg's kitchen table, crying as though he'd never stop, while she gently stroked his hair and silently cursed her strange, anti-social twins who'd only wanted to experiment.

Chapter 2

It was the middle of July and Charles knew that unless he took some holiday and got started on painting the outside of his house he was going to have to pay someone else to do it. With his future as a solicitor in the balance this was an expense he had to avoid.

Meg, unaware of the trouble at work, resented Charles' refusal to take them all away on holiday, feeling certain that it was because he didn't like spending time with the twins. Without even Catriona to talk to – David's condition was little better than that of a newborn baby and her sister spent every waking hour at the hospital – she became more and more dissatisfied and bad-tempered.

Orlando and Olivia were quite content. They didn't like going away to the seaside where they had to mix with other children, and they loathed Charles' company, so staying at home suited them. It also suited their plan.

The plan had occupied a great deal of time since they met the stranger in the park. His whispered instructions to Orlando hadn't been very precise, but they knew that they mustn't let him down and immediately began plotting. They watched a lot of television but most of the things they saw were quite impractical. They read books but they were even worse. Finally they started going through the daily newspaper, and that was far more rewarding. The papers were full of possibilities.

On the first Monday of his holiday, Charles had an early breakfast before fetching his ladder, paints and brushes from the garage. He then started to check all the window frames and sills. One of the frames at the front of the house had rotted and would need replacing; most of the others could be patched up for another year and the twins' window was the best of all. A quick sand down and two layers of paint would have that looking as good as new. Because it was the easiest job on his list he decided to tackle it first.

He didn't like heights and was very careful to make certain that his ladder was secure before he began to climb it. This was easy enough with only sandpaper in his hand but would be a great deal trickier with paintpot and brush. For the first time he wished that their house wasn't quite so large. A bedroom in the roof was no fun at all when you came to decorate.

The twins stood by their window and watched as his face appeared over the sill. Charles was startled by the sight of their weird eyes staring out at him but managed a strained smile as he began to rub at the woodwork. Naturally they didn't wave back. They simply continued to stare.

The day was rapidly getting warmer. Charles decided that once he'd finished the rubbing down he'd leave the actual painting until late afternoon, otherwise the sun would cause the paint to blister and ultimately flake off. Wiping a hand over his forehead he took a deep breath. It really was a horrible job, and the twins' presence on the other side of the glass didn't help. Whenever he looked into their bleak, unfriendly eyes he felt that he'd paid a heavy price for his past indiscretions.

Eventually he was nearly finished, but one small area remained to be done which necessitated the opening of the twins' window. He tapped on the glass; they continued to stare out at him.

'Open the small window,' he mouthed.

Their expressions didn't change.

'Can you open the small window for me? I need to rub it down.'

They looked away from him and began to turn their backs.

Charles banged on the glass. 'Open the bloody window!'

Orlando spun round and with incredible speed his right hand shot out as he unlatched the large window and flung it wide open. With an ear-splitting scream of horror Charles felt the ladder sway away from the wall. He flung himself desperately forward, reaching out to grab at the roughened woodwork, but Orlando was already there — waiting.

The ladder reached the boy's hands before it touched the wall. For one brief moment Charles' terror-filled face almost touched Orlando's and the man began to gibber, frantically begging the child for help, but help was the very last thing on Orlando's mind. As he pushed at the ladder with all of his strength he looked Charles in the eye and for the first and last time in his life smiled at his surrogate father.

Olivia ran to the window and watched as the ladder swung away from the house, remaining upright for one short tantalising moment before falling backwards with gratifying speed until it crashed on to the concrete barbecue area that, for Charles and Meg, had been one of the main attractions of the house.

'Look where he's landed!' exclaimed Orlando. 'He was always complaining that he didn't spend enough time on the patio. Well, he can stay as long as he likes now!' The twins gave one of their rare bursts of laughter.

'Sshh!' cautioned Olivia. 'It's time for part two of the plan.' They exchanged knowing looks, moved to the door, counted to three and then flung it wide open.

'Mummy! Mummy!' screamed Olivia as she pounded down the stairs. 'There's been an accident. Daddy's had a fall.'

Even as Meg leapt to her feet and began dashing to the garden she registered the strange fact that Olivia had called Charles 'Daddy'. In the shock and horror of what followed this thought was temporarily driven from her mind; later on it returned.

This time the twins didn't bother about the ambulance when it came up their drive. Instead they remained in their room and watched as Charles' broken body was removed from the patio and taken away to the mortuary. He was completely covered by a red blanket.

'I wonder what he looked like under that blanket,' mused Olivia.

'All floppy and covered in blood I should think. His bones must have been smashed to pieces.'

'Daddy will be pleased,' said Olivia. 'Now he can come and live with us.'

'He's got to marry Mummy first.'

'Has he?' Olivia wasn't too clear about marriages and how they came about. 'Does he fill in a form?'

'No! He has to make Mummy want him.'

'*We* already want him.'

'We're not going to be his wife,' said Orlando patiently. 'It's Mummy who matters now – just for a little while.'

'Did you tingle when you pushed the ladder?'

Orlando considered the question for a moment. 'No, not really. I did it for Daddy, not for me. If I'd cut his head off or something like that I would have tingled, but not after pushing a ladder. I didn't even get to see the blood.'

'We could always go and look at the patio. There might still be some marks on the concrete.'

As they descended the stairs they found themselves face to face with Charles' parents. The woman had obviously been crying, her eyes were heavy and red-rimmed, while the man looked utterly dazed. He stared blankly at the children.

'Where's Mummy?' asked Olivia.

'At the hospital. Your father's had an accident. She asked us to tell you that she'll be back soon.'

'Can we go outside and play?'

'I'm afraid not. There are . . . That is, the police are examining some of the garden. Why don't you watch television?'

'Why are the police in the garden?' asked Orlando innocently.

'Because . . .'

'Yes?'

'I'm sorry, your mother will have to explain,' he said abruptly, and then put an arm round his weeping wife.

'Everyone's crying these days!' Olivia felt thoroughly exasperated.

'They can't help it. That's the way they're made.'

'I'm jolly glad I'm not like that. I hope the police don't clean the concrete before they go.'

'I don't suppose they will. Let's put a video on. How about a Tom and Jerry cartoon?'

'If you like. Perhaps this time the mouse will get eaten for a change.'

They were still watching television when Meg returned home. She had never felt so weary. It had been a ghastly experience seeing her husband's remains, and she assumed that the only reason she wasn't hysterical was because the full horror hadn't yet sunk in. She hoped it was that because

23

despite herself, at the back of her mind, was the realisation that at last she was rid of him.

Not that she'd wanted him to die like he had, that was gruesome beyond belief, but she had frequently imagined living without him; enjoying the freedom that his death would bring. The strain of their life together had filled her mind day after day. Even the birth of the twins hadn't eased the revulsion that her marriage caused her. But now, once she'd recovered from the shock, she could begin to live properly again.

She glanced in at the children and Orlando twisted round to face her. 'Where is he?' he asked casually.

'Your father?'

'He isn't our father.' Olivia's response was automatic.

They wouldn't mind his death at all, realised Meg. They wouldn't feel any sorrow. If anything they'd be pleased too, and unlike her they wouldn't trouble to disguise it.

'He's dead,' she said shortly.

'We thought he must be, didn't we, Olivia? He fell such a long way.'

'He was painting your bedroom window.'

'And he fell. We saw him. The ladder stood up straight before it fell and you should have seen the way he looked at us! He couldn't believe it was happening.'

'You watched him fall?'

'Yes.'

Both the children were looking at her now and their faces were shuttered. They seemed to be waiting for something but she didn't understand what it could be, unless they were interested in what she was going to say. But why should that interest them unless they'd been involved in some way?

She remembered Olivia shouting out that her daddy had been hurt. Olivia, who had never acknowledged Charles as her father, had obviously been out to impress. She pictured the twins standing at their window watching Charles at work. Could they possibly have opened that window and accidentally knocked him backwards? She doubted it. But they could have done it deliberately which would explain Olivia's attempt at a normal childish reaction...

Whatever had happened it was over. If the twins had been involved she didn't want to know, because if she knew then Dr

24

Tinsdale was utterly wrong and she was right which meant that all her fears about their real father would begin again, now that it was too late. Nothing could be done to change their parentage, they had to be accepted for what they were.

'Mummy!'

Meg jumped. 'Yes?'

'When can we have Daddy to live here?'

Meg's mind was still with Charles and the question seemed so ridiculous that she didn't know how to answer it. 'Don't be silly, Olivia. I've already explained that your father's dead.'

'Aren't you going to marry again?'

After life with Charles? thought Meg in disgust. 'No. I shan't ever marry again.'

'Why not?'

'Because no one would want to take on you two for a start!'

Orlando walked up to her, putting his head on one side as he examined her carefully. 'You're not sad either,' he said emphatically. 'I don't think *you* liked him very much.'

'He was my husband, of course I liked him,' she said automatically.

'You aren't crying. You'd cry if you really used to like him.'

'I'm not the crying type. Why don't you go outside and play?'

'Grandpa said the policemen were there.'

'Not any more.'

'Good! Come on, Olivia.'

Alone in the room, Meg put her face in her hands. The twins were right, she wasn't sad, and that meant that she was no better than them. Perhaps she shouldn't be blaming the unknown father for their lack of emotion − it could very well come from her. But she had loved Charles once, in the beginning, before she found out.

By September Meg had almost forgotten what life with Charles had been like. It wasn't as though they'd led a busy social life, so she didn't suffer the numerous social rejections that many young widows experience. Neither had they shared a bedroom, which meant that there was no empty side of a double bed to cause anguish every night. In fact by the time he died, Meg and Charles had shared little more than a surname, the twins, and an ability to fool all the people all the time.

The only difficulty was that Meg found it difficult to play the part of anguished widow very well. She knew that while some people — including Miles and Catriona — admired her for the way she was getting on with her life there were others who felt she wasn't as shattered as convention demanded. Naturally Charles' parents were among the latter group.

The twins weren't upset but they were distinctly edgy. They developed a habit of trailing their mother everywhere, their peculiar eyes following her wherever she went. Catriona said that they were terrified of losing Meg as well as Charles but Meg knew this wasn't so. No, whatever the reason for their eagle-eyed surveillance it wasn't concern for her safety. Her whereabouts obviously mattered to them a great deal and she wished she could find out why.

One mild October day they nearly drove her mad as they wandered behind her from room to room. When she came out of the toilet and found them sitting by the door she decided that she couldn't stand it any longer.

'What *is* the matter with you two?' she demanded.

'We want to go out,' said Olivia.

'Out where?'

'To the park.'

'You mean to say you've been following me around since July because you wanted to go to the park?'

'No, but we want to go today, don't we, Orlando?'

'Yes. We want to sail my boat.'

'All right. Go and fetch it and we'll stay there until lunchtime. After that I want to be left in peace.'

As they made their way along the leaf-covered pavements, Meg reflected upon all the things that had happened since they last went to the park with the boat. Quite apart from the pleasure of living a strain-free life of her own she'd found that without Charles she didn't worry about the twins so much. They weren't like other children, she knew that, but somehow the difference didn't trouble her as greatly as it had. They weren't doing anyone any harm, and if they chose to spend most of their time alone together it didn't really matter because soon they'd start school and then they'd learn to socialise.

Despite the pleasant weather they had the park entirely to themselves, or so it appeared. Meg couldn't see the man in the grey donkey jacket who was standing behind the trees that lined the park. Standing and waiting, just as he'd waited for the past week. Waiting for the children to come.

'You sit down, Mummy,' said Orlando. 'We like sailing the boat on our own.'

'Well, don't go in the water. It's quite deep in the middle.'

'We know that!' Olivia could be devastatingly scornful when she chose.

'Fine. Then I'll have a rest on the seat.'

Once she was comfortable Meg let her mind roam back to the early days of her marriage. How naïve she'd been, and how eager to take the blame for everything that went wrong. Charles had been fifteen years older than her and a man of the world; she'd naturally blamed herself. What a waste, she thought, remembering how her self-confidence had diminished from month to month. Even now she wasn't as sure of herself as she should have been. Sixteen years with Charles weren't that easy to shrug off.

All at once her reminiscences were shattered by an ear-splitting scream from Olivia. Meg jumped up and saw Orlando climbing out of the pond, coughing and spluttering as he wiped mud from his eyes and mouth.

She hurried over to him, but it was only when she got near that she saw the blood spurting from his left wrist. She couldn't understand why there was so much, or why it was such a dark red.

The man moved very quickly. He ran across the grass from his hiding place and by the time he reached the boy had torn off his tie. Before Meg could say a word he had taken hold of the child's arm, raised it high in the air and was binding the tie as tightly as possible just above the left elbow.

Orlando wasn't crying but his eyes were frightened and Olivia looked ready to pass out. 'Do you have a car here?' snapped the stranger brusquely.

'No, we walked because . . .'

'Then we'll use mine. You'd better direct me to the nearest casualty department. He needs prompt medical attention.'

'What's he done?'

'Severed an artery.'

Meg's stomach lurched and she instinctively reached for her son. However Orlando wound his right arm tightly round the stranger's neck and didn't even glance in his mother's direction. The man was walking briskly away from the pond leaving Meg to hurry after him, Olivia's hand clutched tightly in her own.

Obeying his instructions she slid into the back seat of the large Volvo estate, then carefully took Orlando on to her lap. Olivia sat quietly next to them, her eyes never leaving her twin's face.

The stranger drove fast and well. Ignoring the 'No Parking' signs he parked in the ambulance zone by the casualty entrance, then took Orlando back from her and hurried through the swing doors. He moved so fast that Meg narrowly missed being hit in the face as they swung back towards her.

'What happened?' she asked Olivia as they entered the waiting room.

'He let go of the doors.'

'To your brother!'

'He fell.'

'What was he trying to do?'

'Reach the boat. The wind took it away from us.'

'There isn't any wind today.'

'Then it must have been my burp!'

'I told you both not to go in the water.'

'He didn't mean to go in, he lost his balance.'

'If this man hadn't been around, Orlando could have died.'

'If he hadn't been there it wouldn't have happened.'

'What do you mean?' asked Meg sharply.

Olivia's eyes widened. 'Nothing! I didn't mean anything.'

'Yes, you did, and I want an explanation. Did he push Orlando?'

'Mummy, he wasn't anywhere near us!'

'Then what did you mean?'

Olivia had now had time to work out an explanation. 'I only meant that if the man hadn't been there we wouldn't have come to the hospital in his car, or been able to save Orlando. None of that would have happened. That's what I meant.'

Meg wasn't satisfied but the stranger's return distracted her. She looked up at him, anxious for news.

'They're seeing to it now. Don't worry, he'll be fine.'

In her relief Meg felt the prick of tears behind her eyelids and tried to blink them away.

'You said you weren't the crying type!' shouted Olivia.

'When did I say that?'

'After *he* died. You didn't cry once when that happened and you said . . .'

'Your mother's had a nasty shock,' said the stranger. 'Leave her alone.'

To Meg's surprise her daughter mumbled an apology before walking away to find a comic. The man sat down next to her. 'My name's Ashley Webster,' he said quietly. 'I believe we met once before in the park.'

'I'm Meg Marshall, and I'm so grateful! I don't know how to begin to thank you. I wouldn't have known what to do. I didn't even realise that it was an artery he'd cut.

'I was once a medical student. It's still useful now and again.'

She looked carefully at him, taking in the thick grey hair swept back off his forehead, the dark eyebrows, intelligent grey eyes and wide mouth with a rather thin top lip. He was very attractive, although there was an air of cool reserve about him that discouraged over-familiarity. Despite the grey hair she didn't think that he was much over forty. His face was relatively unlined and there was a compact strength about him rarely found in older men.

'Met before?' she repeated slowly. 'I don't remember.'

'Your children were talking to me on the bridge, and then they didn't want to go home.' He laughed at the memory, a short, harsh sound.

'Of course! What a coincidence.'

'It certainly is,' he lied smoothly. 'I rather think this is the casualty sister coming to check up on your son's medical history.'

He was right, and by the time she'd finished Meg felt thoroughly inadequate because the events of the morning had driven all memories of tetanus shots and allergies out of her head and she feared she'd shown herself to be a very slipshod mother.

When she was finally allowed to see Orlando he was lying on

a high metal cot, his arm heavily bandaged and resting in a sling. His eyes were slightly unfocused and he didn't seem too sure of what was going on, but he did remember Ashley.

'Where's . . .?'

'Mr. Webster's waiting with Olivia.'

Orlando frowned. 'Who's Mr Webster?'

'The man who brought us here.'

Orlando's lips curved in a smile. 'That's our daddy!'

Meg didn't contradict him, reasoning that the painkiller he'd been given had confused him. 'You gave me a terrible fright,' she said gently. 'How do you feel now?'

'All right. Why were you frightened?'

'Because you'd cut yourself so badly. There must be a broken bottle at the bottom of that pond.'

'Didn't you know I was going to be all right?'

'Not at first.'

'How strange! I keep forgetting that you can't . . . My daddy's red.'

'Red?'

'You know, his colour's red. I've never seen red before. I suppose it's because he's special. Will I be red when I grow up?'

'Yes,' she assured him, and went to fetch a nurse.

Half an hour later they were on their way home. Orlando was now far more alert and Meg decided to put his shocked ramblings out of her mind. When they drew up at the house the twins sat quite still in their seats.

'Olivia, you can get out on your own,' said Meg. 'I'll bring Orlando.'

'We want our . . . Mr Webster to come in.'

'I don't think that Mr Webster will want to waste any more time with us.'

'I'd be delighted to come inside for a moment,' he said politely.

'Are you sure?'

'Quite sure!'

Because she had gone on ahead with the children, Meg didn't see the brief smile of triumph that flickered across Ashley Webster's face as he finally stepped inside the twins' home. He had waited a long time for this moment, but the wait had been worthwhile.

Chapter 3

'What's your Ashley doing over Christmas?' asked Catriona as they sat in Meg's kitchen writing their Christmas cards.

'He isn't my Ashley, and I haven't a clue what he's doing.'

'Haven't you asked him?'

'No, and neither has he volunteered the information.'

'He never volunteers a thing, does he? Miles says he feels like an interrogator when he tries to make conversation with him.'

'Tell Miles not to bother. If Ashley wants to talk, he'll talk. Why are you in such a bad mood?'

Catriona sighed. 'Because they're letting David home for the holiday.'

'But that's lovely! Surely you didn't want him staying in hospital on Christmas Day?'

'Why not? He won't know it's Christmas; he doesn't understand anything. It's like having an overgrown baby to look after.'

'Oh, Cat, I'm ...'

'It's horrible! I know I shouldn't say this but he makes me feel ill. When he sits in that ghastly wheelchair dribbling and making those awful noises, I feel physically sick. I can't stand it, and I don't know how Miles can be so patient and caring.'

'But the hospital say he might improve. Miles is probably hoping that with a lot of attention ...'

'*Might* is the operative word. You've seen him. There's nothing there any more. He's like a blank slate.'

'But ...'

'I want him to go into a home.'

'What does Miles think about that?'

'He won't consider it. He's being totally unrealistic. He's even buying David a football kit for Christmas! A football kit when the boy can't sit up on his own! I want another child, Meg.'

'To replace David?'

'Yes! Is that so wrong? I want a baby who'll grow up. I want to hear a child round the house again; a proper child, not poor David who doesn't even realise I'm his mother.'

'You don't know that. The specialist said . . .'

'Him! He's totally useless. When you were having trouble with the twins I thought you were ridiculous contradicting the experts and saying they didn't understand. I remember telling Miles that they were bound to understand the children better than you. What a laugh! They don't understand anything, and what's worse they won't listen. "Have patience, Mrs Carson", or "Give David time, Mrs Carson", that's all they can say. I could train a parrot to repeat all that rubbish.'

'I feel dreadful about it,' confessed Meg. 'If Orlando hadn't been so stupid none of this would have happened. I only wish I could do something to make up for it.'

'I don't blame Orlando any more. David could have slipped and hit his head; it isn't as though the spade did the damage. It's just one of those things. Besides, you've had a worse tragedy this year. At least I've still got Miles.'

'It's easier when the person dies. I wouldn't have coped very well had Charles been left a cripple.'

'Sometimes I wish David was dead. That's terrible, isn't it?'

'I'm sure it's a perfectly normal reaction, but don't mention it to Miles.'

'I won't. We hardly ever talk anyway. He's so busy studying David's every movement, and then looking it up in some book he's bought to see if it's genuine progress, that he hasn't got time to talk to me.'

'I think that Ashley will be visiting his children over Christmas,' said Meg, changing the subject before Catriona began airing her ever-increasing grievances against Miles.

'I forget he's been married. What's he got, two boys?'

'A boy and a girl; the boy's ten and the girl thirteen. They live in Scotland with their mother, Helena.'

'Why did the marriage break up?'

'He's never said. His work takes up a lot of time, perhaps his wife resented that.'

'What kind of research does he do? The splitting the atom kind?'

Meg laughed. 'No! He works for a drug company and specialises in testing new products before licences are applied for.'

'Does he experiment on animals?'

'I don't really know, but that's the usual way they do these things, isn't it?'

'It is in horror films! Are you very keen on him?'

Meg hesitated. 'I don't know. He's very attractive – well, I think so – and he can be amusing, but he's rather secretive.'

'How do you mean?'

'It's hard to explain. He never discusses feelings.'

'Men don't.'

'I don't mean in depth. Ashley doesn't discuss them at all. I haven't any idea what he thinks of his children, or even why he keeps seeing me. He never tells me that he likes me. I suppose I'm meant to assume it by his presence, but sometimes I'd like to be told.'

'What about the twins?'

'They think he's the cat's pyjamas.'

'But what does he think of them?'

'He likes them. He did actually say that they were two fantastic children and a great credit to me.'

'Is it serious then?'

'Not yet, and I'm not sure that I want it to be either. I'm enjoying my independence at the moment.'

'Well, if he wants to join us all here on Christmas Day then he's very welcome, but you'd better warn him about David.'

'I'm not mentioning anything at all unless he brings the subject up.'

Three days later Ashley did just that. They'd been in to town to buy some decorations and a few last minute presents and when they returned he offered to put up the streamers. 'Are you staying here for Christmas Day?' he asked casually as Olivia hopped around beneath the ladder singing an off-key 'Hark the Herald Angels Sing'.

'No, we're going to Catriona's.'

'Is that a regular arrangement?'

'We always went when Charles was alive, but it won't be the same this year.'

'You'll miss him.' It was a flat statement.

'Yes, although that wasn't what I meant. The thing is, David will be there.'

'Who?'

'My nephew, I told you about him, he . . .'

'I hit him over the head and he went simple,' called Orlando from the kitchen doorway.

Meg spun round. 'How can you say such a thing? Really, Orlando!'

'It's true. I did hit him and now he's . . .'

'You shouldn't sound so pleased about it. You've ruined poor David's life, the very least you can do is sound apologetic.'

Orlando's face turned sullen. 'I didn't know what would happen.'

'I'm not saying you did, but most children . . .'

'I'm not most children.'

'You're certainly not!' said Ashley ironically. 'For a start you talk like a ten-year-old.'

'Do I?'

'Yes.' There was a strange hint of warning in Ashley's voice, and Orlando glanced apprehensively at Olivia. 'Hasn't anyone else commented on it?' The twins shook their heads.

'They don't mix with other children a lot,' explained Meg. 'I suppose that because they didn't talk at all for so long I've simply been grateful to hear their voices. I didn't realise they were advanced.'

'There's no law against it, but their school might get a surprise next year.'

'We won't talk the same there,' declared Olivia.

'Good idea. To get back to Christmas, I had rather hoped you'd all spend a few days with me.'

'Yes!' shouted the twins. 'We will!'

'Don't be silly,' said Meg irritably. 'You don't know anything at all about where we'll be for Christmas.'

'We do, we've seen . . .'

'I wanted to take you all to visit my mother,' said Ashley quickly. 'She lives in Scotland.'

34

'It's rather a long way,' said Meg doubtfully.

'We could travel up on Christmas Eve and come back on the 28th. That will probably be long enough.'

'But . . .'

'I'd like you to meet her, Meg. Surely you want to get to know my family? After all, I know yours.'

'That's different. Catriona and Miles live on the doorstep. I didn't take you along and make a formal introduction.'

He studied her with surprise. 'You're not anxious to meet my mother?'

'Should I be?'

'Most women would be curious, and keen to make a good impression.'

'Why should I want to make a good impression on your mother?'

'Why indeed!' He seemed amused by her attitude, amused and not at all displeased. It wasn't until he was leaving that he brought the subject up again. 'Will you come to Scotland, Meg?'

'I don't know. Poor Catriona's got David and . . .'

'You have your own life to lead. She does have a husband.'

'I know, but right now Miles doesn't see things the way she does and if I'm there I can probably keep things on an even keel.'

'It doesn't sound like much fun for the twins.'

'If Orlando hadn't hit David he'd still be a normal little boy.'

'So the twins have to endure a miserable Christmas as penance, is that it?'

'No!'

'That's how it sounds to me. Well, suit yourself, but I'm disappointed. I was looking forward to taking you all home.'

'Scotland isn't your home, you were born in Bristol.'

'If I were a romantic soul you'd cut me to the quick with your down-to-earth statements.'

'Since you're not, I take it I suit you quite well?'

Ashley moved closer to her, putting his arms round her waist so that she was looking up in to his face. 'That's right, you suit me very well indeed,' he murmured, and then he began to kiss her. By the time he finally left, her mouth felt swollen and bruised and she'd agreed to go to Scotland.

'Are we nearly there?' asked Olivia for the twentieth time.

'Only ten more minutes,' promised Ashley.

'Why hasn't your mother put up Christmas decorations?' asked Orlando.

'How do you know she hasn't?' There was silence from the back of the car.

'You'll probably find you can't get in the front door for holly and mistletoe,' laughed Meg. 'Perhaps that will teach you to keep your imagination under control.'

'Everyone looks very cold,' noted Orlando.

'It's always cold here.'

'Then it's lucky I brought my bed socks!' joked Meg.

'You'll have me to keep you warm,' whispered Ashley. She blushed. They weren't yet lovers and she hadn't imagined that a holiday at his mother's would provide the ideal setting for such intimacy.

'That's what you think,' she responded with a smile, but he didn't smile back at her.

All at once they swung into a long, winding gravel drive and came to a halt outside a vast, bleak mansion that only just missed being a castle. Meg drew in her breath in surprise.

'What did you expect? A mud hut?' queried Ashley.

'No, but you must admit this is something out of the ordinary. Come on twins, out you get.'

Suddenly Ashley caught hold of her arm. 'My mother's a little strange at times, particularly where my father's concerned. If you don't understand what she's saying just let it pass. She gets confused.'

Meg, who was beginning to wish they'd stayed at home despite David, nodded briefly. An old woman suffering from senile dementia wasn't likely to be any more stimulating company than a brain-damaged five-year-old.

Surprisingly the woman who answered their ring was quite young, certainly only in her early sixties, and extremely smart. Her suit was plain but expensive and she was carefully made up, with tinted hair that framed her face in attractive half-curls. She wasn't in the least like Ashley in appearance; there was a gentleness about her that helped Meg relax, and her eyes were a light brown with none of her son's penetrating quality in their gaze.

'I didn't think you'd really come,' she said shortly, although she smiled at the twins as she spoke. At least she began to smile at them, but when they looked up at her the smile froze and a look of shock mingled with fear crossed her face.

'Well, we did,' replied Ashley shortly. 'And this is Meg. Meg, meet my mother.' The two women shook hands. 'And these are the twins. Orlando and Olivia, meet my mother. Mother, Orlando and Olivia.'

The children politely held out their hands. Mrs Webster stared at them without moving but a muscle jumped in the side of her neck and her eyes were bewildered.

'Thanks, we will step inside. It's freezing here,' he said sarcastically. His mother continued to stare at the children. Ashley brushed past her and Meg followed, leaving the twins on the front step.

The hall was vast and cold. It smelt of beeswax polish and home-made bread. It was also virtually bare. There was only one chair and a small antique table to be seen. There were no Christmas decorations.

Eventually Ashley's mother came indoors. She murmured, 'You must call me Lily,' to Meg and then began showing them the various rooms. They were all large, but whilst they were well furnished there was an air of desolation about the entire house that depressed Meg. The lack of colour didn't help. Most rooms were a combination of browns and greens, but that wasn't all. There was nothing homely anywhere. No family atmosphere and, as Ashley had warned, it was freezing cold. In fact, Meg was amazed when she accidentally touched one of the old radiators and found it scorching hot.

'I'm afraid it isn't possible to keep the house warm,' said Lily as she began to lead them upstairs. 'It used to be, but after my husband ... The house was never the same again after he ...'

'When did he die?' asked Meg sympathetically.

'Die? Did Ashley tell you his father was dead?'

'Yes, that is ...'

'I wish to God he were,' she said bitterly and increased the speed of her steps.

'She isn't pleased to see us,' said Olivia loudly.

'Of course she is.'

'No, she's not. She's all yellow.'

'What on earth do you mean by that?'

'Yellow, like a canary.'

'It isn't polite to say that someone looks like a canary.'

'I didn't say that, I said she's yellow. The colour *yellow*!'

'Don't shout!' snapped Meg. 'And be quiet, you're talking nonsense.'

'This is your room, Mrs Marshall,' said Lily Webster, throwing open a heavy wooden door. 'I hope you'll find it comfortable.'

'I'm sure I will, and please call me Meg.'

'The children are next door. They can share your bathroom, although there's a hand basin in the corner.'

'Where am I to sleep?' asked Ashley blandly.

'In your old room, unless you wanted your father's?'

Meg was shocked by the expression of pure fury that flashed over Ashley's face. His mouth tightened and his eyes were colder than she had ever seen them. His normal pallor increased, emphasising the four o'clock shadow round his jaw.

'I wouldn't dream of using Father's room.'

'As you wish. I'll be downstairs when you've finished unpacking.' She added to a startled Meg. 'There's cold ham and salad when you're ready. I thought it best as I wasn't sure what time you were arriving.'

'Thank you,' smiled Med. 'We're very grateful.'

Orlando had wandered further along the landing and was busy pushing open another of the heavy doors. 'Ugh!' he shouted, quickly drawing his head back. 'That's a yucky room.'

'Come out at once,' ordered Meg. 'Your bedroom's here.'

'That was my father's room,' Ashley told the boy. 'Don't you like it?'

'It's very strange. I mean, it's yucky and yet it's kind of tingly. Do you know what I mean?'

Ashley's eyes glittered. 'Yes, I know very well what you mean.'

'I thought you would. It's cold in there too.'

'It's a cold house. I did warn you.'

38

'That room's got a different sort of cold in it.'

'Quite possibly.'

'Come along,' shouted Meg, who'd missed the entire conversation. 'I want to get you changed. Mrs Webster has a meal waiting.' With one final fascinated glance at the strange room the twins obediently went to get ready for tea.

'I'm starving!' announced Olivia, beginning to run down the stairs ahead of everyone else. Just as her foot touched the bottom step she halted, gazing at the hall floor in terror. Meg, walking immediately behind, accidentally bumped into her immobile daughter.

'You could have broken my neck stopping like that! Hurry up, you're the one who's starving.'

Olivia shook her head and opened her mouth but all that came out was a peculiar gurgling sound. Meg pushed past her, closely followed by Ashley and Orlando. Ashley was the first to turn and look at Olivia and he quickly moved in front of her, preventing Meg from witnessing the petrified expression on her daughter's face.

'It isn't there!' he whispered urgently. 'You're seeing things. Keep walking. There's nothing to stop you.'

'But she's ... You and Mummy just walked ...'

'*There's nothing there. For God's sake keep moving or you'll ruin everything*!'

Startled by the intensity in his voice she looked him full in the face and at once realisation dawned and relief flooded over her. 'Sorry!' she said gaily. 'I got mixed up. I thought it was now.'

'What's going on?' asked Meg, holding out a hand to her daughter.

'Nothing. I made a mistake. What's for tea?'

The cold meal was served by a middle-aged woman in an old-fashioned pinafore which fascinated Olivia. As they ate, Mrs Webster kept up a running list of questions. They disconcerted Meg since they were all deeply personal onces concerning her marriage to Charles.

'I don't suppose you want to re-marry,' she remarked to the younger woman. 'Men are nothing but trouble. After the things Ashley's father did it was impossible for me to become a normal part of the community again. Naturally they've never wanted me – I can quite appreciate that – but why should I be driven away? It wasn't my fault. I've become resigned to living the life of a hermit but I resent it. I bitterly resent it.' Her face twitched with annoyance.

Meg glanced at Ashley. He'd never said much about his father except that he'd died when he was a young boy. She wondered what crimes he could have committed that accounted for his widow spending forty years segregated from society while his son denied his very existence.

'I don't like you,' said Olivia suddenly, her light eyes staring challengingly at the older woman. 'I think you're horrid.'

'Olivia! I'm so sorry, Mrs Webster, I . . .'

'Please don't apologise. I don't like your daughter very much either. She reminds me too much of . . .'

'Is there a dessert?' demanded Ashley.

'Naturally. What was I saying?'

'That Olivia reminded you of someone,' said Meg helpfully.

'Yes, but it's quite ridiculous. How could she possibly be like . . . At my age all children look alike.'

Not true, thought Meg. She's changed her mind about telling me, that's all. And she wondered who the unknown person was and why she couldn't be told about them.

'Has Ashley talked much about his father?' the older woman continued. The twins glanced at her son and saw his eyes narrow.

'No, but then he can't remember him very well. He was only about two when he . . .'

'Ashley was exactly six months old when he last saw Robert.'

'Well, that explains it. What could he have to tell?'

'A great deal. I'll enlighten you tomorrow, after you're rested.' She shot a malicious glance at her son who continued to eat his ice cream and entirely ignored her. 'He's like him,' she went on. 'Not in looks, but in character he's exactly the same. A cold fish. Haven't you found that? There's no warmth in my son, Meg.'

And no kindness in you, thought Meg. She pitied Ashley his childhood. It wasn't surprising that he wasn't demonstrative, but she would teach him in time.

'You must meet Helena, his ex-wife. I've told her you're

40

here. She's very anxious to see you. I doubt if she'll bring my grandchildren. They don't care for their father.'

Meg winced and glanced at Ashley, but his face was quite expressionless.

'I like him,' said Olivia loudly.

'He isn't your father.'

'Yes, he is.'

'Darling, don't be silly,' said Meg gently. 'Just because he lets you call him Daddy that doesn't mean he's really your father. Your father's dead. You know that.'

'Ashley's my daddy,' said Olivia stubbornly.

Lily Webster gave the child a curious stare, and as the evening progressed she glanced more and more frequently at the twins. Finally it was time for them to be put to bed and Ashley insisted on going upstairs to help.

'Nasty old bat, isn't she?' he said pleasantly. Orlando laughed.

'She certainly isn't a doting mama! Why's she so bitter about your father?' Meg asked.

'I told you, she's a bit peculiar in that respect.'

'She seems sane enough. Why did you say he was dead?'

'When will she really – ?' began Olivia.

'Have you brought your bedtime book?' interrupted Ashley. 'If so I'll read you a chapter. Meg, why don't you go down and keep Mother company? I'm sure she's dying to get you on your own. You might as well hear the worst. I don't intend to come here again.'

'You didn't have to come here at all.'

He gave a slightly unpleasant smile. 'But I did. I wanted her to see the twins.'

'And I thought the visit was for my benefit!'

'Your's too, of course. I mean, the three of you make up the package. I can't have the children on their own, can I?' He laughed but Meg felt uneasy.

'How long have you known my son?' demanded Lily the moment Meg entered the room.

'Not long. Just over eight months.'

'You'd never met him before that?'

'No.'

41

'Extraordinary.'

'What's extraordinary about it?'

'Your daughter looks exactly like Ashley's father.'

It was at that moment that the suspicion first took root in Meg's mind, a suspicion that would gradually increase and intrude more and more into her daily life, but Lily Webster had no way of knowing this for the younger woman was careful not to react before her.

'Well?' demanded Lily as the silence continued.

Meg shrugged. 'I don't think there's anything I can say, except that it seems an amazing coincidence. I take it your husband was fair-haired?'

'Naturally, but it's the eyes that are identical.'

'You mean he had strange eyes as well?'

'How right you are to call them strange! When I first met him I found them attractive, but they're not really, are they? They're almost lifeless.'

'Orlando's are the same.'

'True, but he lacks your daughter's essential coldness of spirit.'

'I hardly think that Olivia . . .'

'Is she an affectionate child?'

'I suppose not. She and Orlando have both had problems with communication, but they're much better now.'

'What a lovely expression! When Ashley was young he was labelled anti-social. I don't suppose your children are any different, but a rose by any other name.'

Meg was becoming annoyed. 'I thought it was your husband the twins reminded you of, not Ashley.'

'My grandchildren take after their mother, thank heavens! They're nice, affectionate children and I think Helena is very happy with her life these days.'

'That's nice,' said Meg feebly, and was highly relieved when Ashley entered the room.

'What are you talking about? Anything interesting?'

'Your father.' Lily Webster's voice was malicious. Ashley stood perfectly still, his eyes flicking from one woman to the other. 'And you,' she added.

'How boring. Haven't you got your whisky out yet?'

'I was waiting for you to join us.'

'I'm here now.'

'Then get the bottle. I can't understand it, you know.'

'Understand what?'

'The resemblance between Olivia and your father.'

His hand looked perfectly steady as he poured the drinks but his body was rigid with tension. However, he kept his voice even and calm. 'Meg and I have only just met so unless her husband was born on the wrong side of the family blanket any resemblance is purely coincidental, as they say at the start of all the best stories.'

The atmosphere in the room became increasingly awkward and Meg drank her whisky as quickly as she could before excusing herself on the grounds that the journey had exhausted her.

Ashley said that he'd probably go to bed as well, but his mother poured herself another drink, seemingly distracted by her thoughts. She scarcely acknowledged Meg's goodnight and looked considerably older than when they'd arrived.

Meg had expected to fall asleep at once but the strange room with its high ceiling and long, heavily curtained windows felt alien and she tossed and turned in increasing discomfort. Her travelling clock showed two-thirty a.m. when she heard her door open and Ashley tiptoed gently in.

'Not asleep?'

'No, and I really am tired. I wasn't making excuses.'

'Perhaps you're cold. Shall I try and warm you up?'

Meg didn't know whether he was serious or not. Until their journey to Scotland he had never given any indication of wishing to make love to her, yet now – under the worst possible circumstances – he suddenly seemed keen. 'What about your mother?' she asked hesitantly.

'I don't think she'd want to do it!'

'I meant . . .'

'I know what you meant.'

'Ashley, I'd rather wait.'

'Why?'

'Well, the children are next door and your mother's around. I'd never be able to relax.'

'Vociferous in your pleasure, are you?'

'Don't make fun of me. Surely you can see that now isn't exactly the best possible moment.'

43

'I'm afraid I can't. Don't you want me to make love to you?'

'Of course I do, only not here.'

'Then we'll use my father's room.' By the light of the bedside lamp his eyes seemed to gleam with amusement at the thought.

'Ashley, please.'

As soon as the pleading note entered her voice he lost interest. His eyes were cool again and he looked at her with a marked absence of desire. 'You women are all alike. I suppose next time you'll have a headache.'

It was such an unfair remark that she couldn't believe she'd heard him right. 'If you're equally insensitive the next time then yes, I most definitely will have a headache. Goodnight, and please close the door quietly.'

His face lightened. 'That's more like it! Helena was so unspeakably feeble our life was no fun at all. Of course you're right. We'll wait until we're back south, or even until we're married if that's what you want. At least you look warmer now. Your cheeks are quite flushed!'

'Married?'

'What did you expect? That we were going to live in sin?'

'I don't know if I want to marry you!' she said incredulously. 'You've never seemed . . . I didn't imagine you felt that deeply about me.'

'I'm afraid I'm not too good at putting my feelings across, as I'm sure my mother will tell you, if she hasn't already. You'd better let me know whether you do want to marry me or not. Take your time. I don't suppose you want to make another mistake.'

'Who said anything about Charles being a mistake?'

'You mean you were blissfully happy with him?'

'No.'

'Quite! Goodnight again.' This time he did leave, closing the door quietly behind him.

Meg felt so stunned and strung up that she was quite sure she wouldn't close her eyes at all, but suddenly it was eight o'clock and the twins were hammering on her door demanding to be allowed into her bed.

'I'm hungry, Mummy,' said Olivia. 'Can we go downstairs?'

44

'Not until I'm dressed, then we'll go together. I'm not sure what time Ashley's mother gets up.'

'I'll peep over the banisters and listen. She might be making porridge with salt. That's what Daddy says they eat in Scotland.'

'He *isn't* your father!' Meg shouted, but Olivia had gone leaving Orlando standing in the doorway uncertain whether to follow his twin or talk to his mother. He decided to stay where he was.

'Why do you keep saying Ashley isn't our daddy?'

'Because he isn't. Your daddy fell off a ladder and died.'

'That was only Charles.'

'He was your father.'

'Will you swear?' demanded Orlando. 'Will you put your hand on a bible and swear that Charles was really our daddy? That it was his seed which . . .'

'Orlando!'

'What?'

'Nothing really. I'm just surprised you know so much about making babies.'

'Will you swear?'

Meg stared into the peculiar opaque eyes of her son and the lie died on her lips. 'No,' she whispered at last. 'I won't swear.' The boy looked gravely at her. 'It's too silly,' she added. 'I'm your mother and . . .'

'You won't swear in case God strikes you dead.'

'There are some things that you're too young to understand.'

'Mummy!' screamed Olivia, hurtling back into the room. 'Mrs Webster's asleep at the bottom of the stairs.'

'She's what?'

'Sleeping in the hall, but her face is all funny – like this.' She twisted her mouth up, stuck out her tongue and opened her eyes until they were wide and staring.

'Stop it!'

'That's what she looks like. I'm good at faces,' she added modestly.

Alerted by Olivia's shout, Ashley passed the bedroom door. 'Stay there!' he snapped. Meg assumed he was referring to the children and followed him to the top of the stairs. Even from there it was obvious that she was dead. Her head was twisted at an unnatural angle and her tongue was sticking out just as Olivia had demonstrated.

Ashley quickly went and touched his mother's forehead. 'She's stone cold. Must have been dead for hours. I could have stayed with you last night: she wouldn't have heard a thing!'

'How can you joke at a time like this?'

'I wasn't making a joke. She reeks of whisky. I suppose she tripped over that damned rug. I warned her about polishing the floor underneath it but she was fanatically houseproud. Much good it did her. I'd better go and phone for the police.'

Suddenly Olivia tapped her mother lightly on the shoulder. Meg nearly jumped out of her skin. 'What are you doing here? Get back in the bedroom.'

'Is she dead.'

'I'm afraid so.'

'Good. She was horrible.'

'Don't talk like that. She wasn't in the least horrible. She made us very welcome, and besides, when people die you don't ...'

'She was only an old woman, Mummy.'

Meg stared at her daughter who looked blandly back at her. 'I'll forget you said that, Olivia. Obviously after a nasty shock like this ...'

'I didn't have a shock,' said Olivia scornfully. 'Yesterday evening I did, but not today. You can't be shocked by the same thing twice.'

Meg was still trying to make sense of that remark when the local police arrived.

Late in the afternoon, while Ashley was at the undertaker's, Helena Webster came to call. She came alone, leaving her children with a neighbour. She also came with a purpose. 'My mother-in-law wanted me to talk to you,' she said as she walked in to the house. 'Now that she's dead I feel doubly responsible.'

'Responsible for what?' asked Meg, leading the short, rather washed-out woman in to the living-room.

'Warning you.'

'What about?'

'Ashley.'

Meg noticed that Helena's hands were never still. They were constantly interlacing one with the other or rubbing together. 'I can't imagine what you need to warn me about concerning Ashley.'

'Don't marry him!' Helena blurted out. 'Once you're married it's too late. He changes. When we were courting he was very nice. So kind and thoughtful, really almost gentle. I couldn't believe what followed.'

'How do you mean?'

Helena stepped closer. 'I don't know how to say this but he was ... the physical side of marriage became ... It wasn't nice,' she concluded firmly. 'It wasn't nice at all. Of course I knew all about his father, but I never thought ...'

'Who are you?' asked Orlando rudely, pushing his way in to the room. Helena stared at him with a mixture of shock and terror.

'This is Mrs Webster,' explained Meg. 'She used to be married to Ashley.'

'Poor Daddy! She's pale pink. That means she's ...'

'Be quiet! Go and play somewhere else. Mrs Webster wants to talk to me.'

He scowled at the woman who was still regarding him with a kind of hypnotised fascination. 'Go away!' he shouted as he left the room. 'We don't want you here.'

'I'm sorry,' apologised Meg. 'I can't think what came over him.'

'Who is he?' whispered Helena. 'I've never seen him before. I've seen others of course, but not that one.'

'Others? What others? Orlando is my son.'

'Your son?'

'Yes, and he has a twin sister, Olivia.'

Helena's face changed dramatically. All the concern and sympathy vanished and now she was looking at Meg with thinly disguised contempt. 'I've wasted my time,' she said flatly. 'You shouldn't have let me keep talking. You obviously know all there is to know about my ex-husband. Presumably you're the same type and it doesn't worry you.'

'Type of what?'

'How long have you been his mistress?'

Meg's temper flared. 'I don't know why you think you've

got the right to come here insulting me but you might be interested to learn that I am not Ashley's mistress, and furthermore I never will be.'

'How did you have the twins? By immaculate conception?'

'I'm a widow. The twins' father died last summer.'

Helena shook her head. 'That can't be true. The twins are his, they must be!'

'I hadn't met Ashley when the twins were born.' At least that was true, thought Meg with relief, but her mind was in a turmoil.

'Go into the village,' murmured Helena, starting to move nervously towards the door. 'Find the Farris family and take a look at their oldest boy. Promise me you'll at least do that.'

'Why?'

'I don't understand what's happened, but I'm beginning to believe that you're not a willing part of it. If you go there at least you'll . . .'

'*Go away!*' shouted Olivia, bursting in to the room. 'Leave my mummy alone.'

Helena's eyes were nearly starting out of her head with terror. 'It isn't possible! She's exactly like . . .'

'You're going to die soon,' continued the little girl. 'Your silly car will be squashed and they'll have to scrape you off the road. Then they'll put all the pieces in a plastic bag and put the bag in a coffin because that's all that will be left of you. And then your children will come to live with us and they'll hate it! They'll cry every night.'

'Get out!' ordered Meg. 'Wait in your room until Ashley gets back.'

'I've finished now,' retorted Olivia sweetly, and without another word she walked gracefully from the room.

'Mrs Webster, I must apologise. I don't know what's got into the children today.'

'Don't take my children to live with you,' begged Helena, her eyes filling with tears. 'They're petrified of their father. They wouldn't be able to cope. Please, as a mother yourself you must understand.'

'But nothing's going to happen to you,' laughed Meg. 'Olivia was simply being horrible.'

'You really don't understand a thing do you?'

'Apparently not, but I'm prepared to listen.'

'I'm home,' called Ashley, striding into the room with a smile on his lips. It died the moment he saw Helena, to be replaced by a look of withering hatred that shook Meg to the core. His ex-wife averted her eyes.

'I only came to offer my sympathy,' she murmured. 'I'll miss her.'

'I'm sure you will. All those hours of malicious gossip gone forever. You might as well move away. After all, what is there for you here now that she's dead?'

'I belong here,' she said fiercely. 'I was born in this village.'

'That's right, and here you'll doubtless die as well.'

With a strangled sob Helena brushed past him and dashed out of the house, leaving the front door open behind her.

'What did she really want?' he demanded.

'I think she just needed someone to talk to.'

'About what?'

'You, mainly.'

'If I want a testimonial I shan't call on her. She's a frigid little troublemaker. Marrying her was the biggest mistake of my life.'

'Why *did* you marry her?'

'There weren't many girls round here who wanted me.'

'I don't believe you!'

'It's true. Where are the twins?'

'Upstairs, and I want you to talk to Olivia. She behaved abominably to Helena.'

'In that case she deserves a medal!'

'Ashley, it isn't funny.'

'All right, I'll go up and have a word.'

'I thought I might go out for a breath of air.' Meg tried to sound casual.

'Wrap up well, it's freezing cold.'

'I will. What's happening about the funeral?'

'It's dependent upon the post mortem. We needn't stay, I'll come back alone. Funerals are something to be avoided wherever possible. You didn't really know her, did you?'

'I'd like to be here, if only to support you.'

'I don't need any support. I've only got to sing the hymns, not carry the coffin single-handed.'

'I'm going for that walk,' said Meg coldly, and Ashley knew that he'd said the wrong thing. He so often forgot the way ordinary people felt about death, about most things in fact. When it came to emotions he was really working in the dark.

It was only a short walk to the village but despite the cold, Meg took her time. She needed a period of solitude while she tried to make sense of Helena Webster's warnings. She also needed to locate the Farris family. She had no idea how to make contact but she would because she had fears of her own, fears that Helena's visit had merely increased.

At the crossroads she saw a telephone box, but when she opened the door the directory was missing. Slowly she wandered along the path and was so lost in thought that she didn't even see the lad running towards here until they collided and half-fell to the pavement.

'I'm sorry!' exclaimed Meg.

'My head was down,' explained the boy. 'I was pretending to be a transformer and didn't notice you were there.'

Surprised by the lack of a Scottish accent Meg quickly looked the boy in the face, and as a pair of pale blue eyes with filmy-white irises stared back at her she fervently wished that she hadn't. The boy didn't seem surprised by her surveillance; she knew that with eyes like that he was probably used to it. He couldn't realise that she was staring not because he was different but because he was horribly familiar.

'Are you all right?' he asked as she continued staring.

'Yes, thank you. Your face is familiar. Have we met before?'

He shook his head. 'No. My name's Tim Farris. What's yours?'

'Mrs Marshall, I'm staying with Mrs Webster.'

He raised his eyebrows as he absentmindedly rubbed at his skinned knees. 'I though she was dead.'

'She is, but I was staying with her.'

'My mother said she'd died.'

'Yes, it's very sad.'

'Why? She was only an old woman,' and he gave her a reassuring smile. Memories of Olivia's identical comment flooded back. She wondered if she was going out of her mind, or simply dreaming. She hoped it was a dream. 'Mr Webster's my father,' continued Tim.

'Did your mother tell you that?'

'No, she says that Michael's my father, but he isn't. I know he isn't. He knows he isn't too. He doesn't like me much either.'

'What to you mean by either?'

'I mean that I don't like him, which makes us quits. In fact, I hate him.'

'How old are you, Tim?'

'Eleven. Have you met the other Mrs Webster?'

'I've met Helena if that's who you mean,' she said as she began to stand up and brush the mud off her coat.

'She's pretty feeble, isn't she! He was right to leave her. One of my half-sisters is pretty feeble. I might kill her, I'm not sure yet.'

Meg decided that the boy was trying to shock her and refused to rise to the bait. 'Rather a waste of your life if you do,' she said with a smile.

The smile obviously surprised him. 'A waste of *my* life?'

'Why, yes. They'd lock you up forever.'

'Only if they caught me.'

There was a short silence and before Meg could say any more a car horn hooted loudly and there, right beside the pavement, was Ashley's car with him at the wheel. He rolled down the passenger window. 'Get in!'

'I'm not hurt, I . . .'

'I said get in, damn you!'

She wrenched open the passenger door. 'Don't you talk to me like that! What's the matter? I told you I was going for a walk.'

'You were snooping around, weren't you? Snooping around the village trying to find the Farris boy.'

'We bumped into one another.'

'But you were looking for him?'

'Yes.'

'Trust Helena. She's a spiteful little bitch!'

'He's your son, isn't he?'

Ashley shrugged. 'He might be, but on the other hand he might not. His mother wasn't too fussy.'

51

'He says he's your son.'

'The twins say they're mine too. Do you believe them all? Or just the ones it suits you to believe?'

'Why should it suit me to believe Tim Farris?'

'Because it gives you a nice get-out from our relationship. A bastard in the same village as my legitimate children. It's hardly acceptable behaviour, is it?'

'He has the same eyes as the twins.'

'Perhaps it was Charles who misbehaved!'

Meg put out a hand and laid it on his arm. 'You know perfectly well that Charles didn't father the twins, don't you?'

'I must admit it seems probable that he didn't.'

'He preferred men,' she said abruptly.

'To children?'

'To women. I came home early one day and found him in bed with the gardener's son. Until then I'd blamed myself for our pathetic sex life. I thought I wasn't sophisticated enough for him, that I was too inhibited.'

'What happened after that?' he asked quietly, steering the car into a lay-by.

'I told him the marriage was over, but he begged me not to divorce him. He said that a solicitor in his position couldn't afford the scandal.'

'Rather late to think of that.'

'He cried and grovelled at my feet. It was horrible. Finally I gave in, but there was a price: children, and not by him. I didn't want them tainted or flawed.'

'So?'

'So we went to London, paid an exorbitant fee and I became pregnant by artificial insemination, donor unknown.'

'I'm surprised you qualified for the treatment. Physically you were both capable of having children.'

'The specialist was an American running a private clinic. He only took cases who would otherwise have been turned down. He wasn't bothered by the ethics of it all. Your money was your entrance ticket.'

'Did Charles mind?'

'Not at first. After all, marriage was good for his image. And twins as well, that was a bonus. No, he was content until they began to grow up, then the dislike became mutual. It was as though they knew right from the start that he wasn't their father. I know that's impossible but it's how it looked.'

'And?' His voice was soft.

'And what?'

'Don't be evasive, Meg, it's out of character. You think that I'm the biological father, don't you?'

'Is it possible?' she asked, relieved to have it out in the open.

'Highly probable. I thought it was a good idea, a chance for medical science to actually make people happier, more fulfilled. I was an idealist, I suppose. Besides, being in the medical business gives you easy entry into that sort of thing.'

'You did it out of the kindness of your heart?'

Ashley turned and smiled at her. It was a good smile, one of his best, but it still didn't quite reach his eyes. 'Why else?' he asked with a light laugh.

'I don't know, but somehow it frightens me.'

'What does?'

'The fact that you and I have met up. Surely the chances of that happening are pretty remote?'

'Infinitesimal.'

'You didn't know about the twins?'

'Of course not. Even American doctors don't give away that sort of information. Not if they intend to stay in business.'

'I want to go home,' said Meg slowly. 'I won't stay for the funeral.'

Ashley nodded and drove her back to the house. He knew that she would come round on her own, providing he gave her time. Things were working out very well.

Chapter 4

'Why isn't Daddy with us?' asked Olivia as they settled down to sleep in their own bedroom again. 'Hasn't Mummy married him yet?'

'Of course not, stupid! She doesn't want to see him at all for a month. I heard her telling him.'

'Why?'

'Because she's found out that he *is* our father.'

'You'd think she'd be pleased. It means we'll be a proper family at last.'

'I think she's afraid he's not really interested in her.'

'Well, he isn't!'

'We know that, but he doesn't want her to find out. It will be O.K. I've seen the wedding.'

'Why haven't I seen it?' demanded Olivia.

'Because your head's full of rubbish ever since we went to Scotland.'

She pouted and threw her pillow at Orlando. 'It isn't rubbish! I *did* see a man in that cold room. He was sort of faint and he didn't have a colour, but I saw him. He kept standing by the bed and looking down on the woman who was sleeping there.'

'Why?'

'I don't know. He didn't talk. I think he was happy because once or twice he smiled, and he gave a sort of shivery tremble now and again, the sort you give when you feel good.'

'Did the woman have a colour?'

'I think it was pink. There was so much blood on her that I could have got mixed up; perhaps it was really white!'

'Blood? I wish I'd seen that. I love blood.'

'So did the man in the cold room.'

'I took a knife from one of the drawers in Daddy's house. That will be very useful and it wasn't stealing because I know Daddy would have let me have it if I'd asked.'

'Let's use it tomorrow,' suggested Olivia eagerly. 'It's dull without Daddy. We could have a bit of fun with the knife to cheer us up.'

'All right. Now let's go to sleep.'

After ten minutes Olivia spoke again. 'When are we going to meet Boy Blue?'

'Soon.'

'Good! I'm so glad there are lots of us. Are you glad, Orlando?'

'I don't much care. I expect I'll be glad one day, when I'm grown up and need people to talk to.'

'Daddy hasn't got anyone to talk to.'

'That's why he's made sure there are several of us. Now go to sleep.' This time Olivia obeyed him.

The next morning, Meg felt in a bad temper. She was tired from all the travelling, the house was cold and neglected and she couldn't stop thinking about Ashley's true relationship to the twins. She supposed that she should have been pleased; after all they were far better behaved now and she would never have to worry about the wicked stepfather syndrome. If only she didn't have the feeling that it was the children he really wanted and that she — as he himself had once put it — was simply a necessary part of the package.

Then there were Helena's comments about Ashley's legitimate children. Why should one set of children be frightened of him when he was highly popular with others? And what had she meant about his behaviour after their wedding? What had he done to alienate himself from both wife and children? And why should the twins and the Farris boy have strange eyes when, on his mother's admission, his children by Helena looked like her and had completely missed the family trait that their father usually passed on?

But most important of all, as she kept reminding herself, was the question of whether or not she wanted to marry him at all. She didn't think that she did. He attracted her for all the wrong reasons. His cool self-possession was a challenge. She wanted to be closer to him, to see him laugh more and hear his private thoughts, not out of love but out of vanity. She wanted to prove that he needed her because then she'd feel more confident as a woman. After Charles that would make a pleasant change, and she was sensible enough to understand the psychology of her thinking.

No, she was quite certain that she didn't love Ashley and that alone was sufficient reason to refuse marriage. It was just a pity that the twins would be deprived of his company — unless he was willing to let things stay as they were. Then he'd have the children, if it was them he wanted, and not be tied to the mother. It seemed a reasonable compromise.

'Mummy,' said Olivia cajolingly and Meg knew what was coming, 'can we go the park now?'

'Darling, it's Christmas time, the park will be crowded and you know how much you hate having the big children round you.'

'We'll be all right together. *Please*, Mummy. It's so lonely without Daddy.'

Meg's heart sank. 'Very well, I'll ring Aunty Catriona when we get back. She doesn't know we're home but I'm sure she'd like to have us there tomorrow.'

The twins stared blankly at her. It was as though they'd suddenly been struck deaf but Meg knew that it was really because they didn't want to go. Well, she wanted someone to talk to, and they both liked Miles. Or had done, before Ashley arrived on the scene.

It was such a damp day that there were far fewer people in the park than Meg had anticipated. The twins ran off at once to the swings and slides. To her surprise they quickly got friendly with a little girl about Olivia's age who was soon laughing at Orlando's jokes and even holding Olivia's hand. Perhaps they would fit in all right at school, thought Meg with relief as she pushed her hands deep into her pockets and started strolling round the perimeter of the grass.

Orlando and Olivia watched her walk away and then nodded to each other. 'Can you play tig, Beverley?' asked Olivia.

Their new friend nodded. 'Yes, and I'm very quick too.'

'I'll be "it",' announced Orlando. 'I'll count to fifty, then I'll run after you.'

'That's a big number,' said Beverley in surprise.

'Come on!' urged Olivia. 'Let's go to the trees.'

The little girl hesitated. 'I'm not allowed in the trees. I promised Mummy I'd stay here until she got back.'

'I'm with you,' scoffed Olivia. 'Are you a cowardy-custard?'

'No!'

'One . . .' began Orlando.

'Come on!' repeated Olivia, and hand-in-hand they began to run. At that moment Meg glanced towards the play area and saw Orlando waving at her. There were two girls on the swings who she took to be Olivia and friend and so she continued on her walk. It was far too cold just to sit on a bench watching them play.

When they reached the trees Beverley tried to pull back. 'There might be a bad man in there,' she whined. 'I want to go back.'

'We'll hide here, behind this big tree. You are soppy. A soppy spoilsport!'

'I'm not.'

'Come on then, or we won't be your friends any more.'

Poor little Beverley didn't have many friends and she reluctantly followed this vivacious white-haired child deeper into the trees. Together they huddled behind a large oak tree and waited for Orlando to come after them.

He wasn't long. Olivia furtively flapped a hand round the trunk so that he knew where they were, and then he crept up on them from the other side and jumped in front of Beverley.

'Boo!' he shouted. She screamed in terror.

'It's only a game!' he said contemptuously.

'I want to go back to the swings.'

'Show me something first,' he demanded.

'What?'

He told her.

'No! I'm not allowed to. My Mummy says it's rude.'

Orlando slipped a hand into his pocket and carefully drew out the knife. 'If you don't I'll cut your throat.' Beverley began to cry.

Orlando felt a delicious sense of power building up in him. Beverley was all pink and feeble, like Helena. She wouldn't be any loss at all, but she could make him feel good. Really good, probably better than he'd ever felt before. Knowing this he smiled at her. 'Cry if you like,' he said pleasantly, 'it might make things better.'

Olivia glanced across the park and saw that their mother had reached the half-way point. 'Hurry up!' she hissed, and grabbed at Beverley's left wrist as the little girl tried to run away.

Orlando wished that he had more time. More time to watch the tears and the terror on his victim's face, but he knew that his sister was right and so he quickly put out his right hand and carefully slit Beverley's throat from ear to ear.

For one blissful moment he was able to study her terrified and disbelieving expression until she fell with a terrible gurgling sound to the cold, damp ground and the blood flowed slowly out from beneath her.

'Come on,' urged Olivia. 'We've got to get back.'

Orlando stayed where he was, hugging the warmth and the tingling to himself, shivering all over from sheer ecstasy. It had been so good, so incredibly good.

'Quick!' Olivia was almost screaming at him.

'What about the knife?'

'Keep it, they won't come looking at our house.'

'They might,' he said as they ran off together. 'Later on they might.'

'Then hide it in the attic. They won't look there. We're only children.'

As Meg reached the play area she was relieved to find the twins still on the slide, although their friend didn't seem to be around. 'All right?' she called. 'Had enough yet?'

'Nearly, one more go on the swings.'

'Only one, I need a cup of tea! Where's the other little girl?'

'She went off home. She said her Mummy must have forgotten her.'

Meg hoped that the child had got home safely. These days children weren't safe anywhere alone. It wasn't until they were eating their lunch that the police sirens began, and by then the knife was safely in the attic.

The next morning Meg opened the door and found herself facing a policeman on routine house-to-house enquiries. As soon as she saw the photograph she knew that it was the girl the twins had played with and, thanking God that her own two were safe, she invited the policeman into the house.

On the very day that Beverley Adams' mutilated body was found in the woods a tall, handsome man sat behind a large oak desk and carefully studied the couple opposite him. 'You do understand,' he said firmly, 'that I can't guarantee anything?'

The woman nodded.

'And it's expensive,' he added.

'We've got the money.' The man was truculent, on the defensive, but then men in his situation usually were and the man behind the desk gave a cool professional smile. 'We were told by Mrs ...'

'No names!' he interrupted harshly.

'I'm sorry, I forgot. We were told that provided we had the money our ages didn't matter. Is that right? Are we suitable?'

He studied her closely. She was above average height, slim, thirty-five years old and highly intelligent. Yes, she was eminently suitable for what he had in mind, although he didn't know why it worked so well on women of this type. Her husband, fast approaching sixty, wasn't of any importance at all. Not in this clinic. 'It would appear so,' he assured her.

'How soon could it be done?'

'Within the next couple of months. I don't foresee any problems, but of course one can never be sure. I think you should study this form carefully before you sign it. It's really a kind of insurance — for me!' and he gave another smile.

The man looked suspiciously at the piece of paper and read it closely. 'This lets you out completely! Whatever happens — success, failure, complications, additional medical care — you're not responsible for a bloody thing.'

'Quite, but there is the fact that in my clinic no questions are asked. Your background is not investigated. Your previous ...'

'What are you suggesting?'

'Be quiet, Hugh!' His wife shot a placatory glance at the

59

man behind the desk, the all powerful man who could give her what she most desired. She didn't want Hugh ruining it with one of his outbursts of temper. 'We knew all about this,' she reminded him.

'It's a bloody sight more one-sided than I'd expected.' Hugh was not easily appeased.

'We wouldn't be here if it weren't for you!' cried the woman in anguish. Immediately Hugh turned brick-red and fell silent.

'Suit yourself,' he muttered. 'Go ahead if that's what you want. At least we'll get some peace at the end of it.'

Only when they'd both signed the form did the man behind the desk permit himself to congratulate the woman, his smile more personal this time, as indeed it should have been considering the amount of money she and her husband would be paying him over the coming months.

'One final point,' he said politely. 'You are going back to Wales to live after the child's born? I remember you telling me that when we first met, but I realise that a businessman's plans can change.'

'We'll be living in Swansea,' confirmed the husband.

'Marvellous!'

'What's so marvellous about Swansea?' demanded Hugh belligerently. The man ignored him and took out his diary. Between them he and the woman made two appointments and then they parted.

Once he had the room to himself the man went to a large filing cabinet and rifled through the folders. At last he found the one he wanted and took it back to his desk. He hadn't been able to use it for some time but this couple were highly suitable. Smiling with pleasure, he opened the folder.

Inside, stuck to the front cover, there was a large colour photograph of Ashley Webster.

'Why didn't you stay with Ashley and help arrange the funeral?' asked Catriona. She and Meg were alone in the kitchen preparing vegetables, the first moment they'd had to themselves all day.

'He didn't want me there.'

'*I'd* have stayed whatever he said. He was probably only trying to spare your feelings.'

60

'I think I know Ashley rather better than you do, Catriona. When he says something he means it.'

'Are you going to marry him?'

Meg wished that her sister wasn't taking such an interest in everything. She'd come here to escape her own thoughts and ended up being cross-examined in exactly the same way she quizzed herself when alone. 'I've no idea. Why are you so concerned?'

Catriona shrugged. 'It makes a change from cleaning David up, or listening to Miles rabbiting on about the amazing recoveries that have been documented over the past fifty years.'

'Recoveries?'

'From brain damage.'

'He's bound to hope.'

'Why? I don't. I've come to terms with it, but not Miles. Oh no! Miles is convinced that one day David will be the same as other children again, and nothing anyone says to him makes any difference.'

'How does he feel about another child?'

'Dead against, and since he never comes near me any more it would be even more of a miracle than David's recovery.'

'Give him time' urged Meg. 'He'll come round in the end.'

'No, he won't. He's like a lot of easy-going people – incredibly obstinate. I'll tell you one thing, if I were in your shoes I'd marry Ashley like a shot. I think he's very sexy!'

'Do you?'

'Yes. He's got that ultra-cool, controlled personality which conceals a fantastically passionate nature.'

'You read the wrong books!' laughed Meg.

'I read the right ones. Take a look at his mouth. That's a dead give-away.'

'I'd no idea you were such an expert on sex-appeal.'

Catriona put the potatoes in to roast and when she straightened up from the oven her face was flushed. 'Have you slept with him yet?'

'No.'

'More fool you! Surely you're not still celibate in memory of Charles?'

'I think it's *because* of Charles, not out of respect for him.'

'What do you mean by that?'

'Well . . .'

'Catriona!' shouted Miles from the living-room. 'David's been sick.' Catriona clenched her hands until the knuckles turned white. 'I told him not to keep shovelling mince pies down David's throat, but would he listen? No! God, what a bloody awful Christmas.'

When Miles finally ran Meg and the twins home she was highly relieved to get away. The atmosphere hadn't been in the least relaxing, and every time David grunted or rolled his eyes Meg remembered that but for Orlando her nephew would be having a normal Christmas and poor Catriona's life would be happy and fulfilled, just as it used to be before the accident.

'That was yucky!' exclaimed Olivia, throwing her scarf and gloves on to the hall floor.

'Really gross!' agreed Orlando.

'Don't talk like that,' snapped Meg. 'David can't help the way he is.'

'They don't have to keep him on show,' complained Olivia, wrinkling her nose in distaste. 'I mean, how can anyone eat with him slurping and dribbling in the same room? He ought to be put down.'

'You mean put away,' corrected Meg. 'Dogs are put down.'

The twins stared at her for a moment, glanced at each other and tried to surpress their giggles.

'What's so funny? Have I amused you?'

'Yes! When's Daddy coming to see us?'

'How did I amuse you?'

'You though we didn't know about dogs!'

'But . . .'

'We thought,' explained Olivia sweetly, 'that it would be kinder for everyone if David could be put down as well.'

'Like a dog?'

'Yes.'

'You're positively revolting! Go and get ready for bed.'

'When *is* Daddy coming?'

'Ashley will come and see us when he's finished in Scotland. And stop calling him "Daddy".'

'He *is* our daddy. You were wrong making us call Charles our daddy. We're right this time.'

62

Meg looked at the children standing side by side, their waxen skin seeming unreal in the brightly lit room. She wondered whether their eyelashes would ever darken. She hoped so. There was something repellent about the curling, colourless hairs fringing such peculiar eyes. Now that they were growing up, the children were less attractive. They still caught the eye, but for the wrong reasons. They seemed bloodless and cold, and despite their fringes, their high domed foreheads reminded her of alien creatures in second-rate science-fiction films.

'What's the matter?' demanded Orlando. 'Why are you staring?'

Meg jumped. 'Sorry, I was miles away. Hurry up and get ready for bed, please.'

'We are right, aren't we?' persisted Olivia. 'Ashley is our daddy.'

'If you know so much, why ask me?' demanded Meg. They gave a small half-smile and filed out of the room.

Feeling thoroughly depressed, she took the brandy bottle from the cabinet and poured herself a generous measure. She added a splash of soda and then sat down in the most comfortable chair.

The day at Catriona's hadn't been such a good idea after all. It was sad that David's accident had put such a strain on the marriage but probably quite common. Just the same it wasn't the ideal place to go for companionship and festive cheer. Catriona had also surprised her sister by her championing of Ashley. Fancy her indulging in flights of fantasy over his sexual ability while Meg herself gave it very little thought, and when she did consider it generally pictured him as being disinterested and undemanding.

For some time she sat sipping her brandy, dreaming idly of the future. It was only when the clock struck ten that she realised the twins were probably still waiting for her to tuck them in. In case they'd fallen asleep without her blessing she tiptoed carefully upstairs and pushed gently on their bedroom door.

It swung open noiselessly, and they were so engrossed in the paper lying spread out on the floor in front of them that they didn't realise Meg was there. 'We're mentioned,' Olivia was saying, the excitement in her voice intense. 'Look, right here: "Police interviewed the mother of four-year-old twins who played with Beverley prior to her disappearance. Mrs Margaret Marshall, a widow in her mid-thirties, was unable to help but said that her heart went out to the bereaved parents. Police think that the murderer had been watching the play area in Shrublands Park and followed Beverley after she left her two playmates." That's us again, Orlando. We were her two playmates!'

Before Meg could speak Orlando gave a short laugh. It was a terrible laugh, deep, knowledgable and gloating, and the sound of it held Meg spellbound. Ridiculous as it later seemed she was, just for one brief moment, too frightened to make her presence known.

'Does it say what was done to her?' he asked after he'd regained his composure.

'Sort of. It mentions that her throat had been cut and . . .'

'*Give that to me!*' shouted Meg, forcing herself into the room. The children jumped up guiltily and sped into their beds. Shaking with anger and something closely related to fear she picked up the paper and scrunched it into a ball.

'How can you be so callous? Don't you realise that it could have been you? Beverley was murdered. She's dead, and she was probably tortured before she died. If you're old enough to read the details in the newspaper then you're old enough to understand what happened. It isn't in the least amusing, it's just horrible, absolutely horrible!'

'She wasn't very bright,' said Orlando gently. 'In fact, she was a very silly little girl.'

'And you think that means it doesn't matter?'

'She wouldn't ever have done anything with her life,' said Olivia scornfully. 'She was slow and timid, and very disobedient.'

'How do you know she was disobedient?'

'Because she'd been told not to go into the woods.'

Meg stared at her daughter. 'Did she tell you that?'

'Of course she did, when we asked her . . .'

'Not to go!' interrupted Orlando loudly. Olivia flicked her eyes at her twin and a faint flush coloured her face and neck.

'Yes,' she continued quickly. 'When we asked her not to go

64

she said that we sounded like her mummy, but she was going anyway.'

'That doesn't sound like a timid child,' said Meg slowly, her gaze switching from one child to the other as she tried to work out what Olivia had nearly said.

'She was timid about swings and things,' explained Orlando.

'Really? When I saw her on the swing she was going very high.'

'That was me,' said Olivia scornfully.

'It was Beverley. Your coat isn't green.'

'I'd pushed her,' explained Orlando, 'but she cried so I had to stop.' For a few seconds the children and their mother remained silent, they eyes locked.

'You're lying to me,' said Meg at last, 'but I don't know why.'

'We are not!' Orlando sounded highly indignant. 'Why would we lie about a stupid girl who's dead?'

'I wish I knew.'

'You're stupid too!' jeered Olivia, her tongue running away with her yet again. 'You're not special either, you're like most of the others. Of course you stick up for silly Beverley because you think she matters, but she doesn't. She isn't of any importance at all. She might just as well be dead because . . .'

Meg, who had been listening in amazement to her daughter's outburst, finally lost her temper completely. She grabbed Olivia by the shoulders and dragged her from the bed. Olivia screamed and kicked but Meg was oblivious to the pain and forced her daughter over her knees before picking up the hairbrush that was lying beside the bed. She rarely smacked the twins but was suddenly filled with such fury that she forgot it was a small child she was punishing and continued hitting the wriggling bottom until Olivia's indignant shouts changed to pain-filled screams.

It was only when Orlando tried to wrench the brush away that Meg came to her senses. She pushed her son off and threw Olivia back on her bed. Olivia lay quite still. There were no tears on her face but her eyes were as cold as the sea on a winter's day.

'You thoroughly deserved that!' blustered Meg, slightly out

of breath, 'And don't ever speak to me like that again.'

Orlando scuttled across to his twin's bed and pulled her into a sitting position with her back against the headboard. Then he settled himself next to her and narrowed his lips into two thin, bloodless lines. Meg couldn't turn away from the children. She looked into their eyes and saw that the pupils had disappeared. The room began to tilt slightly and she blinked as a mist seemed to fill her vision.

Despite the mist she could still see the twins' pale eyes staring at her and a tremendous weakness suddenly made her hands shake and her knees began to buckle as the floor started to rise up and meet her. There was a rushing noise in her ears and then a high-pitched whistle that threatened to shatter her eardrums with its intensity. She clapped her hands over her ears but it didn't make any difference, the whistle continued and the room spun faster and faster like some mad roundabout until she finally fell unconscious to the floor.

'That was all your fault,' complained Orlando. 'You nearly went and said that *we* took her to the woods.'

'Sorry, I forgot.'

'We mustn't ever forget.'

'I wonder what Mummy thought?' mused Olivia. 'She couldn't have suspected us of killing Beverley.'

'No, but she guessed we'd done something wrong. She's very odd about people dying, isn't she?'

'That's because she's a nerd too,' sneered Olivia.

'She isn't. She's really quite bright for an ordinary person.'

'Ordinary's ordinary!' exclaimed Olivia. You're either special or you're not. She isn't.'

'Do we need her?' asked Orlando. 'If not we could finish her off now.'

'You're being stupid this time. Of course we need her. What about Ophelia?'

'I forgot her,' admitted Orlando. 'In that case we'd better leave her until she comes round.'

'We could practise the burning. Just a little bit, of course.'

'I'm not sure I can do it only a little bit. Suppose it gets out of control?'

'I can do it a little bit. You watch, Orlando.'

Orlando, who tended to get a little tired of his twin's

displaying her superior psychic powers, sighed but watched carefully as she took a deep breath, held it and then glared at her mother with concentrated fury. All the time she stared a pulse throbbed heavily in her blue-veined forehead.

Suddenly Meg gave a whimper and moved her left arm beneath her body, unconsciously seeking protection from her daughter. With a splutter Olivia released her breath and watched closely as her mother's eyes flickered open.

For a moment, Meg couldn't imagine what she was doing lying on the floor, especially the twins' bedroom floor, but almost immediately the memories flooded back and she raised her head slowly until Orlando and Olivia came into her line of vision. They were each in their own bed now, watching with apparent concern as she began to sit up.

'You fell down,' announced Orlando.

'I think I must have fainted.'

'What's fainted, Mummy?' asked Olivia.

'You go all dizzy and weak, and then you just sort of black out.'

'What's blackout?'

'Stop asking so many questions, my head aches.'

'Sorry,' said her daughter, but she didn't sound sorry. Neither, noticed Meg, did either of the children ask her if she were feeling better.

'Did I give you both a fright?'

'No,' said Olivia.

'Yes,' put in Orlando. 'A dreadful fright,' he added, in case further emphasis were needed.

'Well, I think I'm all right now. I'll just ... ouch!'

The twins watched with interest as Meg cradled her left hand close to her body while staring down at the red, blistered flesh.

'What's happened?' asked Orlando eagerly.

'I can't imagine. It looks like a burn.'

An expression of triumph gleamed in Olivia's eyes, but was quickly suppressed and Meg – studying her hand in puzzlement – missed it.

'Perhaps it isn't a burn,' said Orlando. 'Perhaps you hurt your hand when you were beating Olivia.'

'I'd hardly call that a beating. Show me your bottom, Olivia. Let me see if it's marked.'

'No, I won't. It's rude to look at people's bottoms.'

'Suit yourself. Right, it's very late and I'm going to get ready for bed. I'll turn your light off now, and I don't want to hear any talking, all right?'

'Right!' they chorused, and Meg quickly left the room.

Once she was away from the children she allowed the nausea that had been threatening ever since she regained consciousness to take hold, and stood over the toilet bowl retching dryly. It was a mixture of shock and pain that was affecting her, but she couldn't think of a remedy for either. The shock had been caused by the discovery of the children reading the paper and chortling over little Beverley, while the pain was in her left hand, blistered and throbbing heavily.

Eventually she made it downstairs and took a sip of the brandy she'd poured out earlier. Its warmth both comforted and calmed her. Then, just as she was locking the front door, the silhouette of a man appeared on the thick glass. With a cry of alarm she stepped back into the shadows, only to flinch when the bell rang harshly. She stayed where she was, praying that the caller would go away. It was nearly midnight, and if he remained on her doorstep she'd call the police.

Tired of pressing the bell the man raised his hand and rapped loudly on the glass. 'Meg! I can see you're there. Open up, I'm freezing.'

'Ashley!' Almost crying with relief Meg grappled with the safety chain. She was hindered by her burnt hand but finally managed to open the door and fall into his waiting arms.

'What on earth's the matter? Are the children all right?'

'Why don't you ask about me?' she demanded tearfully. 'Why is it always the children first?'

'I can see you're all right so naturally I was worried about the twins.'

'I'm worried about them too, but not about their health!' And she gave a half-sob.

Ashley led her into the kitchen and sat her down by the stove before plugging in the kettle. 'You look as though you need a warm drink. It's lucky I came back when I did.'

Meg nodded, beginning to regain her self-control and wishing that she'd brought her brandy with her. 'How did the funeral go?'

'As well as any funeral can. I've finished there now, I won't need to go to Scotland again.'

Meg accepted the mug of hot sweet coffee and attempted to look at Ashley through a stranger's eyes, but try as she might she couldn't see why Catriona had classified him as sensual. At the moment he looked more like a very annoyed commanding officer.

'Meg what did you mean about worrying over the twins, although not their health?'

'They gave me rather a fright tonight,' she said quietly, and Ashley didn't say a single word until she'd completed her story.

'Let me see the burn,' he ordered when her voice tailed off. She held out her left hand and he gave a low whistle. 'That's a nasty blister. Did you run it under the cold tap?'

'No. How do you think I got it?'

'Had the heater been on in their bedroom?'

'Yes.'

'Your hand must have knocked against the element while you were unconscious.'

'It shouldn't have been that hot.'

'Then it's a friction burn off the carpet.'

'Don't be ridiculous!'

Ashley's eyes narrowed. He didn't like being called ridiculous. 'Very well, how do you think you got it?'

'*I don't know*!'

'There has to be a logical explanation, unless you think the twins did it to you.'

'Of course I don't think they did it! Mind you, they weren't very bothered.'

Ashley gave a short laugh. 'Why should they be? The pain's yours, it's purely academic to them.'

'Most children are sympathetic when people get hurt.'

'How would you know? You've only got the twins to go by.'

'It's common knowledge that children . . .'

'Common knowledge! You sound like the twins when they say "everybody's" got one. The mythical "everybody" and the mythical "common knowledge"! Do you realise you haven't even given me a kiss yet?'

'I'm not in a kissing mood,' she said petulantly.

69

'Pity! Oh well, let's go into the living-room. It's more comfortable and there are quite a lot of things that I want to talk about.'

'Not tonight!' complained Meg. 'My head's pounding and I'm desperately tired.'

'All you have to do is listen,' he said gently. 'Surely you want to hear about my father?'

Indeed she did; she had thought about him a great deal since meeting Ashley's mother, and the more she thought about him the uneasier she became. If Ashley were willing to talk she didn't want to stop him. 'I'll need more coffee,' she warned him as she tried to stifle a yawn.

'I'll keep you supplied,' he promised, and with a quick smile pushed open the living-room door and stood back to let her in. 'I'm afraid it isn't a very pleasant story, but it's something you're entitled to know before you decide whether or not you're willing to marry me.'

As the door swung shut on the adults the two children upstairs crept quietly from their beds and then made their way to the bend in the stairs where they sat down and began to listen. They too wanted to hear Ashley's story. They felt it might help explain quite a lot of things, and they were already at an age when they needed explanations for their childhood was over.

It was an as yet unrecognised fact that Ashley's cold, colourless offspring began to mature very early. But then, they had far further to go than normal children.

Chapter 5

'First of all,' said Ashley slowly, 'I want to apologise for letting you assume my father was dead. The fact of the matter is that's the story I put out for public consumption. He's dead in so far as he won't ever mix with ordinary people again. He's locked up, you see, in a mental hospital. That will be my father's home for the rest of his life.'

'I am sorry,' Meg's voice was gentle despite her surprise, 'It must be difficult for you. Mental illness can bring out some pretty deep-rooted prejudices in people.'

'He's only become mentally ill during the last ten years.'

'But I thought he went away when you were a baby?'

'So he did. He went to prison.'

'Prison?'

'For murder.'

At first Meg didn't think she could have heard him properly. Surely no man with a murderer for a father would put himself forward as a sperm donor. Not if he had any sense of responsibility at all. But if he had, then it meant that the twins' paternal grandfather . . . Her mind refused to continue along that line so she lifted her head and looked Ashley straight in the eye.

'Are you saying that your father killed someone?'

'I suppose I am.'

'Look, either he did or he didn't!'

'He wasn't a mass murderer. It was just a stupid accident.'

Meg began to feel relief. Accidents did happen; she, as Orlando's mother, knew that better than most people. 'Then why call it murder?'

'Because the court decided to call it murder. They didn't understand, but I do. I've read the trial report again and again since I was a teenager and it's plain to me what happened. The trouble was he had a useless lawyer.'

'I think you'd better explain from the beginning,' said Meg. 'You're not making much sense so far.'

'It's very simple. My father was a doctor, and a damned good one by all accounts. He was consultant gynaecologist at the local hospital and way ahead of his time. He'd even published a paper on artificial insemination, although it didn't win him any friends. At that time the medical profession were terrified of being seen to tamper with nature. Twenty years later he'd have been another Patrick Steptoe.

'My mother wasn't interested in his work — she admitted as much at his trial — and reading between the lines I'd say that she wasn't interested in him either. They had separate bedrooms because she said his snoring kept her awake at night. I despise women like that.

'To cut the story short, my father began an affair with the daily help, a twenty-two-year-old girl from the village, and got her pregnant. She was from a strict kirk-attending family and didn't dare tell her parents. Instead, although presumably not with the kirk's blessing, she blackmailed my father.

'He told the court that on this particular morning my mother had gone shopping when Isla called to see him. She asked for ten thousand pounds so that she could go away and start a new life in England. Ten thousand pounds! Naturally he didn't have that sort of money to spare and she said she'd report him to the medical council, see him struck off, discredited etc. He lost his temper and hit her. Then he started shaking her; she tried to get free but slipped and fell, hitting her head on one of the central heating pipes and that was it. She was killed outright.'

Meg frowned. 'But that's not murder! I suppose it was manslaughter but you don't usually get very long for that. Why did they call it murder? And why has he finished up in a mental home?'

'I haven't finished yet.' Ashley's voice was harsh and he looked at Meg with an expression bordering on dislike. 'May I go on?' She nodded.

'Obviously if that had been all there was to it he could have got away with manslaughter. Unfortunately, he tried to cover his tracks. He thought that if he got rid of the body he'd be all right, and being a medical man it was relatively easy for him to deal with the corpse.'

'In what way, easy?'

'He wasn't emotional or squeamish about a dead body.'

'Not even that of his mistress?'

'She was only a daily help!' he snapped.

'Go on.'

'He started to ... That is, he began to dissect the body. Obviously he realised it would be easier to dispose of it in pieces.'

Meg felt sick. She'd heard enough, but Ashley seemed to feel obliged to finish the story. She only hoped that he'd be quick. While she continued to listen the words 'only the daily help' echoed in her brain.

'... and then my mother walked in on him. She didn't wait to find out what had happened, she simply ran screaming off into the village and naturally the police came straight out. He hadn't had time to finish the job and I suppose the room must have looked pretty ghastly.'

'What room?'

'His bedroom. He'd taken her there as soon as she arrived.'

'Why?'

'I don't know,' he said irritably. 'It wasn't mentioned at the trial. His lawyer was a complete idiot. He encouraged my father to plead mental instability. He'd been seen by a couple of psychiatrists while on remand and they'd failed to understand that dismembering the corpse was a perfectly logical step. They chose to see it as a sign of mental illness.'

'If he was badly advised why didn't he appeal?'

'How should I know? It's easy to look back and say how things should have been done, but at the time he didn't have anyone on his side. He got put away for an indefinite period. "Until he was judged safe to be released into society" was how the judge put it. Well, as the years passed he became less and less safe. After all, what did he have left to look forward to? Now he's in a locked ward of a top security prison for the criminally insane − and all because of a low-class tart!'

Meg kept silent. Whilst she could understand Ashley's desire to put his father in the best possible light nothing that he'd said made her feel an injustice had been done. All he'd achieved was to fill her with horror at both the crime and the realisation that her children carried the genes of a murderer.

'Haven't you anything to say?' demanded Ashley.

'It must be terrible for you, but I'm still surprised that he was put away for so long. Was there any other evidence that you've missed out? Anything that made the judge feel your father was a danger to society as a whole and not just this particular girl?'

Ashley sighed. 'Some fool of a pathologist said that in his opinion the stupid girl was alive when she was cut up. Absolute rubbish of course, but it seemed to stick in the jury's mind even though another expert said that he couldn't be sure whether she was alive or dead.'

'I don't want to hear any more.' Meg's voice was faint and Ashley glanced at her is surprise.

'It happened years ago. I know it's pretty horrible but it doesn't affect us. Obviously you had to know, I couldn't very well marry you without being honest, but surely it doesn't make any difference? I'm the same person you've always known. You aren't one of those people who holds the sins of the fathers against the children I hope?'

'No,' said Meg, trying desperately to assemble her thoughts. 'I'm not that ignorant, but I honestly don't understand how, knowing what you do, you could have put yourself forward as a suitable father for numerous children whose mothers were in complete ignorance of your family history.'

'I don't follow your objection.'

'Ashley, you've let women give birth to children whose grandfather was at the very least a murderer, and at the worst clinically insane.'

His eyes glittered. 'You haven't listened to a word I've said, have you? Women are so emotional about things. Try and be logical for once. You surely wouldn't say that because of my father I was never entitled to marry and have a family?'

'Well . . . no.'

'So what's the difference?'

'Recipients of artificial insemination are assured that donors are thoroughly screened. That they're above reproach.

No physical disabilities, and no history of mental illness. I remember being told that.'

'*I* don't have a history of mental illness.'

'You must have lied, and for what? To help childless women? No, I don't believe you're that altruistic. So why did you do it? To get back at women? To pay them out because you felt your mother let your father down? Was that the reason?'

'Well, well!' laughed Ashley. 'That's a very good piece of psychology, but it so happens that I never even thought of that. No, my reason was far more simple. You see, I happen to have abilities, talents if you prefer, that I feel should be passed on. As I never pictured myself living in a house full of children, I decided that this was a far simpler and better way of doing my bit for the future of mankind.'

'What talents do you have that are so important?'

He hesitated. 'Oh, a quick brain; a good head for figures; a certain emotional strength that's lacking in a lot of people; and of course I make very fine coffee!'

'Did you lie?' repeated Meg.

'To whom?'

'The doctors. Did you tell them about your father when you so generously donated sperm?'

'Did *you* tell the doctor, at that very exclusive clinic Charles nearly bankrupted himself for, that your husband, the man who would bring up some other man's child, was an active homosexual who lusted after young men and had to drink himself senseless before he could touch his wife?'

'That's quite different!' shouted Meg.

'In what way?'

'You were perpetuating a family line that was flawed. You did your first year's medical training; surely some of the ethics you learnt there should have told you that what you were doing was wrong?'

'Ethics? Don't be naïve! There wasn't time for ethics, we were too busy learning what pills to prescribe. The assessment was frequently influenced by which particular drug company handed out the biggest gift – not a bribe you understand, but a gift. That's the only kind of ethics I learnt in my first year.'

'I don't believe you.'

'No, well you wouldn't. You only hear what you want to

hear. From the way you're carrying on anyone would think I'd revealed a family connection with Hitler. Crimes of passion happen every day, Meg, and they are *not* hereditary.

'Yes, my father was weak and selfish, but so was Charles. You appear to have forgiven him and been quite happy for him to support you and any children you chose to bear. Why doesn't my father get the same degree of compassion?'

'*Because it isn't the same!*'

Ashley lowered his eyes and shrugged. 'I can see it's pointless saying any more. I shouldn't have told you, but for some ridiculous reason I imagined you'd understand. I didn't allow for the engrained narrow-minded attitude to life that's been handed down from *your* dear departed parents. Well, I've told the truth and I can't take it back. The rest's up to you.'

Meg leant forward, trying to make him understand. 'Ashley, it isn't the fact that your father killed a girl that's upset me. It's your casual acceptance of the murder, your defence of his actions, even worse the fact that you can't see that you were wrong to let women bear children who are descended from such a man.'

'Do you really think that the twins are affected by my father?'

'Yes! I've known for a long time that there's something wrong with them. They're fit and intelligent but they don't have any regard for other people. Remember the way Orlando hit David?'

'Accidents happen to all children.'

'But Orlando didn't care. He wanted to find out what happened when a spade hit a skull and David was unlucky enough to be his guinea pig. Then there's Beverley.'

'Who's Beverley?'

'She was the little girl murdered in the park just before Christmas.'

'I remember. What's that got to do with the twins?'

'I caught them reading about it in the paper tonight.'

'You see! Not many four-year-olds can read newspapers.'

'It's a great pity they can. Ashley, they weren't upset about the little girl, they weren't even indifferent. They told me that it didn't matter because she wasn't a special person.'

'Special?'

'Not particularly bright. They have this peculiar belief that when someone with a less than spectacular I.Q. dies it doesn't matter.'

'And that's my father's fault?'

'No, it's yours. I heard you just now, when you were talking about the girl your father murdered. She was "only a daily help" you said, as though that made it all right.'

'I never said any such thing.'

'You did!'

'I think I'd better go,' he said coldly. 'I'm very disappointed but obviously it's better to finish now before we both say things we'll regret. There's just one thing I would like to make clear: I'm not at all pleased to discover that a son of mine was destined to be brought up by a sexual pervert whose taste ran to very young men, and whose wife kept his secret in order to preserve her façade of contented wife and mother. For Orlando's sake, I'm extremely glad Charles died.'

'But . . .'

'Goodbye, Meg. I hope that one day a suitably taint-free knight appears on your horizon − and that the twins take to him, of course!'

As Ashley slammed the front door behind him, Orlando and Olivia began to scream. Running up to their bedroom Meg found them lying on the floor sobbing hysterically and beating the carpet with their fists. She bent over Orlando and tried to pat his rigid shoulders. 'Orlando, please don't cry like this. What's wrong?'

'You know what's wrong,' he sobbed, gasping for breath between the tears. 'Our daddy's gone away and it's your fault. Now we'll never see him again, and we want to die. We hate you! Go away!'

'I did not send Ashley away. He chose to go. A fact that you must know full well since you've obviously been eavesdropping the entire night.'

'You've stopped loving him,' muttered Olivia. 'He went because you'd stopped loving him.'

'At four years of age you don't know what the word love means. Now, I know that you liked Ashley and you'll miss him but . . .'

'*Daddy! He's our daddy!*' they screamed together.

'All right, I know you like your father but . . .'

'We love him, and we *do* know what it means. It means feeling warm when he's with us and cold when he's not. It means wanting him to be safe and needing him beside us.' Orlando's fury was terrifying and Meg could only blink and step backwards in the face of such pain and hatred.

'Please stop crying,' she said softly. 'I'm sorry if you've been hurt but I don't want to marry your father.'

'Then you shouldn't have had us,' retorted Olivia.

'I didn't know you were his when I had you.'

'You did too! You knew we weren't horrible Charles' children.'

'I am not discussing it with you any more. Your father's gone and that's the end of it. You can cry all night if you like, it won't change my mind.'

'You're like a dried up prune!' shouted Orlando rudely. 'You don't know anything about real life, Daddy said so.'

'In which case he must be very grateful I'm not going to be his wife! Now please get into bed.' Their only reply was to raise their voices and begin screaming again.

Meg was sure that eventually they'd wear themselves out but they continued all night, and at six o'clock she went to make herself a cup of tea. As soon as her kitchen light went on her neighbour came to the back door, leaving Meg in no doubt as to what she and her family thought of the twins being allowed to scream all night.

At seven o'clock she decided to go up and speak to them again, but just as her foot touched the bottom stair the crying stopped. For several minutes she continued to wait but it remained silent so she left them to catch up on their sleep.

At mid-day she took a plate of toasted sandwiches up to their bedroom. They were wide awake and lying propped up on their pillows. For once they didn't stare at her, in fact their eyes were hazy and unfocused. 'I expect you're hungry,' she said brightly. Neither child answered her. 'Toasted cheese and ham, how does that sound?'

'We're not hungry,' said Olivia politely. 'Please take them away.'

'Would you prefer a drink?'

'We aren't thirsty either,' Orlando told her. 'Go away.'

'Well, don't expect any snacks before tea.'

'We won't ever be eating again,' Olivia muttered. 'You needn't waste time cooking because we don't want anything.'

'Fine!' agreed Meg, wondering how long they'd manage to hold out.

Four days later, when neither child had accepted so much as a sip of water, she called the doctor out. Dr. Gifford was tall, well-built and hearty. He had a bluff, confident bedside manner and a merry twinkle in his eye. He was also thoroughly incompetent.

While he examined the twins, Meg explained that they were on a hunger strike and he nodded understandingly, but at the conclusion of his examination he scribbled on his prescription pad, winked at the twins and told them they'd soon be on their feet again.

'Gastric flu,' he told Meg as he hurried downstairs. 'Lot of it about; that's why they won't eat. Their bodies know best. They're getting a touch dehydrated so you'd better keep an eye on them. A teaspoon of water every half hour might be a good idea. And get the medicine made up straight away. That will put an end to the vomiting.'

'They aren't vomiting!' cried Meg.

'It'll stop the diarrhoea too!' he assured her, and then he was away with a crashing of gears and much squealing of tyres. Slowly Meg closed the front door and then methodically tore the prescription into a dozen pieces before throwing it into the pedal bin. She had no idea what to do next.

By evening both children had cracked and bleeding lips, and Orlando couldn't manage to speak. His eyes were half-closed, his breathing shallow. Olivia's eyes were still open but she had hollows beneath her cheekbones and her skin looked dry and scaly.

'Olivia, please listen to me,' pleaded Meg. 'If you don't have something to drink you'll die. Just have a drop of water. One tiny spoonful. Please, darling.'

'Go away. We want to die.'

'I won't let you. I'll have you taken to hospital and they'll put you both on drips. They won't allow you to die. You're suffering like this for nothing. It isn't as though your father knows.'

'Tell him,' murmured Olivia. 'Tell our daddy.'

'I can't!' Meg was nearly in tears. 'I haven't got a telephone number where he can be reached. Look, if you both start eating again I promise that I'll contact Ashley and let him come and see you. Does that help? Will you have a drink if I promise to try and find your father?'

Olivia shook her head.

'What do you want then?'

'We want you to marry him.'

'Olivia, be reasonable. I can't spend my life with someone I don't love just to please you and Orlando.'

'You stayed with Charles without loving him. Daddy's much nicer than Charles.'

'Yes, I know, but I was already married to Charles before I realised . . .'

Olivia put out the tip of her cracked tongue, tried to moisten her lips and then drifted off into unconsciousness.

Orlando's breathing was now so shallow that it was difficult to be certain he was still alive and Meg gave a moan of panic. She had to call the doctor out again. She'd say she'd broken the medicine, dropped the bottle, tell him anything at all to explain their condition, but at least he'd be forced to take them to hospital and once there they wouldn't be able to fight medical science. Like it or not, the hospital would make sure they lived.

As she reached for the phone the front door bell rang and she knew at once who it was. When she opened the door and saw him standing there she felt overwhelming relief, and immediately began to gabble about the twins' condition as she half-dragged him up the stairs.

He stood on the threshold of their room in stunned silence. They looked like two small corpses, and when he summoned up the courage to go across and touch them their skin remained dented after contact. They were as near to death as anyone he'd ever seen and the anguish in his eyes started Meg weeping.

'I couldn't stop them,' she sobbed. 'They just wouldn't listen.'

'I'm here!' he called urgently. 'Olivia! Orlando! It's your father. Come on, open your eyes for me. Livvy! Livvy!' His daughter stirred and moaned quietly as her eyes slowly opened. 'What a thing to do! Come on, little one, take a sip of this water for Daddy.'

She opened her mouth like a small bird in a nest, and with great care Ashley spooned in some of the liquid. 'That's right, just a little at a time. We mustn't overload that poor empty tummy.' Olivia blinked in acknowledgement. 'Now for Orlando,' murmured Ashley, and slowly and patiently he went through the whole routine again.

For the rest of the night he stayed beside his children. Meg looked in now and again but knew that she wasn't really needed. The twins would be fine now that they had their father with them.

After twenty-four hours an exhausted Ashley felt confident enough to leave them on their own. Meg made him up a bed in the spare room and ensured that he slept undisturbed for over twelve hours. She then fed him and tried to thank him for what he'd done.

'It wasn't for you,' he said curtly.

'I know. I'm still in your debt.'

'Don't look so worried; I'm not going to ask you to marry me as repayment. I'm sure we can work something out about the twins. I could have unofficial access or something. That way you won't get a repeat performance of that little drama and I'll be able to stay in touch with them.'

'You make it sound so unemotional.'

'As far as you and I are concerned it is. You made that clear during our last conversation together. I don't imagine anything's changed since then?'

'No, but ...'

'Your obvious repugnance at the thought of coupling with the son of a homicidal maniac drove all thoughts of romance from my head, Meg. Believe me, you're quite safe from any further declarations of love.'

'You took me by surprise that night. I've been thinking and thinking about what you said and ...'

'You haven't changed. Your only concern is the twins, and you don't have to marry me to keep them safe. I'm not that desperate to make you my wife!'

'Can't you understand what a shock it was to hear all those things? All right, perhaps I over-reacted, but most women would have done the same.'

'You're not most women. I thought you were different.'

'I am! If we spend more time together, get to know each other better, then I'm sure that nothing your father did will influence me. The trouble was that we really didn't know each other that well when I came to Scotland with you and afterwards I felt cornered. It was as though I were being pushed into something before I had time to think.'

'Why, Meg,' he said in a deceptively soft tone, 'how horrible for you. Well, put your mind at rest. I won't even lay a finger on you, let alone push you into any corners, until you go down on your knees and beg me to show you what a real man's like. Is that clear?'

It was very clear, and from the expression on his face Meg knew that she had hurt Ashley even more than she'd realised and that he would probably never forgive her. But she refused to be cowed by his anger. Instead she managed a very credible smile. 'In that case, it will be interesting to see how long it takes me,' she said brightly.

Ashley raised his eyebrows in surprise. He'd been expecting tears not cheerful acceptance, and he gave a brief nod of acknowledgment at her strategy. He hoped that she would come round. Possessing her would be very stimulating indeed.

Unaware of the small scene being played out downstairs, the twins sat close together on their bedroom floor and clasped hands.

'We very nearly died!' said Orlando indignantly. 'I told you it was a stupid idea.'

'No, it wasn't. We're still alive and Daddy's back with us again. It was worth feeling poorly for a few days.'

'I felt more than poorly. My legs are still stuffed with cotton wool.'

'It doesn't matter about your silly old legs. Mummy and Daddy are going to get married.'

'Are they really? How do you know?'

'I can see, stupid. Can't you?'

'No, not today. I never see things as well as you, and today I can't see a thing, not even what's for dinner tonight.'

'You're feeble! I can see Mummy in a brown suit and Daddy in grey, and we're both there carrying flowers and things. It's a hot day so it must be summer time.'

'Boys don't carry flowers! You're making it up.'

'I'm not. You're carrying a horseshoe.'

'I suppose that's O.K.,' he said doubtfully.

'Aunty Cat's got green all round her.'

'Perhaps *she* wants to marry Daddy,' suggested Orlando.

'Maybe. I'm wearing a lovely lilac dress at the wedding. I wonder where we'll get it.'

'Who cares!' shrugged Orlando. 'I'm starving. I hope it's boiled eggs for tea.'

'I think it's crumpets or teacakes.'

It was buttered teacakes.

Chapter 6

It was amazing how quickly Ashley's visits fell into a pattern. Promptly at two o'clock every Saturday afternoon he would arrive at the front door. If he stepped inside it was only as far as the hall. Not once did he take so much as a seat on a kitchen chair while he waited.

Olivia and Orlando were usually ready, but on the infrequent occasions when they weren't he would make polite small talk with Meg, discussing the weather or the children. It was a pattern followed by many ex-husbands weekend after endless weekend, only in this case Ashley and Meg had never been married.

When she first realised this, Meg wondered why it didn't seem more peculiar but of course she and Ashley were biologically the children's parents. It was only their own relationship that was unusual, and yet at times Ashley seemed closer to Meg than Charles had ever been.

In April, when the weather started to improve and Ashley was able to take them out for whole days, the children started to ask their mother to go too. She wished that she could; it would have been pleasant to go out as a family and have another adult to talk to while the twins played, but she always refused. It wasn't that she was against the contact with Ashley but she knew very well that since their disagreement his defences were up and she didn't want an awkward atmosphere to spoil things for the twins.

Easter was late that year and for once the weather was kind. Ashley had promised to take the children to the newly opened 'Wonder World', which boasted several 'spine-chilling, death-defying rides for people seeking fresh thrills'. When he called, Orlando shuffled his feet and mumbled that he wasn't sure he wanted to go.

'Why not?' asked Ashley in surprise. 'If you're frightened you can always watch.'

'I'm not frightened!'

'What is it then?'

'I want Mummy to come with us.'

Meg, who was waiting to see them off, was astonished. Orlando hadn't asked her to go, hadn't even been interested enough to tell her about the treat; it had been Olivia who had given her all the details.

Ashley glanced at Meg. 'What's caused this?'

'I've no idea. He hasn't mentioned it to me.'

'I don't care whether she comes or not,' interrupted Olivia. 'All I want is lots of rides on the corkscrew.'

'Tell me about it when you get back, Orlando,' urged Meg.

'No, I want you to watch me.'

'I'm quite sure that Ashley . . .'

'Don't use me as your get-out, Mrs Marshall. I'd be delighted to take you along too, provided you ask nicely.'

'Come on,' urged Olivia. 'If we don't go soon we won't have time to do anything.'

'I suppose I could come,' said Meg slowly, and was flattered to see Ashley's face brighten. He even managed a slight smile.

'That's the spirit! Come on, twins, we'll wait in the car.

As Meg ran upstairs to change, Orlando danced down the front path and leaped into the back seat. 'Was I good? Was I?'

'Very,' approved his father.

'Livvy couldn't have done it as well, could she?'

'No, I couldn't.' Olivia was quite firm about that. 'I can't act for toffee, and I'm never going to either. I shall always say what I'm thinking.'

'I trust you'll learn a little discretion as you get older,' said Ashley dryly.

'It was the only way,' explained Orlando. 'If she didn't ever come out with us how could there be a summer wedding?'

'I didn't think we had to help!' exclaimed Olivia. 'What's the point of seeing into the future if you've got to make it happen? When we see something clearly doesn't it mean that it will happen anyway?'

'How will you ever know? How can anyone ever know?' Ashley queried.

'By not interfering and waiting to see what happens.'

'This was too important to leave to chance,' commented her father, but before the discussion could continue Meg got into the car.

Despite the long journey the visit was well worthwhile. The twins dashed from one ride to the next, their normally pale faces tinged with pink and their eyes glittering with excitement.

The more dangerous and terrifying the ride, the more they loved it. Even the endless queuing didn't put them off. They stood patiently hand-in-hand, their eyes fixed on the excitement that lay ahead. Meg realised that people noticed the children and were fascinated by them, not the emotional fascination that babies have for people but the fascination of something rare and exotic.

Watching them amongst other children she was acutely aware of the fact that they weren't like the rest. Their heads were definitely a different shape. She had always thought of them as fair-skinned but it was really a waxen pallor, and their skin looked too thin, as though it were being stretched beyond its capabilities.

None of this would have mattered if their eyes had been normal but they remained very peculiar indeed. Their eyelashes still hadn't darkened and the chill grey-blue colour was cold and hard. The irises made it worse. They were now an even more milky-white with slightly darker swirls, and the minute pupils exaggerated their peculiarity. There was something intrinsically disturbing about them, and being their mother gave her no sense of pride at all.

What are you thinking about?' asked Ashley, casually putting an arm round her shoulders. 'I've asked you three times if you want a cup of tea and I don't believe you even remembered I was here.'

'I was watching the twins.'

'They'll be all right. I've told them to meet us at the restaurant.'

'I wasn't worried about them, it was just that ... I don't

know, somehow they don't seem normal to me.'

'I thought they were having a great time.'

'Yes, they are.'

'Well, that's the idea of the place. A park where children can have the time of their life providing their parents are rich enough to finance the rides!'

'But they look so odd, especially round the eyes.'

'I'm afraid they've got my father's eyes. Come on, let's get some tea.' A chill ran down Meg's back. She remembered Ashley's mother saying that Olivia's eyes were exactly like her husband's, and the woman hadn't meant it as a compliment. If they both had his eyes, what else had they inherited?

Ashley took hold of her hand. 'It's a good thing you came with us today, you're obviously getting far too introspective on your own.' He had never held her hand before and she was amazed to feel a tingle of excitment go through her. He sensed her reaction and gave her hand a slight squeeze in response.

When they sat down at an outside table his eyes were almost kind and his features seemed less harsh than usual. Of course it was always possible that she was seeing what she wanted to see, just as Ashley had claimed that she only ever heard what she wanted to hear. At that moment it didn't seem too important; it was enough to enjoy being with him again.

Finally at five o'clock they managed to persuade the twins to leave, but only because Ashley promised to go in with them when they got home. 'Can he eat with us?' asked Orlando eagerly.

'If he likes.'

'Would you like to eat with us?' Olivia's voice was amused.

'Yes.' His expression was cool and Olivia quickly looked away. She was still young and rather in awe of him. Naturally that would change as she matured but Ashley had no intention of letting her free of his discipline for some considerable time. He sensed that there was more of his father in Olivia than in any of his other children, and while she was small that was something he had to keep in check.

Having always considered Orlando less powerful than his sister the discussion with the twins after their evening meal came as something of a shock. Just as he was about to start the washing up, Orlando asked him to come to their room.

'I'm helping your mother,' he replied firmly.

'But we *need* to talk to you.'

'Go on,' laughed Meg. 'I know you arranged it between you so that you could get out of any chores!'

'You've guessed,' responded Ashley with a laugh, but there was no trace of humour in his eyes when he faced his children across their bedroom.

'I hope this is important,' he snapped. 'I was hoping to do some courting over the dirty dishes.'

'What's courting?' asked Orlando.

'It leads to marriage.'

'Well, it's *very* important,' Orlando assured him. 'We want to ask you about the tingles.'

'The tingles?'

'Yes, you know, the nice feelings you get when there's lots of blood or someone's being hurt. What are they? And how can I get them more often?' Ashley's mouth tightened and he sat down on Olivia's bed. He hadn't expected anything like this while they were so young. He wondered about Tim Farris, and all the other children approaching their early teens.

'The tingles are simply pleasure. You can get pleasure from all sorts of things. A lovely meal, a beautiful piece of music, a book or a play, or sometimes from being in the company of someone special.'

'Don't be silly,' jeered Olivia. 'I bet you don't get tingles from any of those things.'

'I never said I did. I was explaining that the tingles are different for different people. Pain and blood are not considered normal causes. In fact, society positively frowns on people who get their pleasure in that way.'

'Why?'

'Because there are laws to stop human beings from hurting one another simply for pleasure.'

'Then why get married?' asked Olivia. 'I thought you got married for pleasure. Doesn't the law let you hurt the person you marry?'

'Up to a point, but you're too young to understand all that.'

'Did you hurt Helena? Is that why she's frightened of you?'

'Possibly.'

'At least you didn't kill her,' said Orlando. 'I killed Beverley so that was the end of the tingles. And they took David away to hospital so I wasn't able to hit him again. How can you get lots of blood without killing someone?'

'Did you say *you* killed Beverley?'

'Yes, in the woods.'

'How?'

'With a Stanley knife. I hid it in the loft when I got home, and I remembered to wash it clean. They were the best tingles I've ever had.'

'Where did you get the knife?'

'From a drawer in your house in Scotland.'

'Which drawer?'

'It was in the special room,' said Olivia. 'The room where I saw the man.'

'I didn't know you saw a man.'

'He wasn't *really* there. It was like seeing ahead but the other way round. He'd been there once a long time before I think, and he'd left his coldness behind him. I was feeling the coldness and then I suddenly saw him'

'What was he doing?'

'Nothing much. He was looking at this woman on the bed. He kept smiling, proper smiles − not like yours − and there was a lot of blood around. He didn't have a colour but the woman did, she was pink. Usually only little girls are pink but this lady was. So was Helena.'

'That's probably because neither of them matured.'

'What's matured?'

'Grew up.'

'Was the man your daddy?' asked Orlando.

'Undoubtedly.'

'Lucky him! Why don't I ask him about the tingles?'

'Because he got locked away forever when they found out that he'd killed the woman Olivia saw lying on the bed.'

Orlando's eyes widened in horror.

'Now do you understand,' said his father gently, 'how important it is that you're very, very careful?'

'But we get bored,' complained Olivia. 'No other children want to play our sort of games.'

'I'm sure they don't. I'm sorry, Olivia, but that's the way it is for people like us. Other people don't understand and it's very lonely. I know that full well which is one of the reasons why I've tried to make sure that there are lots of you. As you get older you can all get together and enjoy yourselves, but for the moment you have to be sensible.'

'Do you see colours?'

'Yes, Olivia, but not all the time. If I'd seen that Helena's colour was pink I'd never have married her. Not only was *she* boring, she also produced boring children!' The twins laughed.

'How far ahead can you see?' demanded Orlando.

'When I was your age I was very good at it, but for some reason it's gone away with age. Now I can't do it at all.'

'Can you burn things?'

'Yes.'

'Why can we do these things, Daddy?'

'I don't know,' he confessed. 'It must be some form of heightened psychic ability. I'm sure there are others who are the same but it isn't the kind of thing you can go round asking. "Excuse me, do you like seeing blood? And could you tell me what's for lunch next Monday week?" '

'You still haven't told me how I can have more tingles,' complained Orlando.

'It seems to me that you've had quite enough for your age. You'll have to wait, and even when you're older you can't go round slaughtering innocent people for your own enjoyment.'

'It would only be *ordinary* people.'

'I'm afraid that ordinary people don't take kindly to being killed off for our amusement.'

'They're stupid,' said Olivia scornfully. 'We're more sensible than they are. They cry about things and get lots of drippy feelings about animals and babies in prams. Ugh!'

Ashley felt a momentary qualm. Olivia was so vehement in her scorn that he wondered what kind of a woman she was going to become. 'Olivia, I wanted all of my children to be "gifted", to have your psychic powers and use them to get on in life, but you must remember that it's dangerous to take anything to extremes. Just because you're superior to a lot of people it doesn't necessarily mean that everyone else is worthless. You've got to learn to live with ordinary people and ...'

'I'm not going to have anything to do with ordinary people. They're feeble and boring, aren't they, Orlando?'

'Yes, and they don't like blood.'

'Liking blood could be a weakness in you. Look where it got my father.'

'I don't think he could have been very clever,' remarked Olivia. 'If he'd been really bright he'd have got away with it.'

'You're wrong. It's very difficult to get away with murder.'

'Sometimes, Daddy, you're a bit silly too,' said his daughter. For the first time, Ashley wondered if in his enthusiasm to create his own special family he'd actually made a mistake.

'I'm going down to help your mother,' he said slowly. 'Please don't interrupt us again.'

'How do you get your blood?' demanded Orlando.

Ashley paused in the doorway. 'I'm not hung up on blood, I prefer the ecstasy of pain.'

'Your own?'

'Of course not. Now go to sleep.'

'Other people's pain,' mused Orlando. 'Perhaps I'll try that myself. It's easier than blood.'

'You're not practising on me,' declared his twin as she climbed into bed.

'You were up there ages!' exclaimed Meg. 'Were you able to help with whatever was troubling them?'

'I tried,' responded Ashley, 'but I'm not absolutely certain that I got through.

Grace Thomas felt very uncomfortable. Her back had been aching all day and now she couldn't get to sleep because of the pain. As she turned on her side in search of a better position the pain moved and rippled across her stomach. She drew in a sharp breath and sat up. The baby wasn't due for another two weeks but this didn't feel like the painfree contractions that were meant to precede the actual birth, the 'warming up' process as the woman at ante-natal had called it.

Thirty minutes later there was no room for doubt. This incredibly expensive baby was ready to meet the world. Grace only hoped that Hugh was ready to meet the baby. Considering that artificial insemination had been his idea he had become remarkably hostile to the growing child. She wished that she could discuss his attitude with other women in the same position as herself but that wasn't possible, and she hadn't dared tell the social worker in case the child was taken away from her.

She woke her husband and watched him swing his legs out of bed and walk slowly across the room. 'Hugh, please hurry. The pains are ...' She broke off with a gasp as a fresh contraction seized her. Beads of sweat rolled down her face and her body arched.

'You'd better take a grip on yourself, Grace. According to the books this is the easy part. Aren't you meant to walk about a bit?'

The pains were coming so quickly now that she couldn't answer him. They were terrible and all her breathing practice was useless. There was nothing in her mind but pain. Wrenching, nauseating pain. She stifled a scream and her head thrashed from side to side.

At last Hugh accepted that it was an emergency. If anything went wrong at this stage he didn't know what Grace might do. All she'd talked about for the last nine months was her baby – not their baby, never theirs because of course it wasn't theirs, it had nothing to do with him – and if she should lose it now, well, it simply didn't bear thinking about.

When he ran back to the bedroom to tell Grace that an ambulance was on its way she was grunting and moaning. She looked terrible with her pain-filled face, sweat-covered hair and thrashing body. Not like his tall, elegant wife. How could one child be worth all this? he wondered.

'Hugh, it's coming!' she gasped. 'I can feel it.'

'Calm down, Grace. First babies take hours and hours. Try and relax; that's what all those classes were for, wasn't it?' Her only answer was an even deeper groan. At that moment the front doorbell rang, and with considerable relief Hugh left the room.

Naturally Grace had been right and he, Hugh Thomas, wrong. He was getting used to that. Ever since his affair with his secretary, and that unfortunate infection he'd picked up, the balance of their marriage had changed. He was forever placating her, and forever failing to please.

'Go and make yourself a cup of tea, mate!' urged the younger of the ambulance men. 'It won't be a minute now. Have you rung your doctor?'

'No, I thought . . .'

'Better give him a call. She isn't going to make it to hospital and he ought to be here.'

By the time Hugh had persuaded the doctor that he was needed and then made a pot of tea the house had fallen silent. For one terrible moment he thought that Grace was dead but then, loud and demanding, there came the sound of a baby crying. Not the thin, high-pitched wail that he associated with birth but a lusty shout.

'It's a boy, mate! A smashing little boy!' enthused the ambulance man, himself the father of three girls. 'Always something special about a son.'

There was something special about this one all right, thought Hugh grimly, but he managed a smile and fetched a bottle of malt whisky. Half an hour later the doctor — also full of congratulations and good cheer — had departed and Hugh went into the bedroom. Grace looked more like herself now. Her hair had been carefully brushed, the bed changed, and although obviously tired she looked peaceful and content.

'He's lovely,' she said proudly, 'really lovely!'

'Big?'

'No, 6lbs 2ozs.'

'I don't call that value for money,' he joked.

'Hugh!'

'I wasn't serious.'

'Take a look at him.'

Hugh bent over the cot and drew back with great speed. 'He looks like the Mekon.'

'The what?'

'He was a sort of space creature that sat on a saucer and whizzed around the universe. He was in *The Eagle* comic for years.'

Grace's expression was no longer calm. 'I think that's a disgusting thing to say about our son.'

Your son, he thought to himself — proving once and for all that careful counselling was helpless against genetic prejudice — but he tried to smile.

'I suppose it's because his forehead's so pronounced.'

'All babies have big foreheads.'

'He's damned pale as well, and his hair's white. I thought all babies had black hair.'

'Really, Hugh, he's beautiful. The doctor said he'd never seen such a perfectly formed baby.'

'He would, wouldn't he? We do pay him. If you were on the National Health he wouldn't have bothered with senseless compliments.'

Grace's eyes filled with tears. 'You don't like him! After all I've gone through you don't like him. I hate you! If you hadn't ...'

He hurried over to her and began stroking her forehead. 'Of course I like him, but I've never pretended to be fond of babies, now have I?'

'No, but ...'

'I'll soon be devoted to him. It's just rather a shock. He doesn't look real. His skin reminds me of imitation fruit.'

'Hugh!' The ready tears sprang into her eyes again.

'What are his eyes like?' asked Hugh quickly. 'Blue, I suppose?'

'I don't know. Most of the time they're shut.'

'Oh well, we'll see soon enough.'

'Hugh, do you think we ought to tell that specialist that we're not going to Swansea? He seemed so interested.'

'I don't think it's any of his business where we live. He's been exceedingly well paid for his part in this particular "act of nature". We had to fill in a form releasing him from any responsibility after conception so I don't think further contact is necessary. Besides, Cornwall's a completely new area for us and that's all he was interested in – making sure that we moved away from London. No, I'm not letting him know.'

'If you're sure,' said Grace doubtfully.

'I'm sure. Hey, look! He's opening his eyes.'

When Ashley called round the following Friday evening Meg was feeling very low. She'd spent all the morning at the local primary school with the twins. They were to start in September full-time but had been offered the chance of morning attendance for the preceding half-term. Initially they had both been pleased, and Meg thought the school very pleasant with large, airy classrooms and plenty of activities for the younger children. However, the longer they were in the building the more the twins' enthusiasm decreased. They grew silent and clung together, their arms round each other's waists. When directly spoken to they answered with only a nod or a shake of the head, and when pressed to speak mumbled short, childish responses and kept their heads down, apparently too over-whelmed to look any teacher in the eye.

Once outside they began jumping up and down and shouting abuse at the top of their voices. 'Stupid old school!' shouted Olivia.

'Yucky old teachers!' cried Orlando.

'We don't want to go,' they added unnecessarily.

'Why ever not?' asked an exasperated Meg.

'Because its full of thickos!' cried Orlando. 'Even the teachers are thick. How will we ever learn anything there? We thought it would be exciting but it's horrible.'

'I'm quite sure that most of the children and all the teachers know a great deal more than you two do,' she retorted sharply. 'And if you're so incredibly bright then no doubt you will astound the entire school and be moved up to different classes.'

'Will we?' asked Olivia. 'Are you sure?'

'Yes, but somehow I don't think it's going to be a problem.'

Orlando and Olivia ran off ahead and were difficult for the rest of the morning.

In the afternoon, Meg left them both with Catriona while she and Miles went to look at a new school for David. Miles had discovered small bruises on his son's arms and legs over the past few weeks and was certain that this was due to rough, unsympathetic handling by the staff at the day centre where he was currently being trained. 'Although what they mean by training I can't imagine,' Catriona told her sister just before she left. 'I mean, he doesn't *do* anything. Try and talk a little sense into Miles while you're out; he won't listen to me.'

Meg didn't because she soon discovered that Miles already knew the truth about his son. His initial optimism had now been replaced by a mindless quest for a miracle teacher who would unlock the child's mind with sensitive therapy, but in his heart of hearts he knew that no such teacher existed. This special school that he and Meg were visiting represented his final acceptance of what his wife had known all along: that there wasn't any hope.

'I have to be sure they're kind,' he explained to his sister-in-law. 'If he's completely dependent on them then they must be reliable. The poor little chap's suffered enough already.'

The children Meg and Miles saw all looked clean and well cared for, but the pitiful contrast with the children she'd seen that very morning only increased Meg's depression, and she felt that she'd been very little support to Miles although he thanked her profusely for keeping him company.

'Catriona wants another baby, you know,' he confided as they drew up at his home.

'It's understandable, Miles.'

'Not to me. It seems disloyal to David.'

'But David won't think that. He can't reason things out any more.'

'I can, and even the thought of it makes my skin crawl. No, I'm afraid it's out of the question. I don't want any more children.'

'Is it really because of David?'

'In a way. It's because I couldn't handle pain like this again. Children make you vulnerable, Meg. I can't take any more.' She understood what he meant but felt sorry for her sister.

When Ashley turned up on the doorstep at eight o'clock carrying a box of Thorntons chocolates and a huge bunch of flowers she nearly burst into tears on the spot. It was so out of character for him and she was in desperate need of cheering up. Quite inadvertently Ashley had timed things very well.

'How was school?' he asked the twins as they came downstairs to greet him.

'Lovely!' enthused Olivia.

'Nice!' confirmed Orlando.

'Good. Sleep well both of you.' They went off giggling and pushing like any other children. 'You look a bit tired, Meg.'

'I am. The twins weren't as enthusiastic about school to me as they were to you, and then this afternoon I went to look at a special school for David. I went with Miles and it was incredibly depressing. He used to be such a cheerful, happy-go-lucky person, always ready with a joke and a smile. Now he's quiet and withdrawn and all he wants is to get through life without any more pain. It's such a tragedy and . . . '

'It isn't your tragedy,' he reminded her gently. 'Sit down, I'll pour us both a drink.'

'It's nice to see you but you don't usually call on Fridays. Is tomorrow off or something?'

'No, I just felt like some company. Your company to be precise.'

'Then I must try and cheer up for you,' she said with a smile, and as he handed her a glass of wine their fingers brushed, causing her stomach to turn a swift somersault.

Later on, after a few more glasses of wine, they were somehow sitting next to each other on the settee and Ashley's arm, originally put round her shoulders for comfort and reassurance, began to stray a little. Meg closed her eyes and gave a small sigh of pleasure.

He was very careful not to rush her. Every move he made was slow and calm, and whenever she seemed likely to resist him he would talk quietly, whispering endearments as he skilfully removed her outer clothes. The wine and the heat from the gas fire combined to put Meg into an unusually relaxed mood. She was well aware of what Ashley was doing but was enjoying it too much to stop him. It had been a long time since she had felt a man's hands on her bare flesh, and Charles' inept, half-apologetic caresses had never caused her body to tingle the way Ashley's subtle yet positive movements did.

Eventually she was lying naked beneath him and through half-closed eyes she noticed the intense concentration on his face as his hands travelled lightly over her neck, shoulders and breasts until she wanted something different. She wanted him to hold her more tightly, to lose some of his own self-control and handle her with passion, not detached skill.

With a murmur she took hold of one of his hands and pressed it firmly against her breasts, at the same time moving the lower half of her body so that it pressed against him. Ashley sensed the change in her and responded instantly. Now his hands were gripping her breasts so tightly that flashes of pain – or was it pleasure? – flickered down the length of her body and she felt herself growing damp between her thighs.

Now he bent his head, licking at her nipples until they felt as though they couldn't stand the sensation any longer and she gave a small cry. He closed his mouth over her breasts and as his hands began skimming over the soft flesh of her inner thighs so his teeth tightened on the already stimulated nipples and slowly but insidiously he continued to bite.

Now it was definitely pain that she was feeling, but she didn't mind. It was an exhilarating pain, a pain that stimulated all of her body so that every inch of naked flesh tingled and demanded attention. She pressed more firmly against him, and suddenly he too was naked and her hands quickly found his penis. When her fingers closed round the base he gave a smothered groan and his hands, already moving in circular motions on her pelvis, moved lower as he savagely inserted three fingers into her.

She arched with shock and a surge of ecstasy that continued to build as his fingers moved faster and faster. Just as the tension within her became unbearable he twisted away, pulled her on top of him and then entered her. He was incredibly strong and moved her up and down with an almost angry desperation until at last she felt her muscles tighten and then explode.

With a scream she felt her body jerking upwards away from Ashley. His hands fastened tightly on her waist and he pulled her down on to him again, grinding her hips against him. Then, without warning, he turned so that they were side by side. As he gave his last final thrusts he stared into her eyes as though aware of the fact that for her the pleasure was over and every movement that he made was causing her discomfort.

She tried to pull away, or at least slow his movements down, but he only moved faster and then, to her astonishment, she felt her own pleasure beginning again and as she started to moan with excitement Ashley's face contorted. Burying his head in her neck he bit hard on the tender flesh and only stopped when the final shudders of his climax had died away.

When he finally lifted his head and saw her smiling he knew beyond any doubt that she was finally his.

Chapter 7

'So you've finally realised that I was right!' laughed Catriona when Meg gave her the news. 'When's the wedding?'

'In six weeks.'

'That soon? Well, once you've made up your mind, why should you wait?'

'Part of the reason we're hurrying is because I'm pregnant.'

'Pregnant?' The smile on Catriona's face vanished to be replaced with a look of anger and envy.

'Yes. Obviously it wasn't what we intended but . . .'

'I should have thought you were mature enough to know about birth control.'

'What on earth's the matter?' asked Meg in surprise. 'You wanted me to marry him, didn't you?'

'Don't tell me you're going through with it for my benefit!'

'Of course not, but I thought you'd be pleased.'

Catriona turned away. 'Sorry. Yes, I am pleased; very pleased for you both. It's just that I'm rather touchy about babies right now, and knowing that you hadn't intended to have one . . . You must know what I mean.'

'Of course I do. I'm sorry, Cat, I wasn't thinking properly or I'd have realised how you'd feel.'

'Anyway, I'm sure you're doing the right thing and I know you'll be incredibly happy. I think Ashley's very attractive. If I were free myself, I'd try to take him off you.'

Meg laughed, not for one moment taking her sister's remark seriously. 'We'd like you to come to the wedding but it's going to be terribly quiet. With Ashley's mother and our parents dead we're a trifle thin on the ground for family celebrations.'

'Hasn't Ashley any brothers or sisters?'

'No, his father and mother parted after he was born. He's lost contact with his father.' It wasn't really a lie, she thought to herself. He had lost contact, and it would put an end to any questions Catriona might otherwise have asked.

'Are the twins excited?'

'Madly. Olivia's chosen this lilac silk dress that we saw in a bridal boutique in Richmond. She looks lovely in it.'

'What will you wear?'

'I've bought a gorgeous chocolate-brown suit and a cream silk blouse. I'm trying to match the brown for the accessories but it's taking an eternity.'

'What about a hen night? Are you and I going out on the town before you get tied down again?'

'I'm not really the hen-party type. No, the only thing we're doing before the big day is taking the twins to London Zoo. Ashley asked them what they'd most like to do and that's what they chose. We're going the Saturday before the wedding.'

'Rather you than me. London Zoo's exhausting.'

'I'm quite looking forward to it. It will be a trial run for future family outings.'

'Except that baby will soon make five.'

'Not until the end of December. I only hope I've got more energy that day. I'm like a wet rag at the moment.'

'There's one thing about it,' Catriona pointed out. 'Even the twins can't do much damage at London Zoo!'

Despite David's appalling accident, Catriona – like most people – completely underestimated Olivia and Orlando.

On the morning of the trip, Meg awoke feeling both sick and anxious. She was becoming used to the early morning nausea but anxiety was new to her and she tried to think what could be causing it. Nothing came to mind and it was obvious from the twins' excited faces across the breakfast table that they were full of enthusiasm for the outing.

'What will we see at the zoo, Mummy?' asked Orlando.

'Bears, monkeys, lions, elephants – lots of different animals.'

'Will it be crowded?'

'Probably, as it's a weekend.'

'That's why *he'll* be there,' said a satisfied Olivia.

Meg frowned. 'Who are you talking about?'

'Boy B – No one. It's a pretend game.'

'I didn't think you played make-believe games.'

'Sometimes we do.'

'Well, eat up. Your father will be here in half an hour.'

As usual Ashley was prompt. He looked lean, fit and far younger than usual in his jeans and a brushed cotton shirt which was open at the neck. When her eyes met his, Meg was swamped with a desire to feel his hands on her body, to have her breasts tighten and prickle beneath them as he possessed her with the savage fury she found enthralling and irresistible.

For a moment his face changed; desire showed on his normally impassive features, but then he busied himself leading the twins to the car and putting their coats in the boot so that Meg was able to regain her composure in privacy. She found their mutual sexual attraction so compelling that it frightened her; in fact she half-hoped that once they were married it would gradually assume less prominence in her life. Such sexual dependency seemed wrong, leading as it already was to an uneven relationship, for she knew that whilst he too enjoyed their lovemaking it was of far greater importance to her. But then she had wasted so many years with Charles, and it was an entirely new world that Ashley had opened up for her. A world where she finally felt at home.

Once inside the zoo the children's excitement erupted. They ran round and round in circles uttering shrieks of joy, quite oblivious to the curious glances of bystanders.

'What on earth are they excited about?' asked Meg. Ashley shrugged. It was enough for him to see that they were. At times like this he felt certain his actions had been right; their superiority was plain when he compared them with the other children wandering aimlessly around, grizzling for ice creams or complaining that they were tired. He knew which children he'd rather bring up, and considered that the mothers who were chosen to reproduce his offspring were exceedingly fortunate.

'He's here! He's here!' whispered Olivia to her twin.

'Where?'

'I don't know, but quite close. We'll soon be together. Won't that be fun!'

'Maybe. I'd like to find a girl for myself.'

'I expect you will one day. Mummy thinks we're excited over the animals!' They both laughed.

'Where shall we start?' called Meg.

'Where do most people go?' asked Orlando.

'I suppose that at feeding times most of them are round the sea lions or the big cats. Let's find out what time the sea lions get their next meal.'

'He won't be there,' hissed Olivia in annoyance. 'I didn't see any sea lions in the picture.'

'Acually,' called Orlando, 'we'd rather see the big cats.'

'*Actually* that's fine by me!' laughed Meg, taking hold of her son's hand. It felt fragile and cool, surprisingly so for someone who'd been racing round in circles, but then both the twins tended to be cold-blooded.

There was over an hour to wait before the lions and tigers were fed and during that time they visited the monkey colony — which amused the adults more than the children — the elephants, the giraffes and the bears. Although the twins looked carefully at everything and made appropriate comments it seemed to their mother that they were more interested in the other children than the animals.

'I think they'd have preferred a human zoo,' she told Ashley. He too was puzzled by the way their eyes were perpetually scanning the spectators, especially since they were normally anti-social children, but he decided that they were simply fascinated by the whole atmosphere of the visit. In general they'd led a rather narrow life, especially since Charles died, and probably their behaviour was a perfectly natural reaction. Yet there was desperation in the way their eyes flicked over everyone, desperation and a keen sense of anticipation.

They managed to get to the front of the people waiting for the lions' food to arrive, but as soon as the first buckets of raw meat were carried to the cage doors Meg felt her stomach lurch in revulsion. The sight and smell of the blood was too much for her, and pushing her way free she half-stumbled towards the nearby café with its welcome array of seats. After a moment's hesitation Ashley followed her.

The lions were pacing restlessly up and down the cages, tails

102

swishing furiously, and Orlando was hypnotised by the sight of their food. There was so much blood. It made his skin tingle just to watch.

'He's there!' cried Olivia, nudging her twin with an elbow.

'What?'

'Boy Blue's over there. Look, he's standing under that tree.'

Orlando didn't want to leave the buckets of raw flesh and the glorious sickly-sweet scent of the blood but he knew how important the boy was to Olivia and so he followed her reluctantly through the crowd and along the path to where the boy was standing.

It would have been very difficult to miss him. Taller than the twins, he was exceptionally slender but with a wiry toughness that belied the delicacy of his bones. His snow-white hair was slightly wavy, and even from a distance his pallor was obvious. But, like the twins, far more striking than any other feature were his eyes. They were large and round, more heavily lidded than those of the twins but identical in colour. The irises looked like pools of cream and the light pupils were practically invisible in the daylight.

He stood, as might have been expected, quite alone watching their approach.

Olivia could plainly see the bright light-blue aura surrounding him but it was invisible to Orlando whose powers were not the same as hers. He couldn't see that the boy was blue, yet knew instinctively that he was cold, lacking all emotion, a complete outsider who was having trouble surviving on his own. Doctors and psychologists had already classified him as suffering from a personality disorder, but they had failed to agree on its exact nature. All they could agree on was his quite astonishing callousness. As they drew level with him, Orlando realised that the boy had his father's mouth.

'Do you know who we are?' demanded Olivia, coming to a halt about eighteen inches away from the boy.

'Of course I do.' His voice was scornful. 'You're the twins, Olivia and Orlando. I'm Tristan. I'm nine years old.'

'We're only rising-fives,' laughed Orlando. 'That's what we're called for school — the rising fives!'

'You're red,' said Tristan, his eyes running over Olivia. 'I've never seen a red girl before. Red's for death, you know.'

'What colour am I?' asked Orlando.

Tristan looked carefully at him. 'You're a sort of purple and green mixture.'

'Am I?'

'Yes,' said Olivia impatiently. 'I could have told you that!'

'Why didn't you?'

'You didn't ask me.'

'What does it mean?'

Olivia turned her head and became engrossed in the antics of some nearby penguins.

'Livvy, what does it mean?'

'It means,' said Tristan coldly, 'that you're mad.'

'Cross?'

'No, mad as a March hare. Barmy. Round the twist.'

'*I'm not!*' Orlando was furious. 'Livvy, did you hear what he said?'

'I don't want to talk about it. Where do you live, Tristan?'

'In Middlesex. I'm here with my cousins for the day but I managed to lose them hours ago. They're tacky, really boring and ordinary.'

'What's your mother like?'

Tristan pulled a face. 'Tedious but well-intentioned. I'm her only child so she makes a terrible fuss of me. Her husband's horrible; we hate each other.'

'We're going to live with our real daddy!' boasted Orlando, still smarting over the insult he'd received.

'Liar!'

'It's true,' interrupted Olivia. 'He came and found us when Charles was still alive. He told us to get rid of Charles so that he could be with us while we were growing up.'

The look of envy on Tristan's face was balm to Orlando's hurt pride.

'How did you get rid of this Charles?' asked the older boy in wonder.

'It wasn't difficult,' Olivia assured him. 'We just shoved him off a ladder. It was my idea.'

'It would be,' laughed Tristan. 'That's why you're red, remember?'

'Let's go somewhere else,' suggested Orlando. 'We don't want our mother coming to look for us just yet. She's feeling poorly today. I think it's because of Ophelia.'

'Who's Ophelia?'

'She's going to be our sister. Where shall we go?'

Tristan frowned. 'Let's try the children's corner. We can talk better there.'

In the children's corner a couple of miniature ponies wandered aimlessly round a small paddock; a tame goat kept pestering visitors for food, and large overweight rabbits hopped around the paths. In one quiet corner there was a pen where the guinea pigs were kept at night after running loose with the rabbits during the day, but today one had remained in the pen. It was small, obviously unwell, and stared at the children through sad, watery eyes. The only attractive thing about it was its tufty ginger and black fur.

'I wish I could live with you,' confessed Tristan, his pale eyes flicking round the area, checking that none of his relatives were near.

'We are lucky,' agreed Olivia, 'but you can probably get away with more. Daddy knows what we're like and keeps an eye on us.'

'What sort of things do you like?' asked Tristan.

'The tingles!' shouted Orlando.

'That's all he ever talks about!' complained Olivia. 'If he's not feeling tingly then he gets quite ratty. I think tingles are boring.'

'Only because you hardly ever have them!' retorted her twin.

Tristan's eyes gleamed. 'I like the tingles too. How do you make yours come, Orlando?'

'It isn't easy. I have to find ways of getting blood or hurting people. I cut a girl's throat once and that was great, but Daddy said I couldn't keep doing it or they'd lock me up.'

'I suppose they would. I get mine from sex.'

The twins glanced at each other. 'Sex?'

'Yes! Don't you know about sex?'

'Sort of,' said Olivia cautiously.

'Have you watched your Mum doing it?'

'No.'

'I watch my Mum and revolting Roger. They don't do it very much, but when they do it's great.'

105

'I bet blood's better!' boasted Orlando.

'Why?'

'Just because.'

'You're silly, but then you're only a baby!' retorted Tristan.

'I'm not silly. I bet blood˜frightens you, even if you are nine.'

Tristan glared, his heavy brows drawing together and his lips tightening exactly as Ashley's tightened in moments of annoyance. 'It does not. In fact, I like to drink it!'

The twins were stunned. They stared at this mature nine-year-old wonder from Middlesex and tried to work out if he was telling the truth. Olivia rather thought he was, and her resulting admiration gave her the beginnings of a very slight tingle. She wriggled against the wooden fence.

'How do you know?' she asked pertly. 'Whose blood have you drunk?'

'My own when I cut myself.'

'That doesn't count!'

'Some from my baby cousin when I stuck her nappy pin in her stomach.'

'That's more real.'

'And some from a chicken my uncle killed for lunch one day.'

Olivia glanced at Orlando who shook his head. 'We don't believe you,' she said rudely.

Tristan flushed. He never lied and was anxious to prove as much to this very exciting little girl, the first child with whom he'd ever felt able to communicate.

'Watch this then!' he boasted, and after a quick glance round he bent over the wire fence and picked up the ailing guinea pig. The twins moved nearer, shielding him from public gaze. The animal squeaked lethargically and then froze with fear, its eyes half-shut.

'Go on!' urged Orlando, sensing that this was going to be something he could enjoy as well.

Tristan took a deep breath, lowered his head and then bit through the animal's neck so that the nead lolled forward and blood bubbled up into the nine-year-old's mouth. He sucked noisily for a moment before hurling the carcass away to the far side of the pen.

106

'There you are!' He smiled broadly.

'Your teeth are all pink,' said Olivia dispassionatey, determined not to show how impressed she really was. Tristan hastily licked his teeth with his tongue and then rubbed the back of his hand round his mouth.

'Delicious,' he said casually. 'Now that gave me a great tingle.'

'Me too!' Orlando was delighted. He wished that Tristan lived nearer to them. He didn't fancy drinking blood himself but the sight of it on the dead animal and round his half-brother's mouth had given him a taste of near-ecstasy that made his normal tingles dull by comparison.

'I think *you* must be mad,' announced Olivia, but her flush of pleasure didn't pass unnoticed by Tristan.

He smiled coolly. 'Of course I am. We're all a little mad, didn't you know?'

'Speak for yourself,' snorted Olivia, and she began to hurry away from the children's corner, anxious to disappear before the body of the guinea pig was found.

'You liked me doing that, didn't you?' whispered Tristan in her ear.

'Yes. I'd rather like to marry you when I'm grown up. I wonder if I will?'

'Look and see,' urged Orlando.

Olivia closed her eyes and concentrated hard. The two boys waited with interest. 'I can't see anything at all,' she complained. 'I though I could see as far ahead as I liked but I can't see who I marry. Rats!'

'Can *you* see, Tristan?' demanded Orlando.

'No, I can only look about two weeks ahead. Can you burn things?'

'Yes,' they murmured.

'And move stuff about?'

'No.'

'Can't you?' Tristan pretended to be disappointed but he was really delighted at having a second chance to show off to Olivia. He pointed at a nearby rubbish bin. 'Watch that!'

The twins stared hard. After a few moments the top layer of empty Coke cans and discarded crisp wrappers began to rise up in the air. There was no breeze but they seemed to have a life of

107

their own and whirled higher and higher before shooting off in different directions, finally falling to the ground after about thirty seconds. Tristan continued to concentrate on the bin and soon the entire contents were blowing around, some of the chip containers climbing fifteen feet high before beginning their descent.

'Hey, you kids, what's going on?' demanded an official, and the twins watched Tristan take to his heels and run, leaving them surrounded by falling debris.

'What the hell are you doing?' he shouted. Olivia and Orlando glanced at each other, grasped hands and began to cry.

'Nothing!' sobbed Olivia. 'We didn't do nothing! We're lost. We want our daddy.'

As soon as Meg felt better she and Ashley had returned to where they'd left the twins. Feeding time was over and they should have been highly conspicuous but no one that Ashley asked even remembered seeing them.

'Suppose they've gone off with someone!' exclaimed Meg. 'You should have stayed behind and kept an eye on them. I'd have been all right.'

'If anyone tried to kidnap those two they'd pretty soon realise the error of their ways and return them at top speed!'

'I don't think that's very funny.'

'I'm perfectly serious. Try and calm down. They've probably wandered off exploring. You wait at the café while I make a search; that way if they do come back they won't go off again. Otherwise we could all be wandering around for hours without meeting up.' Meg reluctantly agreed and Ashley set off in the direction of the aviary.

He had only gone a couple of hundred yards when he became aware of pieces of paper fluttering around above him. He glanced at the branches of the trees but they were motionless. Grateful for the unexpected lead he doubled back on his tracks, following the trail of floating rubbish. He heard the twins crying before actually sighting them, but to him their cries sounded forced. There was no genuine distress in the sounds. Sensing trouble he quickened his steps.

As soon as Olivia caught sight of her father she increased her wails.

'There's my daddy,' she hiccuped. 'I want him now. You're a horrid man.' The official, who hadn't managed to get a word in since the twins began crying, looked justifiably aggrieved, and his heart sank at the expression on the face of the man who was bearing down on him.

'What's going on?' demanded Ashley, his voice at its most clipped.

'Daddy! We got lost and then this man came and started shouting at us,' sobbed Orlando, one arm protectively round his apparently terrified twin.

Ashley lifted Olivia up and she buried her head in his neck. Her face felt cool and dry while her breathing was perfectly even, and Ashley knew that he'd been right, she hadn't really been upset. He stared coldly at the official. 'Is this the way you're taught to treat small children when they're lost?'

'Excuse me, sir, but I was told to come here because some children were emptying the rubbish bin and chucking the stuff about. When I arrived your two kids were standing right by the bin. I only asked them what they thought they were doing and they started howling for you.'

'Do you honestly imagine that two pre-school children could be responsible for all this?' asked Ashley scornfully, indicating the litter that was scattered far and wide.

'Not really, but as I say they were the only ones I saw and . . .'

'If they had been responsible, don't you think they'd have run off?'

'Well, I . . .'

'That rubbish bin's completely empty. These two couldn't reach down to the bottom, but I suppose you're too stupid to work that out for yourself.'

'There's no need to be rude. They were watching the stuff flying around, they knew what was going on.'

'Presumably they'd have needed to be blind not to see what was happening! Have you asked them if they saw who did it?'

'I haven't had a chance. They've been yelling so loudly . . .'

'That's what happens when you bully toddlers. I've a damned good mind to report you to head office.'

'I was only doing my job,' repeated the keeper, unable to explain his instinctive distrust of two such tiny children.

Ashley bent down to Orlando. 'Did you see anyone playing with the rubbish? You can tell me, I won't let the man shout at you again.' Orlando gulped, casting an apprehensive glance at the official who felt an overwhelming desire to smack the boy round the ear.

'There were some big children. The boys were scuffling around showing off to the girls and they grabbed handfuls of stuff and threw it around. One of the tins nearly hit Olivia in the eye,' he added for good measure.

'Thank you. Perhaps now you'd care to go off and look for the real culprits while I take these two back to their mother. Unless you were thinking of prosecuting them for being at the scene of the crime?' And he gave a humourless smile that made the official wish he'd never bothered to follow up the original complaint.

'I'll have a look,' he conceded, 'but I'm not likely to find them now. Anyway, they'll only deny it.'

'Quite! A fairly fruitless exercise all round, I fear.' And with one final glance of contempt Ashley took Orlando's hand and walked away. As soon as they were out of the official's sight he put Olivia down and placed a hand on each of the children's shoulders. 'Right, tell me what really happened. Which one of you was responsible for the rubbish flying about like that?'

'Neither of us!' said Olivia furiously. 'It was Tristan. He did it and then ran off.'

'Tristan?'

'Yes, he's Boy Blue. He's nine already, and lives in Middlesex.'

'Boy Blue?'

'I call him Boy Blue because that's his colour. He's one of us; you know, special.'

'Where did he go?'

'Back to his mother. He looked a lot like you; more than we do really. I want to marry him when I grow up, but when I tried to see if I would there wasn't anything there. It was just blank, I couldn't see myself at all. Why was that?'

'I've no idea,' said Ashley absent-mindedly. 'I wish I'd had a chance to say hello.'

'There you are!' cried Meg, and was somewhat disconcerted

to see that Ashley and the twins were considerably less than pleased at her appearance.

'Why didn't you wait where I said?' asked Ashley irritably.

'I was worried about the twins. Where were they?'

'Waiting for an elephant ride.'

'But that's not down here, it's up the other way.'

'We didn't get one,' said Orlando patiently. 'We wanted one but we were in the wrong place.'

'Why did you come down here?'

'Let it drop, will you?' snapped Ashley. 'They're safe and that's what matters.'

Meg nodded. She was too tired to argue and assumed that he was being unreasonable because he'd had a fright over the twins' absence. 'I thought it would be nice if we went to the children's corner,' she said brightly. 'I expect they've got quite a few tame animals there for you to pick up and stroke.'

Olivia wrinkled her nose. 'It's probably all smelly rabbits and goats.'

'I'd rather see spiders and snakes,' added Orlando. 'They feed dead mice to snakes.'

'Well, *I* like tame animals so you'll have to put up with the smelly rabbits for a bit,' said Meg firmly, and ignoring their protests she took hold of their hands and led them along the path they had recently taken with Tristan.

At the entrance a uniformed official politely blocked their way. 'I'm sorry, madam, but there's been an unfortunate accident and this area's closed for the next half hour.'

'What sort of accident?' asked Ashley. Meg had already turned away and the twins were almost out of sight so quick had they been to escape.

The official gave a non-committal shrug. 'Nothing important.'

'Important enough to close you down it appears.'

'One of the guinea pigs died, that's all.'

'A guinea pig? Don't tell me you shut down for a half-hour funeral service every time you lose a guinea pig?'

'Not generally no. Now, if you wouldn't mind, sir?'

Ashley's unease was increasing all the time. First of all the twins hadn't wanted to come here, now it appeared there'd been some kind of accident. It was inconceivable that the two facts were unrelated. As he reluctantly started to turn away he caught sight of a uniformed policeman coming out of the wooden office looking very shaken. Without another word, Ashley followed Meg and the twins; he would find out what had happened eventually.

On the journey home Meg fell asleep but the twins couldn't sit still and kept bouncing around on the back seat. 'A pity about the children's zoo,' said Ashley casually. A quick look in his driving mirror showed that Orlando was now quite still while Olivia's eyes were alert as she leant forward so that he could feel her breath warm on the back of his neck.

'We didn't mind,' she assured him.

'I don't suppose you did, since you'd already been there with Tristan.'

'We hadn't.' Her voice was uncertain.

'Don't lie to me, Olivia.'

'How do you know?'

'I have my ways. You aren't the only clever person in the family.'

'You're just guessing.'

'What happened?' he asked quietly, checking to see that Meg was still asleep.

'We walked about a bit, looked at the rabbits and things and then came out. It was boring.'

'See any guinea pigs?'

'Yes!' enthused Orlando. 'A lovely fluffy one with . . .'

'Shut up!' hissed Olivia, and he immediately sank back into the seat.

'Why did you do it?' asked Ashley.

'Do what?' queried his daughter.

'Whatever it was that happened to the guinea pig.'

'It was for the tingles,' explained Orlando in a rush. 'You know, I told you about the tingles. Well, Tristan gets his by . . . Ouch!'

'What's the matter?'

'Livvy hit me in the stomach. Ouch, that really hurts!'

'You mean you were stupid enough to . . .'

'Not us — Tristan!' shouted Olivia. Meg gave a murmur and her head lolled forward, jerking her awake.

'What's the matter?'

112

'Nothing,' Ashley reassured her. 'I'm afraid Olivia couldn't keep quiet any longer, but you've had quite a nap and we're nearly home.

The rest of the journey passed in complete silence.

'I think it was worth going,' commented Meg when the children were finally in bed and Ashley was about to go back to the house that he'd bought for them to live in after their marriage.

'Definitely.'

'It's funny but the twins have never asked for any kind of pet. Do you think they ought to have one this year? It might teach them a few useful things.'

'Such as?'

'Oh, I don't know: the fact that small creatures need care and attention; a sense of responsibility for something other than themselves. All the books say that children should have pets.'

'I don't think they're ready for that kind of responsibility.'

'Perhaps not,' she agreed, closing her eyes as he pulled her against him and bent to kiss her goodnight.

'This time next week we'll be married,' he reminded her when they finally separated.

'Lovely! Cat's offered to have the twins for the first couple of days, to give us time to settle in the new house.'

'How tactful of her.'

'Do you think it's a good idea?'

'Excellent!'

Unfortunately, fate had other plans for them.

Chapter 8

Their wedding day was cold and wet, a typical English summer's day. Whilst Meg's outfit was reasonably warm poor Olivia's lilac dress was completely unsuitable but she didn't seem to mind, and for once she smiled for the photographs.

Orlando, uneasy in grey trousers, white shirt and dark blue jacket, carried a silver horseshoe and had the anxious look of all small boys who are required to stay tidy and quiet for longer than five minutes.

Ashley looked smart but serious in his brown lounge suit and light green shirt. It was only when they finally exchanged rings that he actually smiled at Meg. She cherished his rare smiles, frequently trying to coax extra ones out of him simply for the delighted thrill that ran through her when she succeeded. She no longer noticed that they still didn't reach his eyes.

Catriona insisted on holding a small reception at her house. Miles was very withdrawn but his wife seemed to be as excited as the bride. Several times Meg saw her sister touch Ashley lightly on the arm, or engage him in intimate chats that caused her to laugh vivaciously, her eyes sparkling more brightly than Meg had seen them since David's accident. If Ashley was entertained he certainly didn't show it; his features stayed set in their normal detached mask of indifference and not once did he return his sister-in-law's smiles.

The twins spent some of the time talking to David. He'd been dressed up for the occasion but took little notice of the people around him. He didn't appear to hear his cousins, but whenever Miles came near the boy's eyes would move towards him. When Meg noticed this she felt that Miles' devotion was

114

paying off. If David were truly a complete cabbage, even his father's presence would be meaningless.

It was Catriona who finally toasted the newlyweds. She had already drunk a great deal of wine and scarcely glanced at her sister, saving every vivacious look for Ashley.

'We all wish you both the very best of luck in the future,' she giggled, waving her glass carelessly in the air, 'and hope that not too many of your blessings are little ones! We think, well *I* think – this doesn't apply to Miles – that Meg's been incredibly fortunate and is quite undeserving of such a gorgeous second husband. If you ever feel the same way, Ashley, then you know where to come!'

Meg flushed with anger. She knew that Catriona claimed to fancy Ashley but a joke together was one thing. An outright proposition on Meg's wedding day was so outrageous that she couldn't think how to respond, except that she had an uncharacteristic desire to jump at Catriona and scratch her face.

Ashley, his left hand resting lightly round his wife's waist, merely curved his mouth upwards and nodded politely. 'Thank you very much, Catriona, for those kind words, but I feel that you've got things the wrong way round. *I'm* the one who's incredbily fortunate to find myself such a lovely, exciting wife and two fantastic children. May I also add that I know for a fact that all our blessings will not be little ones!'

'Cheers!' murmured Miles half-heartedly. As they raised their glasses the telephone in the hall began to ring.

'It's for Mr Webster,' called Catriona's daily help.

'Me?' Ashley was astounded. 'Who on earth knows I'm, here today?'

'It's someone called Susan,' explained the daily.

'That must be my daughter. What on earth can she want?' With a puzzled frown he hurried out of the room and Meg saw the twins whispering together excitedly. She felt distinctly uneasy, certain that whatever Susan wanted to say, it wouldn't be a conventional good luck message. Helena had been so adamant about her children's fear of their father that nothing less than a tragedy could have prompted such a call.

Five minutes passed and still Ashley didn't return. Meg took David to the bathroom while Miles picked aimlessly at the food. Olivia looked at her mother with an expression of triumph in her eyes. All at once Meg was catapulted back in time, back to Scotland and Helena's visit. There had been triumph in Olivia's eyes then too as she had shouted at Ashley's first wife a message that, try as she might, Meg had never been able to banish from her mind. 'You're going to die,' her daughter had prophesied. 'You'll be squashed and they'll have to scrape you off the road.' Silently she began to pray that nothing had happened to Helena.

When Ashley did finally return he was even paler than usual and went straight to Meg. 'There's been an accident,' he said shortly. 'It's Helena, she's dead.'

'No! How did it happen?'

'A multiple car crash on the outskirts of Glasgow. A juggernaut went out of control; she didn't stand a chance. I gather it's taken some time to let me know because there wasn't much of her left to identify.'

'*No*!' screamed Meg, feeling the terror sweep over her as she caught another echo of her daughter's words. 'They'll put your pieces in a plastic bag,' she'd said, and now ... She trembled with horror at the realisation that Olivia had indeed known, had somehow been able to foretell the entire incident.

'For goodness' sake pull yourself together, Meg. There's a lot to be done and I'll need your support. For a start Susan and Ryan will have to come and live with us. There simply isn't anyone else who can have them. I know it's awkward but it's the only solution.'

'No,' said Meg again, but this time she was calm. 'No, Helena didn't want them to come and live with us.'

Ashley's eyes sparked with annoyance but he kept his voice reasonable. 'How on earth could you know that?'

'She told me. That time I saw her in Scotland she said that if anything happened to her she didn't want us to have the children.'

'That's typical of Helena, totally impractical. She didn't happen to suggest an alternative, I suppose? No? Well, since she isn't here to advise us further I shall do what I consider best. The children will come and live with us.'

All the time he was talking his grip on Meg's arm was tightening until she winced with the pain and tried to pull free. 'You're hurting me,' she whispered.

'I thought you liked being hurt!'

Furiously she twisted free of him. 'How can you talk like that when Helena's just died? Haven't you any sense of decency?'

'Trouble, children?' enquired Catriona sweetly, pushing David's chair ahead of her as she crossed the room.

'I'm afraid so. Meg will explain. I've got to get away and make some arrangements. I'm sorry to spoil the day but once your sister's told you all about it I'm sure you'll understand. I'll come back and collect you and the children as soon as I can, Meg, all right?'

Meg turned her head away, hoping that he couldn't see her tears which were a mixture of horror, fear and physical pain. Across the room Olivia lifted her head and her pale blue eyes fixed themselves on her mother. Meg stared back, refusing to look away, until eventually her daughter gave up and bent her head towards Orlando. But she had seen the puzzlement in her mother's eyes and knew that from now on Meg would be watching her very, very carefully.

'How perfectly horrible!' shrieked Catriona when Meg had finished explaining. 'On your wedding day as well. What are the children like? Will they fit in with the twins?'

'I haven't met them. The boy's ten and the girl thirteen, so they're much older.'

'I'm surprised they weren't here for the wedding.'

'They don't have much to do with their father.'

'Didn't,' corrected Catriona. 'From now on they'll be with him all the time.'

'Yes.'

'You must feel very put out. I know I would. After all, it's bad enough starting a new marriage with two children of your own but having to take on two total strangers! If you need any help, I'm always here.'

'I know that. Mind you, I rather got the impression it was Ashley you were hoping to help.'

Catriona frowned. 'What do you mean?'

'Never mind,' sighed Meg. 'It was probably the drink.'

'Are you saying I've had too much to drink?'

'It's the only possible excuse for your outrageous wedding speech. Now, if you'll excuse me I'd like to have a word with the twins.'

Orlando ran up to his mother. 'Where's Daddy gone? I haven't had any champagne yet!'

'Daddy's gone to make some telephone calls. His first wife's had an accident.'

'Is she dead?' asked Olivia innocently.

'Yes, which means that her two children will have to come and live with us.'

'They won't like it.'

'I believe I've heard you say that before.'

Olivia raised her eyebrows. 'When?'

'I'm sure you know when. I expect both of you to be very kind to your father's children when they arrive. They'll be feeling extremely sad.'

'They're nerds!' jeered Olivia. 'They're not like Daddy's other children, they're pathetic.'

'How, may I ask, do you know that?'

'Daddy told us,' said Orlando. 'He doesn't like them, so I don't suppose we will.'

'Of course he likes them. I don't want to hear any more nonsense like that, and if I catch either of you upsetting them you'll be in serious trouble.'

'They're big children,' pointed out Olivia. 'How can we upset big children?'

'Olivia, I am well aware that you can upset anyone you like if you set your mind to it, but remember that I shall be watching you closely all the time.'

The twins started to tighten their mouths, and then simultaneously changed their minds and instead flashed identical, meaningless smiles. 'Of course we'll be good to them,' they chanted. Somehow that was far more terrifying than any number of denials and Meg had to walk out of the room to hide her mounting distaste for her own flesh and blood.

It was seven o'clock before Ashley, Meg and the twins finally arrived home. During the few minutes he'd spent at Catriona's collecting them it had become clear to Meg that her husband didn't wish to talk about whatever arrangements he'd made for Susan and Ryan. She decided to wait for him to bring the subject up.

Surprisingly the twins went docilely to bed, leaving the adults alone for the first time since their marriage. Meg felt slightly awkward, aware that her urgent desire to have Ashley make love to her was somewhat inappropriate considering the events of the day. As a result she couldn't think of a single thing to say and sat silently in the vast living-room like a teenager out on her first date.

'Why so quiet?' asked Ashley, pouring them both champagne.

'I'm not sure what you'd like to talk about.'

'Anything at all. I rather fancied an early night myself.'

'Why couldn't the twins stay with Catriona tonight? That was the original plan.'

'Because, my dear Meg, Susan and Ryan are arriving on the early train tomorrow and I didn't fancy spending the entire day collecting children from different pickup points.'

'It's going to be very difficult for them, isn't it? I mean, the twins are so young and it isn't as though Susan and Ryan are at all used to you.'

'They'll have to adapt. I have neither the time nor the inclination to mollycoddle them.'

'Ashley, they've just lost their mother!'

'You're far too soft-hearted. It's a waste of emotional energy which should be channelled to more useful purposes.'

'Such as what?' she demanded indignantly.

'Come upstairs and I'll show you.'

She had quite expected to find it difficult to relax that night but as soon as his hands touched her body she forgot everything except the sensations he was arousing. His touch was rougher than usual, and some of his movements more aggressive, but she found that she didn't mind. It was tremendously exciting because there seemed to be an element of danger in their passion. She wasn't sure what the danger was but it lurked in the background, waiting to show itself.

In the early hours of the morning she awoke to find Ashley's hands stripping her of the silk nightdress with the split skirt that she had bought especially for their wedding night. He was murmuring gently to her as he eased it down over her hips, but she could tell that he didn't realise she was awake.

Once she was naked he crouched above her and let his mouth stray down her body, licking and nipping softly at the tender flesh of her breasts and thighs. Then his hands moved and

119

roamed lightly over her shoulders and neck, soft butterfly movements that titillated and aroused without any apparent effort. She sighed and closed her eyes again, deciding that she would continue with her pretence of sleep a little longer.

All at once his hands moved to her throat, and now his touch was firmer. His fingers tightened against the pulse spots below her ears and the palms of his hands squeezed against the sides of her neck. Her breathing felt restricted and she tried to turn her head slightly, but immediately his hands squeezed even more tightly, and now she really was choking, coughing and wheezing as she struggled to force air into her lungs.

Ashley took no notice of her movements. Looming above her like a figure from a nightmare he continued to squeeze, and now there were coloured lights flashing behind her eyes and she had the sensation of falling even though there was nowhere for her to go and in reality her husband's body was pressing her deeper and deeper into the mattress as he abruptly thrust himself into her, his movements wild and uncontrolled.

Meg felt certain that she was going to die. She was going to be murdered on her wedding night by a man whose own father was in an asylum for killing a woman. A man who had so enthralled her that she had deliberately put that piece of knowledge out of her mind and allowed herself to become pregnant with his child.

There was a sharp pain in her head and she felt terribly sick. For a moment the thought of retching and choking to death because of Ashley's grip was even worse than simply being strangled. She began to picture her body, the moment when her throat closed and refused to allow her to vomit, the terrible choking that would ensue. She could see it all horribly clearly and gave a final desparate heave, but still she wasn't free.

At that moment she felt Ashley's body buck and tremble with the force of his climax, and immediately he slumped down on her, his hands falling away from her throat, his body a dead weight upon hers.

Shaking from head to foot she tried to move away but he was too heavy and refused to free her. 'Ashley,' she croaked, her voice harsh, her throat raw with pain. 'Ashley, please let me go.' His only answer was a gentle snore.

Suddenly she knew that he had been asleep for the entire

episode. Whimpering with fright she pushed at his body again and again until finally, with a muttered query, he rolled to his side of the bed and his breathing fell into its normal regular pattern again.

Shivering with shock, Meg pulled on a towelling robe and crept to the bathroom. Her white terrified face looked back at her from the mirror in the cabinet and she saw the harsh red finger marks downs the sides of her throat and the vanishing blue tinge to her lips. Dark shadows ringed her eyes and her appearance was that of someone who had quite literally endured a living nightmare.

She stayed in the bathroom for hours, until she heard the twins wake up and start talking. Only then did she feel secure enough to creep back to bed where, contrary to expectation, she immediately fell into a deep, exhausted sleep.

'Meg! Meg, wake up! I've got to collect the children in twenty minutes.' Ashley's voice penetrated his wife's heavy sleep and she struggled to open her eyes. It took a moment or two for her to focus on him, and even when she did there was no immediate reaction of fear. In fact there was relief because he was reality while the rest could only have been a terrible nightmare.

'Are you ill?' he sounded irritable.

'Ill?'

'It isn't like you to lie in bed until ten in the morning.'

'It can't be ten o'clock.'

'I'm afraid it is. The twins have had breakfast, but I warn you I'm not a highly domesticated husband so don't make a habit of this.'

'I'm sorry, I had such a terrible night that when I finally got off to sleep again I just . . .'

'What's happened to your throat?' he demanded, his eyes narrowing as they took in the rapidly discolouring marks round her neck.

Meg put a hand to her throat, wincing as her fingers touched the bruised areas of flesh. 'I thought it was a dream,' she whispered, and now the fear was back and she could no longer meet her husband's gaze.

'Thought what was a dream? For heavens sake explain yourself properly.'

121

'You did this,' she said quietly.

Ashley frowned. 'I did it?'

'Yes.'

'That's impossible! I'd never do anything like that. You look as if someone tried to strangle you.'

'That's precisely what you did do.'

He took a couple of steps back from the bed. 'I don't believe you.'

'Then how do you suppose it happened?' Every word she spoke hurt her damaged throat.

'Why did you let me?' She could hear the panic behind his words but felt no desire to protect him from what he'd done. He had to know, so that he understood why she couldn't share his bed again.

'You did it in your sleep. I woke up to find you making love to me. I thought you were awake, and by the time I realised you weren't it was too late.'

'How did you finally stop me?'

I didn't. It ended when you'd finished.'

'But ...'

'*You nearly killed me!*' she shouted suddenly. 'Do you understand what I'm saying? I was nearly murdered. It wasn't lovemaking, Ashley, it was more like hatemaking and I'm never spending another night in the same room as you again.' Then, at last, she began to cry.

Ashley had listened carefully while she talked, his eyes never leaving her face. He didn't doubt her. Injuries like those couldn't have been self-inflicted. All that he was trying to work out was how he could stop her from ending their marriage before it had even begun. He needed her, not just for the children they would have together but also for the sex. She was his kind of woman and if he could only convince her that she was safe then he envisaged an exciting future for them together.

Her revelation was a shock to him, but he would deal with his own emotions in due course; right now it was Meg who needed reassurance. His brain raced round and round while he tried to come up with any explanation other than the probable truth — that he had inherited his father's insanity. He sat down carefully on the side of the bed. 'Meg, I'm so sorry. I should have realised that I might have a nightmare, only we were . . . '

'A nightmare?'

'Meg, listen to me. Years ago, when I was about fourteen, a gang of village boys got hold of me and started taunting me about my father. They wouldn't let me go and in the end one of them held my head under water in the village stream. I panicked and when he let me go I grabbed him round the throat and tried to throttle him. The other boys pulled me off, he wasn't even hurt, but ever since then if I have too much to drink I seem to regress and live the entire scene over and over again.

'Yesterday, what with the wedding and then the news about Helena, I had more to drink than I realised. For some reason, instead of just dreaming, I acted it out. The only thing I can do is promise that I won't ever drink again, not even a glass of wine.'

'But you didn't only try to strangle me.'

'What do you mean?'

'You were making love to me at the same time. Don't try and tell me that fits in with this childhood memory.'

He shrugged. 'What else can I say?'

'Not much. I don't want you sleeping in here tonight.'

'You're my wife.'

'If I go to the doctor he'll probably help me become your ex-wife fairly rapidly.'

Ashley's first reaction was to lash out, to hit her again and again until she stopped talking forever. He hated her, hated all women for their clinging, deceptive softness that offered so much pleasure then quickly turned to ashes with their whining, unreasonable demands. They were all the same with their silly painted faces and beseeching eyes that positively demanded to be smashed and . . . He pulled himself together with a start. What on earth was he thinking about? That wasn't how he saw women. It certainly wasn't how he saw Meg. Why on earth had he imagined that it was? Surely deep down he didn't . . . ? No, he pushed the thought away. That was how his father must have viewed women, and there was nothing of his father in him.

'Ashley!'

'Sorry?'

'Do you understand why I want you out of here tonight?'

'Yes, of course I understand, but apart from apologising profusely and promising that it won't happen again I really don't see what I can do. The trouble is that my children will need a room each, which doesn't leave a spare.'

'Then you can sleep on the settee. Hadn't you better be on your way?'

'Don't do this, Meg,' he said quietly. 'We've got every chance of being really happy together, don't ruin it before we begin.'

'You don't even look ashamed,' she said bitterly. 'If you'd cried, or asked for help, or simply held me and apologised it might have been different. But no, you look at me as though it's my fault and calmly suggest that the reason I nearly died was because you'd drunk too much champagne.'

'I wanted to hold you but couldn't believe you'd let me.'

'Perhaps you should have tried.'

'Whatever I did was bound to be wrong.'

As she heard him drive away to the station she had to admit that what he'd said was true, but his reactions hadn't been reassuring. He hadn't seemed to appreciate the true horror of the incident, hadn't tried to imagine what it must have been like for her. He'd remained so cool, so self-controlled; and always, at the back of her mind, there was the memory of his father.

In the hour before Ashley returned with his children, Meg dressed in a high-necked blouse and applied careful makeup to conceal the shadows under her eyes. She wanted the children to see her looking her best and desperately hoped that they would eventually settle in and become reasonably happy. She felt that she owed Helena that much at least.

Susan and Ryan's appearance came as something of a shock. Despite Ashley's remarks about them she had still expected some similarity to the twins but there was none. Both the children had fine, mousey-brown hair and were short for their age. Their soft brown eyes were nervous, their faces tense. Ryan's appearance wasn't helped by his National Health glasses with frames held together by a piece of dirty sticking plaster.

'Meet Helena's gift to the wonderful world of children!' laughed their father, ushering them into the hall. 'I apologise for their appearance. Obviously their mother chose all their clothes for them.'

'She didn't,' corrected Susan politely. 'I chose this dress myself.'

'Then clearly you've inherited her lack of dress sense along with her physical characteristics. Where are the twins, Meg?'

Her heart went out to the children in front of her and she glared furiously at Ashley. 'Upstairs playing. Incidentally, Orlando's check shirt is hardly the height of sartorial elegance.'

'At least it's bright; Helena always felt there was virtue in being dull.'

'Come into the kitchen,' said Meg, taking Ryan by the hand. 'I expect you'd like a drink of Coke or lemonade.'

'Lemonade would be nice. We aren't allowed Coke; it rots your teeth.'

'Lemonade it is then. What about you, Susan?'

Susan shook her head. 'I'm not thirsty. I'm sorry but I feel a bit sick.'

'I'm not surprised. You've had a long train journey right on top of the most terrible shock. Most people would feel sick. It's nothing to be ashamed of.'

'Daddy said I was feeble.'

'We can't all be as self-controlled as your father. Once Ryan's had his drink I'll take you both up to meet the twins.'

However, Olivia and Orlando couldn't wait that long. No sooner had Meg got Ashley's children seated than her own two marched into the room, stopping directly in front of the new comers. 'Who are you?' demanded Orlando. 'And why are you drinking my lemonade?'

'This is Ryan, and the lemonade belongs to all of us,' said Meg firmly. 'I told you that Susan and Ryan were coming to live with us.'

'Yes,' said Olivia, with a disdainful glance at the older girl. 'I remember. Their mummy is the one that got squashed by a lorry.'

Both the older children began to cry, although Susan tried very hard to stop her tears. Before Meg could say anything, Ashley came in. 'Not crying again, Susan, surely!'

'Olivia was very unkind,' retorted Meg.

'You both look like Tim Farris,' announced Ryan aggressively. There was a moment's silence while the twins looked questioningly at each other and Meg immediately recalled her collision with the tall ashen-haired boy in Scotland.

'How is Tim?' asked Ashley with interest.

'He keeps running away,' muttered Susan. 'Mr Farris says he wishes Tim would go and never come back. Did you know his sister had died?' Ashley shook his head. 'Well, she did. She fell into the brook and drowned.'

'Feeble' thought Meg. Tim Farris had told her that his half-sister was feeble.

'No great loss as I remember her,' commented Ashley. Olivia laughed.

Meg was horrified. 'You shouldn't talk about people like that, especially in front of the children. You make it sound as though human life isn't important.'

'Not all of it is. I thought I'd take the twins to the park while you get Susan and Ryan settled in.'

'That sounds like a very good idea.'

As she reached the doorway, Olivia turned round and faced the new children. 'We didn't want you to come here,' she said politely, 'and you'll probably be very miserable, but that's not *our* fault.'

Stunned by such calculated cruelty, Meg could only stare after her daughter in disbelief, a feeling that intensified when she heard the sound of Ashley's laughter dying away in the distance.

'I'm sorry,' she said at last. 'I expect she's jealous. She's only a little girl and . . .'

'Tim's like that, too, and Daddy. You're not though, are you?'

Meg looked into two pairs of anxious bespectacled eyes. 'No, Ryan, I'm not like that. Now, let's go and have a look at your rooms.'

It didn't surprise her that they chose to stay there for the rest of the day. She could well imagine their confusion and fear at the thought of facing both their father and the twins. Fortunately she failed to realise that after just one day of marriage she was thinking of her husband and the twins as forming one camp while she and her step-children formed another.

126

Late that night, when all the children were finally asleep, she tackled Ashley over his thoughtless cruelty to his older children. 'I don't understand how any adult could be so unkind, let alone to their own children!' she raged. 'They've just lost their mother. Don't you feel any sympathy for them?'

He had been pretending to read a book but now raised his head and gave her a long, considering look. 'Don't try and turn me into something I'm not, Meg. I've never pretended to be fond of those two upstairs and nothing you say will make me revise my opinion of them.'

'Just because you're not a devoted father it doesn't mean you have to mock and humiliate them. How will they ever get any self-confidence with you continually chipping away at them?'

'They're worthless.'

'Ashley!'

'It's time we got some sleep. May I have a blanket for the settee?'

'Certainly,' she said tightly. 'I'll get it for you.'

He moved so quickly that he was at the door before her. 'May I have a goodnight kiss first?'

'No!'

He put his arms round her stiffening body. 'Come on, Meg. Just a kiss.'

'I don't want to kiss you.'

Very gently he lowered his head and brushed her lips with his. 'Then I won't force you.'

Against her will she could feel her heart pounding as his hands lightly moved down her arms. Her body relaxed a little and at once he pulled her close to him, kissing her temples and the lobes of her ears. 'I want you,' he muttered fiercely. 'Don't you want me?'

She did, but knew that she mustn't give in. Last night she'd been lucky, but the next time it could end very differently and it wasn't only the physical risk that worried her. Ashley's heartless indifference to Susan and Ryan was chilling. How could she want such a man? Yet she did. Even now she wanted him to touch her, arouse her, let her lose herself in ways that were completely new and all the more addictive because she had been so late in discovering the real nature of her sexuality.

127

'No,' she said firmly. 'I need time to think.'

'About what?'

'Us, our future.'

'Our future's fairly predictable. In five months time we'll have a new baby, remember?'

She hadn't remembered, but now that she did she experienced a pang of regret at the over-hasty wedding. The twins were bad enough; Tim Farris sounded equally cold-blooded, and now — thanks to Meg's stupidity — there would be another tainted child for that's what they all were, tainted children.

It was ironical because she recalled telling Ashley how she hadn't wanted to bear Charles' children in case they carried his taint or flaw, but the taint that Ashley passed on was far worse. Charles had paid a small forturne in order that she could give birth to cold, unfeeling children who were descended from a psycopathic killer. Furthermore, she was now carrying yet another of these children and was consumed with lust for their father. She felt utterly ashamed.

'It won't happen again,' he promised as she remained silently lost in thought. 'I'd never knowingly h — '

'Hurt me?'

'I was intending to say injure you. I thought you found some pain stimulating.'

'But I shouldn't' she blurted out. 'What's wrong with me?'

'Nothing at all. You'd be surprised at what goes on in the privacy of bedrooms all over the country.

'It isn't normal. Lovemaking should be tender and caring.'

'Rubbish! Caring, yes. It's important to care about your partner's feelings. But tender? Well, frankly, I'd be wasting my time with you in that respect.'

'I'm so ashamed.'

'You shouldn't be. Just put your romantic novels away and let yourself be natural. Come on, Meg, you want me too. Why deprive yourself?' And he began to unbutton her blouse.

She desperately wanted to stop him, knew that she was being stupid and that if she gave in now he would do exactly as he wanted for the rest of their lives, knowing that she was too sexually obsessed with him ever to oppose him, but when his fingers tightened on her rigid nipples and he began lowering her to the floor her murmured protests changed to moans of desire and her one brief moment of power had gone.

Afterwards, lying in his arms on the floor while he traced the outline of his teeth marks on her lower stomach, she completely despised herself but knew that it was too late. Naturally Ashley didn't spend the night on the settee. However, their sleep was uninterrupted, and as the weeks passed Meg came to believe that providing he didn't drink she was perfectly safe.

Two weeks before the twins were due to start school a hot and heavily pregnant Meg answered a ring at the front door and was flabbergasted to see an all too familiar face. He was taller than when they'd last met, his features less child-like, but there was no mistaking Tim Farris.

'I want to stay,' he said casually. 'Will you let my father know, please?'

'Doesn't he know where you are?'

'I mean Ashley. Your husband is my father. You knew that, didn't you?'

Yes, she'd known, but she certainly hadn't expected to find herself taking in children like some modern-day Dr Barnardo. 'I'd guessed, but I'm afraid you can't turn up uninvited and expect to stay. What on earth will your mother say? You must ring her at once.'

'My father can ring her. She and I aren't talking any more. Where shall I put my case?'

She looked in to the cold, relentless eyes. 'Didn't you hear what I said, Tim? You can't stay here.'

'Why not?'

'For one thing there isn't any room, and for another, children don't go travelling round the country choosing their own home! I'm sure it seemed a good idea when you were lying in bed at night but in reality it can't be done. You'll have to go back to Scotland. I'll ring Ashley now and tell him what you've done. He'll back me up.'

'No!' exclaimed Tim, and he fixed his eyes on Meg. She began to feel weak and dizzy and experienced a strange burning sensation in the middle of her forehead. The baby within her began to move, kicking vigorously, and she knew that she was going to be sick.

When she returned from the bathroom, Tim was watching television with the twins. Meg, frightened by her giddy spell, decided to wait until the evening and Ashley's return.

He was delighted to see Tim, and seemed quite taken aback by Meg's lack of enthusiasm at his arrival. 'He's got a perfectly good home of his own!' she raged. 'There isn't room for him here. Besides, what will his mother say?'

'I've rung her. She doesn't want him back.'

'Why not? She's had him for ten years, why this sudden rejection?'

'She blames him for his sister's death.'

Meg's mouth went dry. 'Was he to blame?'

'How would I know? The police in Scotland certainly didn't think so.'

'*I don't want him either*!' she shouted. 'I can't cope. Once the baby arrives I'll have too much to do; it isn't fair. No normal man provides a refuge for all his illegitimate offspring, it's ludicrous!'

'Thankfully I'm not normal. Oh, Meg, don't be difficult. Tim's a nice boy, he won't give you any trouble and the twins will love him. He might even prove to be a blessing in disguise. He can give them some of the attention that you'll be giving the new arrival. This way they won't feel so left out.'

'What about his schooling? We can't just send him along to the local comprehensive. He's got to have an identity, and I'm definitely not telling people he's your son.'

'Why not?'

'Because they already think you've got all your children under this roof. What explanation can I give for Tim's presence? I don't think we can kill *his* mother off. After all she might come and visit him one day! So what do we say?'

'I'll deal with it,' he assured her. 'I'll see to everything, and I know you'll be as wonderful with him as you are with Susan and Ryan. You're a natural mother, Meg. I appreciate that a great deal.'

'People will talk.'

'Why?'

'Because he's the spitting image of your own step-children!'

'They won't give it a second thought. Lots of children are fair-haired.'

'But he's got the same eyes!'

'I think it's probably best,' he said smoothly, 'if we don't get too involved with other people. Our family relationships are somewhat complex — largely due to Charles' inability to be a proper man — and life will be easier if we try and keep to ourselves.'

'You can't shut the children away from the world, Ashley.'

'I can protect them for a time. That's all they need.'

'Why do they need protecting?'

Ashley raised his eyebrows. 'Haven't you noticed how unlucky they are? Little friends get murdered; fathers have fatal accidents; sisters fall in streams . . . Need I go on?'

Meg stared dumbfounded at him. She couldn't answer because his words had such appalling implications.

That night she went into premature labour and sixteen hours later their child was born.

Despite her hasty entrance she was a healthy child, surprisingly strong for a premature baby. 'She's beautiful!' said the midwife. 'Very striking. Really a most unusual child.'

'I expect she's like the twins,' murmured Meg to Ashley. He'd already taken a quick look at his new daughter. As soon as he saw the pale skin and high domed forehead he knew that once again he'd been lucky and the excitement tingled within him.

'Yes, she is,' he confirmed. Meg turned her head away. It wasn't what she'd wanted; she'd have preferred a normal, brown-haired baby, even if it did grow up to be a despised nerd.

'Have you chosen a name yet?' queried a trainee midwife, busy examining this small, delicate baby who for some inexplicable reason made her feel uncomfortable.

'Ophelia,' said Ashely quickly.

'You can't be serious!' Meg was incredulous.

'It goes well with Olivia and Orlando.'

'She'll be laughed at all through school.'

'I doubt it.'

'Shall I write Ophelia on her name tag?' persisted the midwife.

'I supposed so,' agreed Meg. It didn't matter that much; in

her mind the baby was Ashley's and her name of little importance compared with her personality. When, a few minutes later, Ophelia was put into her arms any slight hope of her being normal vanished.

If anything Ophelia's forehead was even more pronounced than the twins' had been, and there was no vestige of colour on the small face. Not even the occasional red spot or minor blemish that normally mars the features of a newborn baby. Ophelia's skin was waxen and transparent. Her eyes were still tightly shut but when she did open them Meg knew what to expect.

'Well?' asked Ashley.

'Well, what?'

'Don't you think she's beautiful?'

'Not in the least. She's certainly different from most babies, but I imagine you'd have been disappointed with another Susan.'

Putting an arm round Meg's shoulders he gently kissed her temple. 'I'd have been delighted with any child of ours.'

'Sometimes you actually manage to say the right thing in a highly convincing manner.'

'I'm learning!' he laughed.

Meg looked at him and wondered why she remained so obsessed. He was good-looking, but so were a lot of men. His face was hard. There were no softer, redeeming features to it. It was all sharp angles, and the bleakness of expression was redeemed only by the intelligence of the eyes. Yet she was terrified of losing him. She felt a ridiculous urge to cry.

'Ashley, do you love me?'

'Madly!'

'I'm serious.'

'So am I.'

'Can't you think of a better word?'

He hesitated for a moment. 'Insanely?'

She sighed. 'You'd better go now. The children will want to know what's been happening.'

'I'll come back tonight. You'll feel better by then. Try and get some sleep.'

She watched him go and slowly the tears streamed down her face. Madly and insanely were not comforting adverbs.

132

Three days later, Ophelia was taken home. All the children were waiting in the hall like a welcoming committee and Meg was careful to make as much fuss of Susan and Ryan as she did of the twins. She didn't trouble overmuch about Tim. He was only there for Ashley and she felt no affection for him at all. It didn't matter. Tim was too old to need female support; as long as he was near his father he was happy.

'She's super!' enthused Olivia. 'When she's older will you comb her hair forward, Mummy?'

'What a funny question.'

'That's how you hide our big foreheads.'

'True. Well, I probably will. Are you all right, Susan? You look a bit off-colour.'

'She's got a head cold,' said Ashley wearily. 'Don't let her too near the baby.'

'Have you taken anything for it?'

'Daddy said if you coddle a cold it gets worse.'

'Honestly, Ashley! I'll get you a Beechams when Ophelia's in her cot.'

'May I look?' asked Tim diffidently. Meg pulled back the shawl that was protecting her new daughter. 'She's nice,' he said approvingly. 'A proper baby. Not like my half-sister was.'

'How fortunate. Perhaps she'll live to grow up then,' snapped Meg. Everyone was so astonished by her outburst that they remained silently in the hall while she took Ophelia upstairs.

As she lowered her into the carrycot standing next to the bed the baby's eyes opened. For a moment they looked quite normal, but then the light blue became clearer, the irises cloudy and the pupils mere pinpoints. '"O" for Omen,' murmured Meg as she tucked in the sheet and blankets. 'Well, you're in good company.' At that precise moment a trick of the light made it appear that Ophelia actually smiled with pleasure.

Fortunately she was a very good baby. She only cried when she was hungry or wet, and even then it wasn't for long. Within two weeks she was sleeping through the night, and after the early morning feed she would often go back to sleep until ten or eleven a.m.

Ashley had been right about Tim's potential for helping with the twins. There were times when they both resented the demands of their new sister and he was always willing to play board games or take them out for a walk so that Meg could get some rest. She wished that she could warm to him more but it was impossible, so she over-compensated by giving him greater freedom over his bedtime, and also his worrying habit of disappearing on long walks without telling anyone where he was going.

On the 7th September the twins started school. They seemed highly excited, especially with Tim starting at the nearby private school on the same day, but when they entered the building again and found themselves surrounded by crying, screaming, clinging youngsters all using their vocal powers to the full, they panicked.

When the twins panicked they didnt run amok. Instead they stood completely still and retreated into themselves. Their eyes became unfocused, their limbs rigid, and it was impossible to make contact as they always feigned deafness.

Not until the cramped cloakroom had cleared did they come out of their trance. Then, with a quick glance at one another, they hung up their smart blazers, changed into indoor shoes and obediently followed a junior mistress out in to the corridor. They didn't say goodbye to their mother but she stayed until their classroom door shut behind them, in case they gained any comfort from her presence.

When she collected them at lunch-time, after worrying non-stop during their three-hour absence, they looked like children in shock. While other beginners chattered about their experiences, Olivia and Orlando seemed to have trouble with even the simple task of fastening their sandals, and neither of them said a single word.

'Were they all right?' Meg asked their smiling teacher. The smile wavered slightly. 'They were *very* quiet and didn't join in at all. But don't worry — they all settle in the end.'

'Did they cry?'

'Goodness me, no! Nothing like that. They were just ... well, quiet.'

They stayed silent all the way home, but once in the front door they raced round the kitchen hurling playground insults at each other. Then, when they'd finally exhausted themselves, they sat down at the table and looked expectantly at their mother. 'How did it go?' she asked encouragingly.

'I'm hungry,' said Olivia. 'Are you hungry, Orlando?'

'Very hungry. I hope Ophelia's been fed. I don't want to wait for lunch.'

'I'll toast you some sandwiches after you tell me about your day.' teased Meg.

'When I'm hungry I can't talk to people.' Olivia's statement wasn't directed at her mother but at a point some three feet to her right.

'When children don't speak politely to me I can't cook,' she retorted.

'Perhaps I'm not so hungry after all. Shall we go to our room, Orlando?'

It was the beginning of a horribly familiar pattern. A pattern of silence that had led to consultations with the psychologist and Meg had no intention of following that path again.

'You will stay right there,' she said firmly, 'and unless you talk properly to me I shan't let you hold Ophelia tonight.'

Whether they tired of their game or if it was really the prospect of missing this nightly ritual Meg never knew, but straight away Orlando spoke directly to her.

'We don't like school, Mummy. It's full of noise and all the children are pink or pale blue. They've got funny heads as well.'

'Funny heads?'

'Yes. Inside their heads it's just dull grey. One boy — Chris — he's sort of silver so I suppose he's quite clever, but the others are grey.'

'Do you see everything in colours?'

He smiled. 'Most things. Don't you?'

'Not things like the inside of people's heads!'

'Your head isn't grey.'

'I'm relieved to hear it. When you say the children are pink or blue, do you mean . . .'

'Mummy, may we have a sandwich now?'

'In a minute, Olivia. I want to hear what Orlando has to say.'

'You promised! You said that if we talked to you we could eat.'

'All right, I'll start on the sandwiches while Orlando tells me about this blue and pink business.'

'I made it up,' said Orlando flatly.

'It's a game we play,' added Olivia. 'Just a silly game.'

Meg knew that she was beaten and let the matter drop. There'd be other days when she might get Orlando on his own.

By the time half-term came round there was no appreciable improvement in their attitude to school. Meg approached their teacher, Mrs Cusp, and enquired whether or not they'd managed to settle in at all.

Mrs Cusp looked uncomfortable. 'They're very bright children,' she assured her. 'Really quite exceptional. They're both reading fluently, which is more than can be said for most of the children who have been attending full-time. Orlando is good with numbers too.'

'But are they fitting in with the other children? Have they made any friends?'

'I must admit they're somewhat withdrawn. They don't mix, but we've had this problem before with twins. Unfortunately Olivia and Orlando refuse to converse at all. Sometimes they ignore what I say as though they hadn't heard. They're never rude they're just . . . indifferent I suppose you'd call it.'

'I see.' The teacher was only confirming Meg's worst fears.

'Mrs Webster, I don't want you to worry too much about them. They'll be attending full-time after the break and that will probably make a considerable difference. It's always possible that they're simply shy, and of course they do have each other. Unfortunately in a small school like this it isn't possible to split them up, but ultimately that might be the best thing for them both. How did they get on at playgroup?'

'They hardly ever went. After their father died I just let it slip.'

'I do understand. And now there's a new baby in the family. May I peep in the pram?' Meg nodded. 'Goodness, isn't she like Olivia? They obviously take after you.'

'Why do you say that?'

'Why, because . . . That is, I thought you'd remarried?'

Meg flushed at her own stupidity. 'I'm sorry, I wasn't thinking properly. Yes, I suppose they take after my side of the family, but they're not in the least like me.'

'Anyway, Mrs Webster, if things haven't improved by Christmas we'll have another little chat.'

'Thank you,' said Meg, knowing very well that things wouldn't improve and dreading Mrs Cusp suggesting professional advice.

'A whole week off,' enthused Olivia, skipping along beside the pram. 'No more nerds for a week!'

'The teacher says you're both doing very well at reading,' commented Meg. The twins stopped in their tracks. 'What's the matter? She's very pleased with you.'

'That doesn't mean anything. She's not very clever herself.'

'Olivia, she is an adult and a qualified teacher.'

'We might as well be taught by a chimpanzee for all she knows.' Orlando screamed with laughter and another boy who was walking past with his mother pointed at the twins.

'That's them, Mum. They're the funny children I told you about. They don't talk.' His embarrassed mother gave Meg a quick smile and hurried her son away.

The twins widened their eyes and stuck out their tongues like gargoyles on a church wall. 'He's so thick he isn't even grey,' jeered Olivia, but she moved closer to her mother in case any other of her classmates were nearby.

Contrary to Meg's expectation, the half-term holiday passed off quite peacefully. She found that if she kept Susan and Ryan with her and left Tim to keep an eye on the twins then everyone was happy. However, on the occasions when she was too busy to pay attention, Ashley's children by his first marriage nearly always ended up in floods of tears, Ryan weeping uncontrollably for his mother. Despite their misery Helena's children refused to tell Meg what caused their tears.

She didn't mention any of this to Ashley. He wouldn't have had any sympathy for his older children and every time he rejected them, even verbally, Meg found herself less tolerant of this side of his character. It depressed her to think that she could be so obsessed with him, and it seemed logical to avoid confrontation.

Only once during the weeks did she find herself completely unable to cope, and surprisingly it was Tim who caused the trouble. Ever since joining them he'd enjoyed long walks, sometimes staying out for over an hour. Ashley didn't encourage this, saying that if Tim were in an accident they wouldn't know what time to start worrying. They boy had laughed but seen the sense of the remark, and cut the walks down to between twenty and twenty-five minutes after that. Then, on the Thursday afternoon, when Meg went upstairs to collect all the children for a trip into town for winter shoes she found that Tim was missing.

'Where's he gone?' she asked Orlando.'

'Don't know. I want slip-on shoes like Daddy's.'

'Olivia, do you know where Tim is?'

'He's gone for a walk. I want high heels and pointed toes.'

'Has he gone to meet some other boys?' It was a possibility because unlike the twins Tim had fitted in quite well at his new school.

'No,' said Olivia. 'He wanted a walk in peace. I think his head felt swollen.'

'I do wish you two would talk sense now and again. How could his head feel swollen?'

'You know!' cried Orlando eagerly. 'All big and puffy. It means you need some tingles; they always send the puffiness away.' Meg shook her head and searched for coats and boots. Sometimes the twins spoke a language of their own. If she thought carefully enough about what they said she could usually make some sense out of it, but not this time. Puffy heads and tingles were beyond her understanding.

Leaving the back door key in the garage she took the other children into town. They got back at five o'clock but Tim was still missing. Her first instinct was to ring Ashley at work. However, Ophelia started crying for her tea and then Susan had a nosebleed after colliding with Orlando and before Meg had time to turn round she heard Ashley's key in the front door.

'Daddy! Daddy!' chorused the twins, running to meet him with open arms. Meg glanced at Susan and Ryan. They weren't even looking in their father's direction. Susan was concentrating extra hard on the television while Ryan fiddled nervously with a pocket computer game.

'How's life?' Ashley greeted Meg cheerfully, giving her a lingering kiss.

'Tim's missing.'

'Missing?'

'Apparently he went out for a walk after lunch and we haven't seen him since.'

'What do you mean, "apparently"?'

'You've always encouraged him to go off when he felt like it; he no longer considers it necessary to get permission.'

'But he's never been gone this long before. Where was he going, twins?'

They both bit on their bottom lip and looked thoughtful.

'I *have* to know. Where has he gone?'

'He didn't tell us exactly where he was going, but his head felt puffy and he said he wouldn't be back until it was better. If he couldn't find any ...'

'Right! Thank you very much. I think I'll take a drive round the side streets. Hopefully he's making tracks for home by now.'

'Ashley, what on earth do the twins mean by puffy heads and tingles?'

'He must have had a thick head, the sort you get when you're cooped up indoors for days at a time. He needed air, that's all. Good grief, why do you try and make such a mystery out of everything?'

Because it is, she thought resentfully. Because you and your children have a secret life from which I'm excluded and it makes me angry.

It was nine o'clock before Ashley and Tim returned. Ashley's face was grave and he made his son apologise to Meg immediately. She listened to the beautifully spoken words of contrition and knew that they meant nothing. He'd learnt them from Ashley and was repeating them as a parrot would repeat them; they were simply a string of meaningless words.

'Why do you do it?' she asked when he'd finished.

'I guess I miss Scotland. I used to do a lot of walking there.'

'Perhaps you ought to join the Youth Club or something. They're always doing tremendously physical things.'

'Join a crowd of thickos like that? No thanks! I'd rather sit indoors on my own that go out with that crowd.'

'But some of your schoolfriends belong.'

'They're not *my* friends. They like me, that's all.'

'Tim, you must like some of them. Everyone has friends.'

'We don't!' said Olivia complacently.

'No, we jolly well don't,' endorsed Orlando.

Susan looked up from her crocheting. 'I'm not surprised. You're both horrid children!' she shouted, and then ran from the room before anyone had time to react. Ashley jumped out of his chair but Meg caught hold of his arm.

'Let her go. The twins are always teasing her, it isn't surprising she dislikes them. I would in her position.'

'Let go of me,' snapped Ashley. 'She's not getting away with behaviour like that.'

'Why not? You never correct Tim or the twins.'

'Let go of me,' he repeated quietly.

'Not if you're going to punish Susan.'

For a moment she felt a ridiculous sense of fear as his eyes gleamed with temper but then he took a deep breath and returned to his chair. 'You're probably right. Isn't it time *all* the children were in bed?'

Meg felt disproportionately pleased by the incident, incorrectly assuming that she'd begun to teach him how unreasonable he was towards Helena's children. In fact, all she'd done was teach him how to control his temper. She and Susan had come very close to being physically abused.

However, both Ashley and Tim had learnt important lessons that day, and fortunately the news of the discovery of six disembowelled kittens in the park keeper's hut never reached No. 2 Harrowby Drive, otherwise Meg might not have felt so contented.

Chapter 9

Once the twins were at school full-time they appeared to settle in better. Mrs Cusp said they now took an active part in class discussions but were still very reluctant to mix with other children at playtime. Meg, who didn't want any fuss made, accepted this reassurance at face value. As long as the twins weren't disruptive and continued to learn then she was content, and she certainly wasn't going to ask any more questions.

Once spring arrived and the evenings began to lengthen, Tim's desire for solitary walks abated. Meg assumed that this was because he'd started to settle in, but Ashley knew better. The things that Tim wanted to do needed the cover of darkness.

In the middle of May the primary school held their annual crowning of the May Queen, combined with a PTA-run "May Fayre". 'The spelling alone's enough to put me off,' remarked Ashley, surveying a poster brought home by the twins.

'I was asked to run a stall,' confessed Meg, 'but I managed to wriggle out of it because of Ophelia. Even the PTA don't want a mobile toddler beneath their feet.'

'I'm surprised they didn't suggest that I looked after her. Presumably that's why they hold the thing on a weekend.'

'So far you've been conspicuous by your absence. They probably think you're away earning a fortune in Saudi Arabia.'

Ashley continued to read the poster. 'Beautiful baby photo competition. What's that?'

'We've got to take pictures of ourselves as babies to school.

Then the parents choose the prettiest. Livvy and me want separate photos.'

'There isnt any point,' said Meg. 'You were identical babies.'

'Then Livvy can go in for it. Boys aren't meant to be beautiful.'

'Lucky for Ryan!' sneered Tim.

'But unlucky for Susan!' laughed her father.

'They don't have fêtes at our school,' mumbled a flushed Susan.

'It sounds as though they ought to run elocution classes. You're forever muttering.'

'If you didn't jump down her throat every time she spoke, she might be less nervous about talking,' chided Meg.

'Mummy's pets! Mummy's pet!' shouted Olivia. Susan and Ryan picked up their school books and left the room.

'Did you have to do that?'

'Mummy, they're feeble.'

'You think everyone's feeble.'

'No, we don't. Tim isn't; Ophelia isn't; Daddy isn't; Tristan isn't.'

'Who, may I ask, is Tristan?'

Orlando kicked his twin under the table. 'Just a boy we met,' she replied quietly.

'At school?'

'No.'

'He must have been quite someone to meet with your approval. Now go and watch television or something. I want to bath Ophelia in here, and when you two are around she gets thoroughly silly.'

'I don't care to have you correcting me in front of the children, Meg,' remarked Ashley as soon as they were alone.

'We're never private long enough to hold a proper conversation. Besides, I think it's important that Susan and Ryan realise that at least one of the adults in this house doesn't condone the twins' behaviour.'

'We're alone for long spells at night. I'd rather you saved your corrections for then.'

'You wouldn't want to listen at night.'

'How would you know? As soon as we're alone you're

climbing all over me. I don't get time to talk to *you*!'

Meg felt her face go hot. 'That's not true,' she said stiffly. 'I never climb all over you.'

'Not literally perhaps, but you must agree that most of our free time is taken up with activities other than speech.'

'I apologise. I mistakenly thought that you enjoyed it too.'

Now his eyes were dancing with amusement. 'Indeed I do. I've never met a woman who gave me so much pleasure. But the point I'm trying to make is . . .'

'Don't bother. I'll endeavour to have a few headaches from now on.'

'That's stupid. Why make yourself miserable for nothing?'

'You're no better than Charles. He always made me feel over-sexed. Why is it that men are expected to think about nothing else while women should at least make a pretence of occasional indifference.'

'Nobody's asking you to pretend anything. I certainly don't consider you oversexed, I think we're extremely lucky to have found each other. All I'm saying is . . .'

'I know what you're saying.'

'SHUT UP! Kindly let me finish what I want to say. It's ludicrous to tell me that we never have time to talk alone. We do. We have hours and hours when we can talk so if you must criticise me over my relationships with *my* children, then be kind enough to do it in private, before we start amusing ourselves.'

'It's time for Ophelia's bath.'

'You take my point.'

'The only point that is crystal clear to me is that you can't stand Helena's children and take every possible opportunity to humiliate them. I think that's rather demeaning for an intelligent man, and I hate listening to you when you're doing it.'

'Then leave the room until I've finished! Right, shall I fetch Ophelia down?'

It was hopeless, she thought that night when Ashley, worn out by their frantic lovemaking lay asleep beside her. Whatever she said or did he wasn't going to change towards those unfortunate children. It was up to her to compensate them. She found it doubly upsetting because basically they were very nice children, far nicer than any of her own.

The day of the May Fayre was warm and sunny, and even Ashley couldn't think of any good reason to stay away. He insisted that if he was going so was everyone, which meant dragging along a reluctant Tim — who promptly refused to speak to anyone except the twins.

The brown-haired, hazel-eyed seven-year-old who was the May Queen looked wonderfully regal until she tripped over her long train, whereupon she promptly burst into tears while Olivia, who was the youngest of the attendants, had a fit of uncontrollable giggles which attracted the local paper's photographer and meant that the following week her picture appeared alongside the May Queen's and stole the show.

Once the crowning ceremony was completed all the parents flocked to the trestle tables set out round the perimeter of the playing field. There was the usual Tombola, a lucky number stall, some games involving hoops and tennis balls and a marvellously high pile of tin cans on which Orlando spent all his money, paying 10p a time for the privilege of knocking them down with bean bags.

Meg led Ophelia round on reins and paused at the beautiful baby pictures. The photographs were numbered to prevent favouritism, but it was quite clear that one dark-haired baby was outstandingly beautiful. She willingly paid twenty pence to record her vote and resolved to stay around for the result. The winner was going to be the lucky recipient of the Cabbage Patch Doll — to Meg's way of thinking a hideously unattractive toy — which was craved by almost every girl in the school.

'Can't we go home?' asked Ashley at four o'clock.

'No,' scowled Olivia. 'I'm waiting for the Cabbage Patch Doll.'

'You won't win that!' laughed Orlando. 'You looked and you saw who . . .'

'I'm changing things!' she said fiercely. 'That's the whole point of looking. I've been round telling everyone which photo was me.'

'What do you mean she's looked?' asked Meg.

'They're talking nonsense.' Ashley tried to sound disinterested but was actually furious that they could be so careless in public.

144

'Even so, I can't see us getting her away from here without the use of considerable force!'

'Well, I'm going. I'll take Ophelia and the others. You stay with Livvy until she knows she's lost, then bring her home to eat humble pie!'

'We want to stay with Meg,' said Susan and Ryan, edging closer to their stepmother.

'Even better! What about you, Orlando?'

'I'll stay. I'd like to see if Livvy can change things.'

Ashley frowned at him. 'Right, come on, Tim. We'll be on our way.'

Meg resented being left alone to cope with Olivia's disappointment but realised that Ophelia was over-tired and Tim thoroughly bored. It didn't stop her resenting the way Ashley removed himself from any potentially embarrassing scenes. If he found the twins so wonderful she wished he'd do more of the coping.

Eventually the Mayoress stood up to announce the most beautiful baby. She spent several minutes reminding parents that every baby was beautiful in its own way and then finally took out the vital slip of paper.

'The winner of the competition is — ' she paused, smiling down at the waiting children — 'Petra Stanthorpe! Would Petra like to come forward and collect her prize?'

Olivia was stunned. Her lips moved silently while her eyes were at their blankest as a plump, dark-haired six-year-old clambered up the steps and clutched the doll to her chest, her face wreathed in smiles.

'And in second place,' continued the Mayoress, 'Olivia Webster.'

'Livvy, that's you!' whispered Meg, pushing her reluctant daughter forward to collect a furry Koala bear. Olivia's face was expressionless and when she accepted the bear she held it at arm's length, her mouth turning down disdainfully. The onlookers fell silent, quickly parting to let her back to her mother.

For a moment her coldness seemed to affect them all, but then Petra's excited voice rose in the air and the parents were all smiling and talking again while Meg tried to comfort Olivia, explaining that only one girl could win and she was fortunate to have such a lovely bear.

'Pot on the bear!' shouted Olivia, hurling it at Susan. 'You have it, ugly mug. It's the only prize you'll ever win.'

'Stop it!' hissed Meg, trying to drag Olivia towards the school gates. 'You're making a disgraceful exhibition of yourself.'

Olivia twisted free and ran back to where Petra was standing cradling the Cabbage Patch Doll. She stood to attention in front of the older girl and Petra backed away at the look of sheer fury in her eyes.

'Make the most of the doll, Petra Stanthorpe,' she said clearly, her light voice carrying extraordinarily well so that all around them everyone fell silent. 'Enjoy it while you can because you won't have it for long.'

'I will,' said Petra, clutching hold of her mother's skirts for moral support. 'It's mine to keep.'

'*But you're soon going to die*!' shouted Olivia triumphantly. 'You're dying inside now, that's why you're always tired, and you'll be dead before next summer.'

'I won't!' screamed Petra, while her mother stood frozen to the spot.

'Yes, you jolly well will. I can see your coffin: it's white with gold handles, and your mother's crying, and there are gold and white flowers all round, and Mrs Cusp's there and . . .'

'Stop it!' shouted Mrs Stanthorpe. 'Stop it this instant!'

'But it's true!' yelled Olivia. 'It's true, and nothing you say can change it.'

Even as Meg ran towards her daughter, Mrs Stanthorpe's hand shot out and she smacked Oliva hard on the side of the face. She staggered for a moment but then regained her balance and spat at the screaming woman.

By now parents were standing around shouting and pointing and Meg simply grabbed Olivia round the waist, lifted her off the ground and ran out of the playground, through the gates and down the main street until the shouts and screams could no longer be heard. Only then did she put her daughter down.

Before Olivia could speak, Meg took her by the shoulders and shook her backwards and forwards. 'What's the matter with you?' she demanded. 'You must be mad to say such terrible things. You're a wicked little girl. This time even your father won't be on your side. I've never seen such disgraceful

146

behaviour. I'm utterly ashamed, and I don't want to hear another word out of you until we're home.'

'Idiot!' whispered Orlando. 'You've done it now.' But Olivia, almost beside herself with frustration and fury, ignored him.

Once home, Susan and Ryan wisely ran straight to their rooms. Meg marched the twins into the living-room where Ashley and Tim were watching cricket while Ophelia played with her building bricks. 'I think you'd better start looking for another school for the twins,' she announced grimly.

Ashley glanced up. 'What have they done? Burnt the place down?' Meg told him exactly what Olivia had done, and while she spoke Tim too retreated to his bedroom, which was really a converted attic box room. Like Orlando he realised the gravity of Olivia's error, and the possibility of unwelcome repercussions.

'Come with me, Olivia,' ordered her father when Meg finally finished.

'Don't want to,'

The skin on Ashley's face tightened and he fixed her with a look that was far colder than any she could yet manage. 'Do as I say,' he said quietly. This time she obeyed. Sitting her down on her bed he crouched on the floor until their eyes were on a level. 'Were you telling Petra the truth?' he demanded.

'Yes! I don't tell lies.'

'Then you've been incredibly stupid. What will people say when your schoolfriend dies?'

'She isn't my friend!'

'What do you think they'll say?' he repeated evenly.

'Nothing.' Her voice was sullen.

'Oh come along, Livvy, you're a bright girl. They'll all remember today and what you so accurately forecast.'

'So? I'm not going to kill her. It isn't my fault she dies.'

'They will begin to talk about you,' he continued relentlessly. 'They'll point at you in class and whisper about you behind your back. They'll say that you're a witch, that you're abnormal.'

'I don't want to be like other people.'

'And then you'll be watched closely all the time. Watched and watched until you make another mistake, and possibly another and then — when they're quite sure you're not normal — do you know what they'll do, Olivia? They'll lock you away from the world for the rest of your life, just like they've locked up your grandfather. Is that what you want, Livvy? Is it?'

For the first time in years genuine tears filled Olivia's strange eyes and rolled slowly down her face. She shook her head.

'Speak up. I didn't hear you.'

'No,' she sobbed. 'I want to be free.'

'Then learn to control that nasty temper of yours. It's your only weakness so master if before it masters you.'

'Don't let them shut me away!' she whimpered, clutching hold of his sleeve with hands that were trembling. 'Please, Daddy, don't let them.'

'It isn't up to me, it's up to you. Only you can make yourself hold your tongue.'

She wiped the back of her hand over her face. 'What about Petra? Even if I never do it again there's still Petra.'

'I think I'm going to have to have a word with your headmistress. Explain that your were copying some television programme you'd seen and apologise profusely for all the distress caused. That and a generous donation to the school fund might be enough for a time, but if it happens again you're on your own. I'm not jeopardising all of my children just because you can't behave in a civilised manner. You'll be sacrificed, Livvy, for the sake of the others. I have to be fair to you all.'

'I thought you loved me best,' she murmured.

Ashley raised his eyebrows. 'Come on, Olivia, you know better than that. I never expected to hear you talking about things like love.'

'Don't you love any of us?' She was thoroughly shocked.

'Do *you* love *me*?'

Olivia opened her mouth to say that she did and then closed it again. 'I like you,' she said slowly, 'and I want you with me but . . .'

'Precisely, there's always a but, which is how it should be. Emotional clutter is useless, we're better off as we are.'

'I'm sorry about today, Daddy. I won't do it again.'

'Good girl. Now we'll go downstairs and you must apologise to your mother for giving her such a terrible time.'

'Do you love Mummy?' she asked curiously.

Ashley's mouth curved upwards in what was almost a genuine smile. 'Not exactly. What I feel for your mother is far more rewarding.'

'What's it called?'

'Lust, Olivia. It's called lust.'

'That's probably what Orlando feels about blood.'

Yes, mused Ashley. It very probably was.

Thanks mainly to Ashley's visit to the headmistress, Olivia's outburst at the May Fayre was overlooked. He made it clear that she had been punished at home and there it was allowed to rest. Whatever her private thoughts, Mrs Anderson's school came first and since as yet there weren't too many parents willing to pay her fees, she had no intention of antagonising someone with two children at the school and a third due to start in four years time. She therefore smiled graciously and never referred to the matter again. Naturally she didn't forget.

Neither did Meg. She wasn't able to dismiss her daughter's words as mere temper. There had been certainty in Olivia's voice, knowledge in her eyes and triumph on her face when she watched Petra's fit of hysterics. Meg wouldn't feel satisfied until a year had passed and Petra was still alive.

In the meantime, Ophelia was rapidly growing up. She was still extraordinarily well-behaved, never demanding the kind of attention that the twins had required. Catriona continually commented on what a gem of a child she was, and laughingly asked how Meg had managed it.

'I've no idea,' she confessed. 'I think she must take after her father.'

Catriona smiled. 'I wouldn't call Ashley placid.'

There was something about the way she spoke that Meg didn't like. 'How can you say that? You hardly ever see him.'

'Yes, I do. He often calls in to see Miles on his way home from work.'

'Ashley calls in on *you*?'

'Didn't he tell you?'

'No. Why does he need to see Miles?'

'I think he's interested in joining the drama group.'

Of all the lies to choose that was the most ridiculous, and

Meg could only think that Catriona had done it on purpose to get her upset, so she pretended to believe her. 'I hope that doesn't mean I've got to come and watch the plays,' she joked, and had the satisfaction of seeing Catriona's smile disappear. 'How is Miles?' she continued. 'Coming to terms with David's disabilities better now?'

'No, and I can't think why you assume he might be.'

'I imagined that once David was in a good home, Miles might stop thinking about him all the time. An "out of sight, out of mind" situation.'

'Well, you're wrong.'

'And another baby?'

Her sister flushed. 'What are you on about?'

'Has he agreed to have a second child?'

'No.'

'Pity. Still, give him time.'

Catriona started prowling round the kitchen. She seemed strangely keyed-up and moved restlessly from one electrical gadget to another. 'You've done very well for yourself with Ashley. I'm surprised you haven't got an automatic cook, then you'd have absolutely nothing to do except eat grapes and prepare for your nights of bliss.'

'Nights of bliss?' Meg was startled, the memory of the strange, exciting yet terrifying nights that she shared with her husband bringing a flush to her cheeks.

'I assume they are blissful? He looks as though he'd be good at it.'

'I don't want to talk about that if you don't mind, Cat. Some things aren't for general discussion.'

'How funny you are! Most of my friends are only too anxious to talk about their sex lives. Naturally I reciprocate.'

'Poor Miles.'

'Why pity him? I'm the one who has to put up with his infrequent bungled attempts. He used to be quite exciting. David's got a lot to answer for.'

'I'm sure he wouldn't want you talking to me about it, and frankly I'd rather not hear. I happen to like Miles.'

'I like Ashley, so we're one big, happy family.' And Catriona gave a strained laugh. 'How's Ophelia?' she added, crossing the room to where her niece sat with an old board book of the twins.

'She's fine.'

'Has anyone ever said anything about the size of her head?'

'Why should they?'

'Because it's enormous.'

'No it isn't. It was measured when she was born and came within the normal range. Her high forehead makes it look bigger than it really is.'

'Isn't it strange how like the twins she is. I mean, you'd never guess they had different fathers, would you? I wonder who they take after? I don't remember anyone in our family who had eyes like theirs, do you?'

'No,' said Meg, who had been waiting for this ever since she brought Ophelia home from hospital.

Catriona's eyes glittered with malice. 'Tim looks like them, too. Even Miles has noticed that.'

'What do you want me to say?' asked Meg cautiously.

'Tell me the truth, of course. I'm consumed with curiosity. I mean, normally I'd assume Tim was yours too, but since we've never been out of touch for longer than two weeks I know that can't be true. So, tell me what's been going on?'

'Well, I . . .'

'You and Ashley have been lovers for years, haven't you? Go on, admit it. He fathered the twins and poor unsuspecting Charles thought they were his. You're certainly a deep one. I never once suspected you had another man. You always seemed boringly conventional. I quite envy you your secret life.'

'And where does Tim fit in to this theory of yours?'

'I suppose he's Ashley's by some other liaison. Mind you, it's surprising Susan and Ryan are so different. Well, am I right?'

'No.'

'But I must be! You can't pretend it's all one big coincidence. I'm not that gullible.'

'They are all Ashley's children,' admitted Meg slowly, 'but I never met him until after Charles died.'

'What on earth do you mean?'

'Charles was a homosexual. He didn't like making love to women. He preferred teenage boys.'

'I don't believe you.'

'I caught him with one in our own bed one day, otherwise I don't suppose I'd have believed it either.'

'Where does Ashley fit in?' asked Catriona in bewilderment.'

'I'm afraid I threatened to expose Charles unless he allowed me to become pregnant by artificial insemination. I didn't want *his* children, you see. I couldn't let him near me again, and besides I'd have been afraid of a boy inheriting the same perversion.'

'It isn't a perversion, they can't help it.'

'I think it's a perversion. Anyway, as a result I went to a private fertility expert and for an outrageous payment I became pregnant by an unknown donor. A donor who later turned out to be Ashley.'

'You mean you met him by chance? Without knowing that he was the twins' real father?'

'Yes.'

'I don't believe it. Oh, I believe you didn't know,' Catriona continued scornfully, 'but not Ashley. He must have deliberately tracked you down.'

'Why? I'm not the only woman who's borne his children. Why try to find me in particular?'

'Perhaps you were the only widow.'

'But why would he want to marry me?'

Catriona looked questioningly at her sister. 'Perhaps there's something special about the children you bear him?'

Meg swallowed nervously. 'Only their eyes,' she said as lightly as possible. 'Apart from that they're like any other children.'

'I hope that's true,' murmured Catriona to herself. 'What about Tim?' she added aloud. 'Why is he here?'

'Since I'm being completely honest I might as well admit that he's Ashley's son by a woman in Scotland. His step-father quarrelled with him and he ended up on my doorstep.'

'My word, your husband's put himself about a bit, hasn't he! Not only a sperm donor but a philanderer as well. It's an incredible story. Fancy Charles being gay!'

There was then an awkward silence which continued through their lunch of soup and sandwiches. Bitterly regretting

152

her honesty, Meg switched on the television news just in time to see a picture of the country's first test tube triplets flashed on the screen.

The two sisters stared at each other in disbelief for it was like looking at Ophelia in triplicate. 'Mother and babies are all said to be doing well,' concluded the announcer with the slightly simple smile that newsreaders assume when talking about babies or animals.

Meg put down her sandwich and tried to stop her hands from shaking while Catriona kept staring at the screen as though she could summon back the picture by sheer willpower. Across the room Ophelia's eyes widened as she stretched out her arms in a gesture of recognition.

Suddenly Catriona jumped to her feet. 'I'd better get home,' she gabbled. 'I haven't started preparing dinner yet and Miles and I are due out by seven.'

'As you like,' murmured Meg distantly. As soon as she had the house to herself she went to the telephone and dialled a once familiar, never to be forgotten number.

'The Grantley Clinic. Can I help you?' enquired a pleasant voice.

Meg hesitated, wondering whether or not to give her name. 'Yes. That is, I've been given your number by a colleague of my husband's and I wondered if I might make an appointment to see the doctor?'

'What is the name of this colleague?' The voice was sharper now.

'Webster,' said Meg quickly. 'Mr Ashley Webster.'

'And your name?'

'Townhill, Mrs Mary Townhill.'

'One moment please, Mrs Townhill.'

The few minutes that she was left waiting seemed interminable but eventually the receiptionist returned. 'That seems to be in order. The doctor could see you on Friday week at eleven forty-five if that's convenient?'

'That's fine. Thank you very much.'

'Thank you for calling.'

Meg slammed the receiver back and clenched her hands together. Dr Grantley would probably recognise her once she got there but he'd scarcely dare to throw her out without first listening to her. She only hoped that he didn't contact Ashley before her appointment, because he would reveal that he didn't have a colleague called Townhill and then she had no doubt that her appointment would be cancelled.

The next ten days crept by, but finally she was on her way to London. Catriona had Ophelia for the day, the twins were being collected by Tim, Susan and Ryan had their own door key, and she would be back before Ashley, who seemed to be working later and later. Or so he said. Once this interview was over she was going to ask him about his visits to Miles, but that could wait. Dr Grantley couldn't.

As soon as she walked in to the Harley Street consulting room, Meg knew that she'd been right to give a false name. Dr Grantley's expression was far from welcoming as he waved the nurse out of the room, politely remaining standing until Meg was seated.

'I'd expected a Mrs Townhill but your name isn't Townhill, is it?'

'No.'

'You're Mrs Marshall.'

'I *was* Mrs Marshall.'

'Why the deception?'

'Would you have seen me if I'd given my true name?'

'Possibly, if there were problems that you and your husband needed to discuss then I would willingly have seen you together.'

'I'm no longer married to Charles Marshall. I'm now married to Ashley Webster.'

Roger Grantley had spent many years perfecting the art of disguising his true emotions but the astonishment on his face would have been laughable under any other circumstances, and the fear that replaced it was equally plain. 'I fail to see why you gave a false name even if you have remarried,' he said. His tone unconvincing.

'You wouldn't have let me in the door if I'd given my true name.'

'Why ever not?'

'Because Ashley Webster was the donor whose sperm was used to fertilise me.'

The gynaecologist was recovering now and managed an

154

avuncular smile. 'How would you know that? Even if your husband *is* among our donors — and I'm not saying that's true — you have no way of knowing that he fathered your twins. No way at all.'

'He and I have a daughter of our own now.'

'How nice for you both.'

'She's exactly like the twins.'

'Plainly your children take after you.'

'And all three of them are exactly like my husband's natural son by another woman.'

'Indeed?'

'Yes, indeed. Furthermore, the children aren't normal.'

'My dear Mrs Webster, donors are most carefully screened. If we were ever at any time given proof that one of them carried some hereditary taint, then he would no longer be used. We do have certain rules, you know.'

'Actually I didn't know. I've been doing some research at our local library and as far as I can tell you have very few rules indeed. Possibly clinics funded by the National Health have some, but a private practice like your own can do virtually what it likes.'

'Nonsense! It is widely accepted that no donor may be used more than ten times — in fact we are legally obliged to refrain from using them 'more often — and all blood samples are subjected to the most rigorous tests.'

'That may well be the law but I don't believe that you abide by it.'

'Come now, why would we wish to break such a law? There is no shortage of donors and . . .'

'I believe that you're a friend of my husband's from his days at medical school. For reasons best known to himself he's anxious to father a lot of children, far more than could be achieved by normal methods, and you're helping him.'

'Why would I do such a thing?'

'I'm not sure, but it could be connected with his research work. He's busy checking the safety of new drugs. If you are involved in that field then a favourable report from my husband would be invaluable.'

Roger Grantley's face darkened. 'I'm surprised that a mother-of-three has nothing better to do with her time than invent such nonsense.'

155

'Did you know that Ashley's father was jailed for life for killing a girl he'd made pregnant?'

'What rubbish! His father died in ...'

'His father is still alive, but too mad to be allowed out. He's insane, Dr Grantley. A psychopathic killer.'

'If Ashley Webster were a donor for our clinic we would ...'

'And my children are insane.'

There, she'd said it. She'd managed to voice the fear that had been steadily growing over the past months.

'In what way, Mrs Webster?' If he was shocked he certainly wasn't showing it this time.

'Well, they ... They don't seem to understand that it's wrong to hurt people. Orlando hit my nephew with a spade one afternoon and ...'

'Not a unique incident among young children!'

'And now David's a cabbage, a growing boy trapped inside the mind of a six-month-old baby, and Orlando doesn't care! Both he and Olivia seem to think that other people are of no importance.'

'At their age people aren't.'

'They say strange things as well.'

The specialist was regaining his confidence. He could deal with trivial fears like these.

'What kind of things?'

'The twins see everyone as having a colour. I don't know what it means, but they do. And then sometimes they talk about the future as thought they know what's going to happen.'

'Tell me, Mrs Webster, are you under the doctor for any kind of nervous strain?'

'*No*! Why won't you listen to me?'

'I am listening, but there isn't very much to hear.'

'Then a father who kills doesn't automatically exempt a donor from consideration? You don't mind perpetuating a line of killers?'

'We rely upon the donor's integrity when giving us personal details.'

'More fool you.'

'Medical students have high moral standards.'

'You told us that when we first came to you. Charles didn't

agree at the time. I'm afraid the General Medical Council might not agree with you either. Surely you have some responsibility towards the women who come to you? A brief background check wouldn't be that time-consuming.'

'It isn't required by law.'

'Well, it damn well should be!'

He shrugged. 'Possibly, but on the whole most of this kind of work is left to the discretion of the medical profession. Our work is controlled not by laws but by the high standard of medical ethics in this country.'

'Very laudable I'm sure, but you're not even British, are you? You're an American.'

'And Americans have lower moral standards?'

'They're more interested in making a lot of money quickly.'

'How very indignant you sound, and I find that amazing. Shall I tell you why?'

'I don't imagine I can stop you.'

'When you and your first husband came to me you had only decided to have a child one month earlier, am I right?'

'Yes, but . . .'

'And your husband was physically capable of fathering children himself?'

'Yes.'

'Do you know how long most couples who apply for help of this kind have been trying for a child? Approximately ten years. Ten years of waiting, hoping, and undergoing humiliating tests while they make love to a hospital time-table. And after that they wait another two or three years before they get an appointment at a clinic, and even then they have to undergo up to six months' intensive counselling and investigations by social workers before they're accepted as suitable.'

'What's all that got to do with the way you're behaving?'

'Let us be frank, Mrs Webster. Both you and your first husband knew perfectly well that you stood no chance at all of undergoing artificial insemination under the normal system. You didn't qualify. You didn't come within the guidelines so carefully laid down by your beloved National Health.'

'No, I realise that, but Charles was told . . .'

'Precisely! He was told that for a fee, an admittedly high fee, you would be treated *and no questions asked*. Which was

157

fortunate for you because a homosexual husband is possibly even less suitable to be a surrogate father than a murderer's son is suitable to be a donor. One might almost say they deserved each other.'

'We trusted you.'

'Just as I trusted you both to give me frank personal details. It's regrettable that none of us proved worthy of such trust.'

'Even if we were wrong, what you're doing is worse. I saw those triplets last week. They were Ashley's. Three more tainted children. Yes, Charles and I were wrong, but you take advantage of people like us. People with personal problems who . . .'

'Did you know that shortly before your husband's death he'd been literally caught in the act with his office junior? A lad of seventeen.'

'That's a lie!'

'I'm afraid not. His future with the company was in serious jeopardy. One might even say that his death was fortuitous coming at such a time. I'm sure your insurance company would be interested in the details. It makes suicide such a strong possibility.'

'Charles didn't kill himself. He wouldn't have done anything so drastic. He would have known that I'd stand by him and . . .'

'I'm only telling you how it would look to an outsider. I'm sure you knew him best.'

'You're trying to blackmail me.'

'What a ridiculous suggestion. I have no need to stoop so low. My strongest weapon lies with you yourself.'

'I don't understand.'

'If, as you say, Ashley Webster's ancestry is so flawed then why on earth are you married to him? And why have you borne him another child? I'm astounded that you can bear even to share his bed, and this astonishment would undoubtedly be felt by anyone else listening to your preposterous story.'

'I didn't know at first!'

'But you know now. Do you intend to leave him?'

Leave Ashley. These days the thought no longer crossed her mind. She was only concerned about his children, not him. How could she ever live alone after what Ashley had taught

158

her? She was certain that no other man would be able to satisfy her the way he did. She was totally addicted to their peculiar dark sexual practices and eager to progress. How could she possibly leave him now?

'Mrs Webster?'

She stood up. 'I don't think there's much point in my saying any more, but if you continue allowing my husband to father children I think you'll have cause to regret it. When his children grow up, go out into the world and probably inter-marry — since no record is ever kept to prevent such an occurrence — it will be too late for anything except regret. I only hope that one of them crosses your path.'

'Nothing that I've heard today makes me think there's anything wrong with your husband's *children*.'

'Only his wife?'

'I didn't say that, my dear lady.'

'You didn't have to. I'll see myself out.'

Two minutes later Roger Grantley picked up his telephone and dialled Ashley's business number. It would be up to him to make sure that his wife didn't repeat her accusations outside the safety of the Harley Street clinic. Not that Ashley was very amenable to pressure from the specialist, but if it were true about his father then Roger Grantley himself had been manipulated and in those circumstances he felt rather more willing to lean on his friend and colleague than usual.

Exhausted, dispirited and aware of the fact that she'd failed to make any headway at all — mainly because of another of Charles' terrible secrets — it was a thoroughly bad-tempered Meg who collected her youngest daughter from Catriona.

'Did you buy much?' asked her shopaholic sister with a radiant smile.

'No. You're looking more cheerful than you have for ages.'

'That's because I'm happier than I've been for ages.'

'I'm glad someone is. Come here, Ophelia, let's get back home before your father arrives. What's happened, Cat? Something good?'

'Something fantastic — I'm pregnant again!'

'Oh, Catriona, I'm so happy for you! Is Miles pleased too?'

Catriona smiled to herself. 'Not really, but who cares? I'm happy, and that's what counts.'

159

'Well, he can't be that unhappy. It does take two to tango.'

'Indeed it does. I'll ring you tomorrow, Meg.'

If Meg hadn't felt so downcast she might have taken a little more notice of her sister's strange laughter when she agreed with Meg's statement, and seen the gleam of envy in her eyes when she watched her set off for home — and Ashley.

Chapter 10

For several weeks Meg waited in fear of Ashley being told about her visit to the Grantley Clinic, but as time passed and nothing was said she began to believe that for some reason of his own the specialist had decided to keep silent.

There was one small incident that made her wonder, but on reflection she decided that she had made more of it than necessary. It occured late one night as she lay naked beneath Ashley's hands, her flesh leaping in anticipation of the pleasure that awaited. He had been arousing her gradually for nearly an hour, amused as he always was by her attempts to hurry him, and when he finally moved his hands towards the light riding crop that was kept concealed in his bedside drawer and she moaned with the mixture of terror and desire that he always elicited he suddenly stopped, touching her delicately on the breasts.

Startled by the tender gesture where none was anticipated her eyes flew open and she found that he was looking down on her thoughtfully. 'You really love it, don't you?' he murmured.

Meg didn't answer.

'Tell me,' he urged. 'Tell me how much you want it.'

This was something new, and she found herself unable to reply. She was still ashamed of her own passions, as he well knew, and to vocalise such desire was beyond her.

'Tell me or I stop!' he teased, smoothing her hair off her forehead. She wriggled impatiently against him but he moved his body away. 'Tell me,' he repeated.

'I want you,' she whispered, closing her eyes to blot out the satisfaction she knew she'd see in his face.

'No you don't, you want what I can give. You want to be hurt.'

She refused to speak another words.

'Say it. Say that you want to be hurt.'

She shook her head. Nothing on earth would make her admit her weakness aloud.

Ashley waited several minutes and then gave a harsh laugh. 'It doesn't matter. We both know that's what you want. After all, what other reason could you have for staying with me?'

At that moment she was certain that he did know about her visit. That Roger Grantley had told him everything, including the damage that her continuing relationship with Ashley was doing to her case against him.

Later, as she stood beneath the shower hoping that the hot water would soothe her aching body, she decided that she'd misunderstood. It had simply been a new variation of the cat-and-mouse games that he enjoyed so much. Surveying her bruised and discoloured buttocks and thighs she realised that such enjoyment wasn't at all to her credit, but try as she might she couldn't resist the rapture he allowed her to experience. At times like this she wished she could discover how many other women shared her tastes; the answer might make her feel less unnatural. On the other hand it might not.

Apart from that night there was never anything said that could be remotely construed as relating to her confrontation with the doctor. The summer passed, then a damp and dismal autumn, until finally it was nearly Christmas and at last she felt safe.

All of the children were involved in school productions for the last week of term. Tim was to narrate a modern version of the virgin birth written by his class; Susan and Ryan were in their school carol concert and the twins were in a traditional primary school nativity play.

For over a week Olivia talked of nothing but playing the Virgin Mary. Everyone in the family, including her twin, explained that she wasn't likely to get the part but Olivia ignored them.

'I will play Mary, I know I will,' she responded loftily to all their warnings, and so when she finally came home to say that

162

she was one of the angels, Meg quite expected a full blown temper tantrum.

Amazingly enough Olivia took it very well. 'I don't mind,' she assured her mother. 'I *will* be Mary on the day, you wait and see.'

'In that case you won't need an angel's costume!'

'No, I won't.'

'I'd better make you one anyway, for the rehearsals,' said Meg diplomatically. Olivia nodded, plainly humouring her mother for the sake of some peace.

Three days before the performance Olivia positively danced all the way home. 'Petra's off sick! Petra's off sick!' she shouted.

'Who's Petra?'

'She won the baby competition,' said Orlando gravely. At once Meg's heart missed a beat and she had to take slow breaths to keep herself under control.

'What's wrong with her, Livvy?'

'Don't know, but she's off sick. Yipee!'

'Why the pleasure?'

'Because she's meant to be Mary, stupid!'

For a moment Meg stared at her daughter, but eventually the cold glare from the ice-blue eyes defeated her and she turned away. 'Dear God, please let Petra get better and come back to play Mary,' she prayed silently. Nothing more was said. However, on the day of the play Olivia left her angel's wings at home. 'I won't need them,' she said pertly. 'I'm going to be Mary.'

By two p.m. the school hall was packed with parents and young siblings. Ophelia sat quietly on her mother's lap and stared about her. She seemed to know that this was Olivia's day and she was a privileged spectator.

'Excuse me, but do you know how the little girl is who was to play Mary?' Meg asked her nearest neighbour, after spending ten minutes plucking up the courage to speak.

'Petra Stanthorpe?' The woman lowered her voice. 'Haven't you heard? She died yesterday, poor little thing.'

Meg thought she was going to faint.

'It was leukaemia,' confided the woman. 'Very quick. They only found out about a month ago. And do you know the strangest thing of all?' Meg shook her head. 'Last May, at the Fayre, I heard another little girl telling Petra she was going to die. I said to my husband, it really makes you wonder when something like that happens. I mean, how could another child have known? Everyone said it was just a childish outburst of temper, but even then I felt it was more. She was so certain.'

'That's dreadful,' mumbled Meg, pretending that Ophelia's nose needed blowing.

'I tell you one thing: I wouldn't want to be the other girl's mother. What must she be feeling like right now?'

Like death, thought Meg to herself. She's feeling like death.

The nativity play was excellent. There were the usual minor accidents — a king was tripped up by his own page; an angel's wings got caught up in one of the screens; Joseph dropped his lantern — but somehow that only added to its charm. The children were all so intense and self-conscious, taking pride in their performances as they waved at their parents or grinned at classmates.

Except for Olivia.

Olivia gave a flawless performance as the Virgin Mary. She moved with the grace of a natural performer, she gazed at the plastic baby Jesus as though it were the most precious thing she'd ever held, and she never once looked towards her mother and sister. She was, as Meg was forced to admit, truly outstanding.

While Meg was eating the compulsory mince pie afterwards, Mrs Cusp actually came and congratulated her on Olivia's performance. 'She was wonderful, and at such short notice too. I expect you've heard about little Petra?'

'Yes, her poor parents.'

'Terrible, isn't it! We have explained to the children. The headmistress doesn't feel death should be brushed under the carpet so to speak, but I don't think they've really taken it in.'

'Probably not,' agreed Meg.

At that moment Olivia joined them. 'Hello, Mummy. Did you enjoy it? Was I good?'

'Yes I did, and you were very good. Everyone was good.'

'I was the best.'

'You were certainly one of the best.'

'I was *the* best. Mrs Cusp! Mrs Cusp!'

164

Her teacher turned and smiled down at her. 'Yes, dear?'

'Now that Petra's dead may I have her Cabbage Patch Doll?'

Mrs Cusp stared blankly into the cold eyes and swallowed hard, unable to find any words.

'I did come second,' continued Olivia, 'so really I ought to have it. It will only be wasted if I don't.'

Meg wished that the floor would open up and swallow her, preferably taking Olivia too, but since it seemed unlikely to oblige she grabbed her daughter by the arm and pulled her out into the corridor, not caring what other parents thought.

'Olivia, you're a horrible, horrible child! I have never heard such . . .'

'What's the matter? What have I done?'

'What have you done? How can you even ask?'

'*Because I don't know!*' screamed her daughter. 'I only asked for the Cabbage Patch Doll.'

'Petra is dead and your first reaction is to try and take her toys away. Olivia, you must be out of your mind!'

'Well, I knew she was going to die. I can't pretend to be sad and surprised when I've known for ages, can I?'

Meg knelt down on the hard floor and put her face close to Olivia's. 'How did you know?' she hissed. 'Tell me how you knew.'

'Because I looked, of course. It's like going straight to the end of a book, you cheat by skipping a bit, but it's jolly useful. If I hadn't known I wouldn't have made nearly such a good Mary, but I've been practising secretly in my bedroom for weeks now.'

Meg straightened up. 'Have you told anyone else about this?'

'No, I'm not allowed to, it's a secret. *Oh!*' And she clapped one delicate hand over her mouth. 'I shouldn't have told you either.'

'Now it's too late, I'm afraid. Fetch Orlando, we're going straight home, and tonight I'm going to have a long talk with your father.'

'No, Mummy, don't. I'll be in trouble. He warned me not to show off. He said it would be dangerous.'

'He was right.'

'But he'll punish me. I'll be sacri-something just for the others, and the others aren't as good at it as I am so it isn't fair. Please, Mummy, don't tell on me.'

Fortunately for Olivia there wasn't time for Meg to discuss it with Ashley when he got in because it was open night at the twins' school and both he and Meg were going. Meg didn't like leaving all the children alone in the house, so in the end Tim accompanied them to the school so that he could supervise the twins. Susan and Ryan stayed at home with Ophelia.

'After this,' Meg said grimly to her husband, 'I want a word with you about Olivia.'

He nodded, guessing that the child had given herself away again and wondering what he was going to say, but the dreaded discussion was never to materialise.

'I'm so very sorry,' apologised Mrs Cusp when she finally managed to see them over an hour late. 'Unfortunately some of the parents simply refuse to stick to their ten minutes.'

'You should keep a timer by you and when the buzzer sounds their time's up,' joked Ashley, smiling his most boyish smile at the woman whom he knew full well must be in a position to question some of the twins' behaviour. 'How's Orlando's work coming along?' he continued smoothly. 'He's an excellent reader but some of his number work leaves a lot to be desired.'

'Not really, Mr Webster. Orlando is way ahead of the rest of the class in all subjects; in fact I sometimes wonder whether he's getting sufficient stimulation.'

'I'm sure he is. If he became too advanced then his second year would be boring. It's something of a Catch 22 situation.'

'But a very pleasant one! I rarely find a bright boy who's willing to work. Girls are different, they nearly always work hard, but the boys prefer to get by with the minimum of effort.'

'And Olivia?' asked Meg.

Mrs Cusp's face changed. 'Olivia's English work is excellent, as is her art and P.E. Her number work is slightly below average, mainly because she isn't interested.'

'But?' queried Ashley.

'I'm sorry?'

'You sound as though there's more you'd like to say.'

Mrs Cusp took a deep breath. 'You're right of course. Unfortunately I don't know how to phrase this without causing offence.'

'Just tell us what's bothering you.'

'Olivia is a social misfit.'

Meg and Ashley glanced at one another. 'In what way?' asked Meg.

'In every way! She refused to take part in any team games this term, and when we work in groups on the P.E. equipment she wanders where she likes. Unfortunately the other children dislike her so intensely that they're only too pleased when she goes away.'

'What does Orlando do?' asked Meg.

'He does as he's told. It's surprising, but when Olivia's at her most trying he simply disassociates himself from her.'

'Apart from P.E. on her own, what other forms does her anti-social behaviour take?'

'Mr Webster, this isn't easy for me because in all my thirty years of teaching I've never come across a case quite like it, but your daughter is both untruthful and spiteful. She pulls other children's hair, pushes them to the ground, hides their lunch boxes and even — on one occasion — bit a classmate. Whenever she's disciplined for these offences she simply denies them.'

'Do you think she's taking the blame for other children's disobedience as well as her own?' asked Meg, more for the sake of appearances than because she felt it likely.

'No. I never take other children's word for anything. Olivia is only reprimanded when one of the staff knows for certain that she's misbehaved.'

'You're saying she's disruptive?'

'That's an understatement! I've tried to make allowances, but the incident concerning little Petra this afternoon was typical of the kind of behaviour that's commonplace with her.'

'What incident?' asked Ashley.

'I'll tell you later,' murmured Meg.

'Frankly, the school feels that your daughter needs some kind of psychiatric help. You see, her lying isn't confined to trying to escape trouble. She's always telling ridiculous stories to the other children, stories that they find frightening. I've had over half a dozen complaints from parents about these tales tonight.'

'What kind of stories does she tell?' asked Meg.

Mrs Cusp hesitated. 'She pretends that she knows what's going to become of all the children. I suppose it's a kind of twisted fortune-telling because she certainly never tells them anything good.'

'Surely the parents could tell their children to ignore her,' remarked Ashley acidly.

'If it weren't for the unfortunate incident at the May Fayre then I'm sure they would, but after that ... Well, you can imagine how people feel.'

'Olivia is a bright five-year-old,' said Ashley slowly, 'and it seems likely to me that she's as bored with the work here as Orlando. Under the circumstances she's livening life up by behaving badly, trying to make herself the centre of attention through unpleasant behaviour rather than good. It's a common enough problem with intelligent youngsters, and if the school doesn't feel that it can cope then I will withdraw the twins. I do not consider that any psychiatric counselling is necessary.'

'I fully realise how upsetting this must be,' said Mrs Cusp sympathetically, 'but don't you think that their father's death may have affected the twins?'

'Hardly. Neither of them liked him.'

'Ashley!' Meg was horrified and her face showed it. Ashley curled his lip and remained silent.

'Perhaps you'd care to see the headmistress?' suggested Mrs Cusp after a prolonged and awkward pause.

'Not particularly.'

'She is fully acquainted with all the facts.'

'We'll come back another day. I can see Olivia standing outside and we've got two others somewhere. It's time they were in bed at home.'

'Very well, Mr Webster, but I'm afraid the situation can't be ignored.'

'You seem to have ignored it quite successfully until tonight.'

'Yes, but the incident this afternoon emphasised how wrong we've been to allow her so much freedom. If I hadn't heard her

168

myself I would never have believed that any child could be so callous.'

'Come on, Ashley,' urged Meg. 'We'll telephone Mrs Anderson tomorrow.'

Ashley's face was grim. 'You were entrusted with the care of the twins, Mrs Cusp. Any deterioration in their conduct since they arrived at the school can only be because you don't know how to handle them.' Mrs Cusp didn't answer. In the private sector of education there were some things that were better left unsaid.

'Where are Tim and Orlando?' demanded Ashley as Olivia ran to greet him.

'Looking round. Did you see my art work! It's very good. I keep getting stars for art.'

'But not, unfortunately, for tact and sociability.' Olivia stared at her father silently. 'Did you hear me, Olivia?'

'I don't know what you mean. Orlando! Tim! We're going now.' The two boys came running along the corridor. 'I suppose Orlando got all the praise,' she continued. 'Mrs Cusp likes him; he's teacher's pet.'

'Yes, she's very pleased with you, Orlando. And so am I. You're behaving very intelligently.'

'What about me?' demanded Olivia, grabbing at her father's hand.

'You are a very stupid little girl who ought to know better.'

'Why? What have I done? I can read well. I can . . .'

'Be quiet! I'll talk to you later.'

Olivia took one look at his face and fell silent. Suddenly her acts of bravado at school didn't seem quite so clever.

'You're quiet, Tim,' commented Meg when they got home. 'You haven't said a single word this evening.'

'I'm all right, but it was boring waiting around.'

'You're very flushed,' she continued. 'Do you feel ill?'

'No, just tired. May I go to bed now?'

'Of course. Would you like an asprin?'

'I said I'm not ill. Are you deaf or something?'

Meg glanced at her husband. Tim was usually rude towards her when she was alone but never in the presence of his father. However, he got away with his mistake because tonight Ashley had too much on his mind either to notice or care how Tim behaved.

It was nine-thirty before the children were in bed, and even then Meg didn't like to raise the subject of Olivia's behaviour. Ashley looked so furious that she was sure she'd only make him angrier, and she knew it was important for all of them that he should listen calmly to what she had to say.

'Fancy coffee, or a whisky?' she queried.

'Whisky, please. How could she be so stupid?'

'Mrs Cusp?'

'Don't be more foolish than you can help! Olivia.'

'I don't think she's being foolish, I think she's being honest.'

'Precisely!'

'But Ashley, why does she . . . ?'

The sharp ring at the front door was immediately followed by a hammering on the wooden panels. Ashley hurried to see who it was. 'Can't you wait a minute?' he called irritably, and as he opened the door was amazed to find two uniformed policemen standing on the step, their identification cards already outstretched.

'What on earth do you want?' he demanded ungraciously.

'If we might come in, sir?' suggested the Sergeant. 'We're talking to all parents who were at the Heathfield Preparatory school this evening between the hours of six and nine. You and your wife fall in to this category I believe?'

'Why, yes. You'd better come in to the living-room.'

As soon as Meg saw the policemen she was afraid. It was totally illogical but the fear swept over her until her hands trembled and she had to clasp them tightly in her lap to conceal the fact. 'What can we do for you?' queried Ashley politely, but he didn't invite them to sit down.

'What time was your appointment to see Mrs Cusp?' asked the Sergeant.

'Six forty-five,' replied Meg, and watched the constable write it down in his notebook.

'And what time did you eventually get in to see her?'

'Eight o'clock. Surely she's told you that?'

'Just checking our facts, sir.'

'What's wrong?' asked Meg. 'Has something been stolen?'

'Not exactly, madam. Where did you wait from six forty-five until eight?'

'In the corridor.'

'Together?'

'Naturally.'

'You were together all the time?'

'Of course. We sat next to a fair-haired man and his wife who had the appointment after ours. We all talked about the amount of time we were wasting.'

'Do you know their name?'

'I'm afraid not, but their daughter's called Samantha.'

'Did you have your children with you at the school, Mr Webster?'

'Some of them. We took the twins and Tim. My other two children remained behind with the baby. We hadn't expected to be gone very long.'

'Quite so. How old are the twins?'

'Five.'

'And Tim?'

'Twelve.'

The Sergeant nodded. 'Did either of you notice a dark-haired girl of medium height dressed in a pink skirt and jumper?'

'Medium height for what?' asked Ashley.

'Sir?'

'For a three-year-old? A ten-year-old? What age is the child in question?'

'Six, sir. She was six.'

'Yes, I saw her,' interrupted Meg, unaware that he'd used the past tense. 'She was skipping in the corridor outside the girls' cloakroom. She had short white boots on and they made quite a noise.'

'At what time was this?'

'Soon after we got there, about ten to seven I suppose. Is she lost?'

'She's been murdered, Mrs Webster.'

'Murdered? But that's impossible! Murdered in the school?'

'I'm afraid so. She was found in the stationery cupboard with her throat cut. She'd also been sexually assaulted.'

Meg remembered little Beverley whose throat had also been

cut, but tried to push the ridiculous suspicion out of her mind. Even if Orlando could have cut a child's throat he couldn't possibly have sexually assaulted her. Despite this she was trembling from head to foot.

'That's terrible,' said Ashley, politely compassionate. 'But I fail to see how we can help you any further.'

'I don't suppose you can, sir. No, all we're trying to do is find out where everyone was and precisely when the little girl died. The pathologist thought it could have been as early as six-fifteen, but your wife's evidence shows it has to be later. That's a considerable help, we're very grateful.'

From the look in Ashley's eyes he didn't share their sentiments but he took them to the door and expressed his regret for a second time before walking slowly up the stairs to Tim's bedroom. He tapped lightly on the door, 'Tim, are you awake?'

'No!'

'Let me in. I want to speak to you.'

After a few seconds delay his oldest son opened the bedroom door and glared mutinously at his father. 'What do you want?'

'I want to talk to you about a nasty incident at the school this evening.'

'What happened?'

'A little girl was murdered.'

'So?'

'And assaulted.'

'Well?'

'And stuffed in the stationery cupboard.'

'I'm surprised there was room. It was chock full of . . .'

'Thank you, Tim. I trust you can come up with an alibi when the police return, as return they undoubtedly will in due course. Once they find out who you really are they might contact the police in Scotland and hear about that accident to your half-sister. After that, given that policemen here have regrettably suspicious minds, they just might start putting two and two together.'

Tim's face was cold. 'Of course I've got an alibi.'

'May I enquire what it is?'

'I was with Orlando all the time.'

'Were you? Then no doubt he had some quite exceptional

172

tingles. Are you relying on him to keep you out of trouble?'

'Yes. He's popular at school. They'd never think of him protecting someone who killed little girls, any more than they'd think of you having a father who did the same.'

'Save the insults, they're meaningless to me. All I want for you children is that you grow up safely and do well in life. I'm not going to try and tell you what's right and wrong, it's different for all of us, and I'm not going to pass judgement but I must admit that I hadn't anticipated quite such a ferocious blood lust as seems to consume you boys.'

'She wasn't important. Orlando said she couldn't even read.'

'It was a pointless and risky killing. I'm disappointed in you.'

He dropped his head. 'I'm sorry. I was so bored.'

'All right, get to sleep. I'll talk to Orlando over breakfast.'

Downstairs, Meg was still sitting where he'd left her. She looked anxiously up at him. 'What did he say?'

'Who?'

'Orlando.'

'I haven't been talking to Orlando. Good grief, woman, you don't think he did it do you?'

Her laughter was strained. 'Not really, but there's always been something about the murder in the park that bothered me, and hearing that this little girl's throat was cut too I suddenly wondered if . . .'

'He's only five, Meg. Sexual assault's beyond even Orlando!'

'Then why did you go upstairs?'

'To talk to Tim.'

Tim. Her eyes widened with shock and she began to shake her head slowly from side to side. 'Not Tim! Not Tim as well! Ashley, what's wrong with your children. They're not human. they shouldn't be allowed to . . .'

He put a reassuring arm round her shoulders. 'Meg, Tim didn't do it either. Orlando was with him all the time. You're overwrought again.'

'Again?'

'Yes, I decided that you must have been overwrought the day you visited Roger Grantley, that's why I never brought it up. Mind you, I was furious at the time. You could have ruined everything.'

'What is there to ruin?'

'My plan,' he said softly. 'My special plan.'

'If your plan is to populate this country with your maladjusted children then I hope I did ruin it. Can't you see that it's your children who are second class citizens, not everyone else's! They're not special at all, they're simply mad. They take after your father. They . . .'

'*Stop it*! You're shouting loud enough to wake Ophelia. If anyone in this house is unbalanced it's you. I've never heard such rubbish. Perhaps they do like unusual things, but who are we to question that? I'd scarcely call either of us normal!'

Meg's stomach churned. 'That's why I make a good mother for them, isn't it? Because of my . . . Because I like . . .'

'Violence? Yes, it is. You strengthen an already strong strain.'

'But I don't hurt other people. It isn't the same at all!'

'Please, don't bother justifying yourself to me. I'm quite happy with you. Now, I suggest that you take a hot shower and get to bed. You look exhausted, and I want you to be there when I talk to Orlando over breakfast. Once you've heard from him perhaps you'll stop imagining that Tim's some kind of psychopath.'

Meg had her shower and a drink of hot milk before going to bed, but it didn't help. She couldn't fall asleep and pictures of little Beverley and the dark-haired girl at the school danced before her eyes, becoming confused until they no longer had proper faces but instead were simply female forms dripping with blood that flowed from deep gashes across their throats. She was relieved when morning came.

'Shredded wheat please,' demanded Tim at breakfast. Meg watched Susan hand it over before she'd finished helping herself.

'Wait until Susan's finished, Tim!' she snapped.

'I don't mind waiting,' Susan assured her.

'Why aren't you at work, Daddy?' asked Orlando cheerfully.

'I overslept. Tell me, Orlando, how did you and Tim keep

yourselves amused at school last night?'

Olivia glanced briefly at her twin and then kept her head bent over her toast.

'Well, we sort of played about. We peeped in the classroom and looked at all the paintings and books.'

'Why wasn't Olivia with you?'

'She was playing in the sand tray.'

'And you didn't do anything else at all? Nothing that some people might consider wrong?'

'No, not really.'

'And Tim was with you all the time?'

'Oh, yes.'

'I think you did do something wrong.'

Orlando scuffed his feet beneath the table. 'Not *very* wrong.' Meg wondered what her son would consider very wrong.

'I want to hear about it.'

'Mummy won't want to hear at the breakfast table. Nor will Simple Sue and Rotten Ryan!'

'Tell me,' insisted Ashley. Meg glanced at Tim but he appeared quite unconcerned.

'We did go and look at the fish in the tank.'

'Yes?'

'And I said to Tim that they looked like the fish at the beginning of that James Bond film. The one where the man gives his cat a goldfish to eat. Then we sort of talked about the film. I said I didn't think the cat really ate a live fish because I didn't hear it crunch, and Tim said it probably wouldn't crunch because there aren't any big bones. Then we argued a bit and finally Tim took one of the fish out of the tank and ate it.'

'*He ate it while it was alive*?' shouted Meg in disbelief.

'He had to, Mummy, otherwise it wouldn't have been a proper test.' Susan pushed her cereal bowl to one side and left the table. She was quickly followed by her brother. Meg wished she could run after them but she had to stay. She needed to hear it all.

'Anything else' asked Ashley.

'It didn't crunch!' Orlando admitted ruefully. 'I lost the bet, so now he's got my biggest marble.'

175

'Perhaps he swallowed it whole,' suggested Olivia. 'I bet he did. He's a rotten cheat at everything, even snakes and ladders.'

Finally Meg's stomach refused to stand any more and she had to make a frantic dash for the bathroom. She knelt over the toilet bowl retching until there wasn't anything left but still she couldn't stop.

'Are you all right?' asked Susan timidly. Meg nodded.

'Will you keep us safe?' asked Ryan nervously. 'We're rather frightened of Daddy's other children.'

Meg rinsed her face in cool water and turned to face the only other normal human beings in the house. 'Yes,' she assured them, 'I'll keep you safe.'

'Promise?' insisted Ryan.

'I promise.'

Brother and sister turned and went off to school, pathetically reassured by her meaningless statement.

For Meg the scene at breakfast had proved highly significant. Regardless of what else Ashley's children might have done she was never again able to feel any genuine affection for the twins. Once they realised this they dismissed her from their lives by ignoring her, just as they had once ignored Charles. Remembering Charles' fate, Meg lived in a perpetual state of fear.

Chapter 11

'You look washed out, Meg,' said Catriona, letting her sister in the front door. 'Ophelia keeping you up at night?'

'No, she's very good.'

'Then what's the matter? I've never seen you so pale.'

Meg shrugged. 'I'm just over-tired. The children are more difficult now they're getting older, and when I am in bed I can't get to sleep. My brain won't switch off.'

'You ought to see the doctor.'

'He can't help,' Meg said, remembering the silence at the breakfast table that morning. These days only Susan and Ryan ever spoke to her when Ashley was absent, and they were too timid to say very much.

'Change to one who can. I'm glad you've come, I really wanted to talk to you.'

'Why?'

Catriona laughed. 'Don't sound so suspicious. Can't a girl speak to her sister if she wants to?'

'You're not a girl. Besides, I'm surprised you don't talk to Ashley.'

'He doesn't call any more,' said Catriona slowly.

'Perhaps he's given up the idea of drama. I'm not surprised. He can get plenty at home without paying an annual subscription!'

Over coffee, Catriona chatted about her pregnancy and how much she wanted a daughter, none of which required any participation from Meg. However, as the morning passed Catriona began to steer the conversation round to what she really wanted to discuss.

'It's amazing how alike the twins and Ophelia are, isn't it? I mean, you don't usually find brothers and sisters who are virtually clones of one another. And then there's Tim. He must have looked the same when he was young, Why, even now there's a strong resemblance.'

'Yes, it's odd,' admitted Meg.

'But not all of Ashley's children are alike, because there's Susan and Ryan to consider, and by no stretch of the imgination could anyone say they resembled the others.'

'Different mothers,' retorted Meg, wondering why her sister was still so interested in Ashley's children.

'Tim's got a different mother.'

'Well, I don't know why it is. Perhaps Helena had incredibly strong genes that she passed to her children while mine are incredibly feeble and don't show at all. What does it matter?'

'I suppose it doesn't, but it's interesting. Do you think that most of his children look like yours?'

'It appears so. Those triplets we saw on television certainly did.'

'Were they his?'

'I imagine so. That's the trouble with having a child by artificial insemination, you never know when you're going to come across a relation. It's a horrible feeling.'

'Do you mean he might have fathered hundreds of children?' Catriona sounded appalled.

'Not legally. Legally he's only allowed to father ten through the fertility clinic. Mind you, he can father as many as he likes in other ways.'

'He'd need a lot of spare time to rush round seducing enough women to make any significant difference.'

'I wasn't suggesting that he had to court the potential mothers. Since you're interested you might be intrigued to learn that there's nothing to stop him putting an advert in a paper offering to help childless women.'

'You're joking!'

'I am not. If Miss X and Miss Y, who live together in blissful manless harmony, should desire a child to make their "family" complete obviously they wouldn't have a dog's chance of getting one through an adoption agency or infertility clinic, but there's nothing to stop them taking advantage of

178

some generous male who wants to help increase the number of people on our already over-populated planet.'

'You mean men can go round selling themselves?'

'I've no idea if they charge. The point is, there's nothing to stop them and no records will be kept to keep track of their offspring. Technically all such children are illegitimate. The father's name won't appear on the birth certificate.'

'But what happens when the children grow up?'

'Precisely! What happens is that they grow up like all other children, only without being aware of their true parentage. If Olivia happened to fall in love with a blond-haired Adonis in her teens, and if his mother was Miss X or Miss Y, then they'd marry without knowing they were actually half brother and sister.'

Catriona frowned. 'Surely you're wrong? That's ridiculous. It's against the law to intermarry.'

'The way things are going, in another twenty years or so it will be impossible to enforce that law. Now that everyone feels it's their God-given right to have a child, donors will be used more and more. I mean, those test tube triplets were born to a woman with damaged Fallopian tubes and a husband who was infertile! If people like that start having children where will it end? Nature won't have a chance of balancing things out any more. I can imagine white-haired children with strange eyes standing in a line from John O'Groats to Land's End!'

'Do you think that *most* of Ashley's children look like that?'

'I've already said yes.'

'Poor Ashley,' joked Catriona, but her eyes were troubled.

'Why poor Ashley?'

'He won't dare be unfaithful to you in case he makes his women pregnant and gives the whole game away.'

'If Ashley were unfaithful to me it would only be to have more children.'

'How can you say that?'

'Because I suit him better than other women.'

'My word,' jeered Cat, 'you are complacent.'

'I'm not,' said Meg quietly, 'I'm utterly ashamed.'

Surprisingly her sister didn't take her up on the statement, merely changed the subject.

'How was Catriona?' asked Ashley when he got home that evening.

'Very well. She's positively blooming with this pregnancy.'

'Good for her. Tim, answer the front door, will you?'

Tim was back in seconds, sounding nervous. 'It's the police. They want to see you, Meg.'

She went into the hall and found a woman police constable and the Sergeant who had called on them the first time. 'Yes, Sergeant?'

'I'm sorry to trouble you but we did rather want to talk to the children about the open evening.'

'That was weeks ago. They won't remember anything now.'

'It's surprising what children can recall. Is that your oldest boy who let us in?'

'That's Tim. He's staying with us.'

'A relation?'

'Yes.'

'A nephew perhaps?'

'No.'

'What then?'

Meg sighed. 'He's my husband's natural son.'

The W.P.C. made a note on her pad while the Sergeant pulled a sympathetic face. 'I'm sorry.'

'He isn't. He thinks the world of his father.'

'Where does his mother live?'

'Scotland. Would you like to come into the living-room?' she added, sensing that they were moving on to dangerous ground. Ashley's expression was far from welcoming as he gestured for them to sit down. The policewoman remained standing, pencil at the ready, but the Sergeant settled himself in Ashley's chair, glancing around at the assembled children.

'Which of you two is Olivia and which Orlando?' he joked.

'I'm Orlando,' said Olivia coldly. The Sergeant laughed.

'And I'm Livvy,' added Orlando.

'Very good! Well, I'm Sergeant Phipps. I understand that young Orlando here didn't play in the sand tray on open night.'

'Nor did I,' said Olivia.

'A lot of people saw you, young lady.'

'Not in it they didn't. I played *with* it.'

'Well . . .'

'Or possibly *by* it, but certainly not *in* it!'

'Olivia!' snapped Ashley and she fell silent.

'You're correct, of course. To continue, you young man did not play *by* the sand box.'

'No, I was with Tim.'

The policeman glanced at the older boy. 'All the time?'

'Yes, we looked at paintings and things.'

'Which painting did you like best, Tim?' asked the Sergeant suddenly.

'The one of Herod having the babies killed.'

'Which room was that in?'

'Class Three's.'

'Fine. Orlando, didn't you run out of pictures to look at? Your parents were gone a long time.'

'Yep, then we looked at the fishes.'

'In the aquarium?'

'Are there any swimming round loose?' asked Olivia innocently, only to be silenced by a glare from her father.

'Yep, in the tank.'

'And you just watched the fish swimming around, did you?' The question was too casual and Orlando far too bright to miss the significance of this.

'No, we sort of played with them.'

'How do you play with fish?'

'We picked them up — just for a minute or two — and then put them back. Except for one.'

'What happened to that one, Orlando?'

'Tim pretended to swallow it, like a trick on the television, but instead of it sliding up his sleeve it fell on the floor. It looked pretty dead so we flushed it down the toilet in case we got into trouble.'

'They boys' toilet?'

'No, we used the girls' toilet because it was nearer, didn't we, Tim?'

'Yes,' murmured Tim, keeping himself out of the line of the Sergeant's vision.

'Did you see any of the girls while you were flushing the unfortunate fish on to the great pond in the sky?'

Orlando hesitated. 'I think so,' he said at last. 'There was one girl by the door. She had a pinky sort of dress on and told me we couldn't go in the girls' toilet.'

'What did you say to that?'

'I said "Mind your own business".'

'Very sensible! I must say I'm quite relieved to have found out what really happened to the missing fish. One of the mothers saw your little illusion, Tim, and really believed you'd swallowed it. Do you want to be a magician when you grow up?'

'No, I want to be ...'

'Yes?'

'I'm not sure. I can't see too clearly yet.'

'See?'

'What I want to do.'

'Quite! Right, we'll be on our way. I'm sorry to have bothered you again but we're no nearer finding out what happened to that poor girl than on the day she died and so we're going over and over original statements and adding little bits from the children themselves.'

'Naturally you have to do all you can,' said Ashley smoothly.

'Where did Tim live before coming here, sir?' Ashley told him and the Sergeant left, but the W.P.C. hesitated a moment, her eyes on Olivia.

'Was there something you wanted to say?' she asked her gently.

'I was looking ...'

'Is it about the school open evening?' ashed Ashley quickly.

'No, Daddy.'

'Then don't waste the lady's time.'

'It wasn't anything,' Olivia assured her. 'Nothing special, really.'

When the police car drew away, Ashley turned on his daughter. 'I suppose you were about to tell her who she was going to marry, or how many children she'd have!'

'Sort of.'

'I wish you'd learn to keep your mouth shut.'

'Ashley!' Meg hated him speaking so crudely to a child.

'And you shut up too!' he told her furiously. 'Keep out of this; it doesn't concern you.'

'She is my daughter.'

Olivia stared at her mother in silence.

'I'm sorry if you don't like it, Olivia, but facts are facts. You're my daughter.'

Olivia turned to her father. 'Tell her she's right. I *don't* like it.'

When Ashley started to laugh it was the last straw. Meg left the room in a fury. If Ashley found the children so witty and entertaining then let him look after them. Taking down a small case she threw in a few necessities before collecting Ophelia from her cot. Then she packed for the baby and walked downstairs.

'I'm going to stay with Catriona,' she said calmly, enjoying the look of astonishment on all their faces. 'It's obvious that I'm nothing but one of your despised peasants who's stupid enough to cook and clean for you while you ignore me, Well, this particular peasant is rebelling. When you feel that you can treat me civilly, I'll come back.'

'Don't be ridiculous!' Ashley's voice was gentle as he walked over to take her hand.

'I'm not. I'm being realistic.'

'What about us?' cried Ryan in a panic. 'We don't want to stay without you.'

'You're *my* children,' said Ashley sharply. 'You stay with me.'

'No! We don't like it here. We want to go with Meg.'

'I won't let you. Shall I ring for a taxi, Meg?'

Tim moved round behind Susan and tugged sharply on her hair. When she cried out her father didn't even check to see what had happened. 'Stop grizzling, Susan. I can see it's time I toughened you up a little. Meg must have been spoiling you both.'

'Baby!' jeered Tim. 'Cry-baby! Grizzleguts!' And he poked a finger sharply in her ribs.

Susan screamed and ran to Meg. 'Don't go! Please, don't leave us here. You know they'll hurt us.'

It was being done on purpose, Meg knew that. Tim didn't normally bother to abuse Susan or Ryan physically, making fun of them verbally was good enough sport for him. Even so she hesitated.

'Ophelia,' said her father quietly, 'Mummy's going away.

183

Say goodbye to the twins.' Opehlia stiffened and tried to throw herself out of Meg's grasp. Then she began to cry: loud indignant wails of fury which increased in volume while she stretched out her arms towards the twins.

There was no way that Meg could leave them like this; she'd really known that all along. Physically she was free to go. No one would stop her, no one would drag her back to the house, but she couldn't live with herself if she left Helena's children at the mercy of Ashley's dangerous and souless offspring.

Placing Ophelia on the floor she watched the twins run up to her and begin patting her face. 'All right, you win. But I refuse to put up with being ignored day after day.'

'You didn't tell me they were ignoring you,' protested Ashley. 'Besides, they're only children.'

'Try telling that to the little girl in the pink skirt! I'm going to bed. Goodnight.'

Hours later, when Ashley joined her, Meg was still awake. She waited for him to speak but he didn't, simply leant over, kissed her on the forehead and turned away. 'Ashley,' she murmured.

'Yes?'

'Do you believe in the soul?'

He groaned and rolled on to his back. 'What a time to ask me!'

'But do you?'

'No, I think it's a fancy name for a conscience.'

'It hasn't got anything to do with conscience. It's the special part of us that makes us unique, the part that . . .'

'Our fingerprints make us unique.'

'It's the part that makes us cry at the opera and enjoy good paintings. The unseen essence that's an inner part of us.'

'My inner parts consist of lungs, intestines etcetera.'

'Ashley, please. I'm serious.'

'I know you are.'

'Then you don't believe in it.'

'As a matter of fact I do. But I believe that, like our tails, we no longer need souls. Presumably they were useful once. I don't know why but there must have been a reason. Now they're obsolete. I'm convinced that the people who do well these days are the ones fortunate enough to be uncluttered by all the emotional baggage that accompanies this soul.'

'Are you one of the fortunate ones?'

'I'm pleased to say that I am, and so too are most of my children. That's partly why they're special. And they'll do very well indeed for themselves, you'll see.'

'You think that this lack of soul is progression?'

'Naturally.'

'Well, you're wrong. If the children are anything to go by it's regression to the times when the strongest exploited the weak and amusement consisted of barbaric entertainments like gladiator fights where the main excitement came from spilt blood.'

Ashley laughed. 'You're so intense! This is all speculation, and I don't really believe that *our* children are that special, they're simply more realistic than most. Definitely less spiritual — but I hardly think that matters!'

'It does, Ashley.'

'You're not particularly spiritual yourself, you know,' he murmured as he began to kiss her neck and shoulders.

'I am! I don't like hurting anyone.'

'But you like me to hurt you. I don't think I could do that very well if I was highly spiritual.' By now his mouth had closed over her engorged nipple and his teeth were grazing it, lightly at first but then more and more firmly until the tip was scarlet and her breasts aching with desire.

'No, I definitely don't think of you as spiritual,' he continued, his fingers moving between her thighs and parting her pubic hair. 'This is a distinctly earthly pleasure. And it is a pleasure, isn't it?' His fingers were no longer light and teasing but hard and strong. Meg's body was tense with anticipation, her breath coming faster and faster until she screamed aloud as he thrust his thumb deep inside her while his fingers dug into her tender flesh.

There were tears in her eyes because she hadn't been ready but the pain quickly remedied that, and then he was on top of her, his hands now gripping her shoulders as he moved his hips forward and back while constantly increasing the pressure of his hands.

The tension in Meg's body was almost unbearable. She moaned for him to do more, to help her climax more quickly.

Immediately he moved his hands and closed them round her throat. He was lost in his own rhythm now, unaware of her needs, driving towards his own goal. His eyes gleamed with excitement and his hands tightened convulsively, just as they'd tightened on their wedding night, only this time he hadn't been drinking.

The poundings in Meg's ears warned her that she was in danger. She tried to tell Ashley but the words couldn't escape; she tried to twist free, but it was impossible. He was laughing now, looking down at her terror-filled face and laughing. Her eyes began to bulge and he shouted his ecstasy aloud. She was dying and he would actually achieve his ambition to shoot his seed, his chance of future life, into the body of a dying woman. It had always seemed such a potentially marvellous irony, and now he would savour it for himself. Now . . .

At that moment the telephone began to ring.

The extension by their bed was deafening in contrast to the silent, fear-filled struggle that had just been acted out. It brought Ashley back to reality and he immediately removed his hands from Meg's neck. Then he picked up the receiver, hoping that her harsh gasping sounds couldn't be heard by the caller.

Coughing and choking, Meg fell out of the bed. But for the telephone she would now be dead, that was undeniable, and she had only herself to blame. She had wanted more: more pain, more exquisite torture than he had ever given her before, and he had granted her wish. How could she blame him? It was no good telling herself that a normal man wouldn't have reacted that way. What was normal in such situations? How many women would behave as she did? No, it wasn't his fault, but she was still terrified.

'That was Miles,' he said calmly, replacing the receiver. She nodded, still unable to speak because of the restriction in her throat. 'Your sister's had her baby — a little girl. He didn't sound all that thrilled about it. Do you know what they're calling her? Cindy! Like some stupid doll.'

Meg gulped, coughed again and managed to croak a few words. Ashley frowned. 'What did you say?'

'I said Catriona chose that name ages ago.'

Ashley continued to frown. 'Have you got a bad throat?'

186

Meg blinked. Didn't he remember? How could he possibly pretend not to know? She shook her head.

'You sound terrible. If you're no better in the morning then stay in bed.'

'You did this!' she gasped. 'Look at the bruises on my throat.'

A memory tugged at him but then disappeared into the rapidly swelling fog that was obscuring every thought. 'I don't remember,' he said slowly. 'I honestly don't remember.' It was the first time Meg had ever seen him look frightened.

'But you've done it before.'

'When?'

'On our wedding night! You said it was the champagne.'

'Did I?'

'Yes!'

'I suppose I felt I had to give some explanation. It isn't true, of course. Drink doesn't make me . . . Tell me what happened this time.'

Meg rested her head against the pillows. 'It was partly my fault. I wanted you to do more, to . . .'

'I don't supposed you asked me to strangle you?'

'No, but I . . .'

'I'm going back to Scotland, he said abruptly. 'I must go back.'

'Why Scotland?'

'I want to talk to people who saw my father. Doctors, psychiatrists, people like that. I need to know more about him to see if you're right, in which case I've made a terrible mistake.'

What he was saying sounded logical and convincing but Meg didn't quite believe him. Certainly he wanted to find out more about his father's condition, but as to admitting he'd made a mistake, well, she found that very unlikely.

Due to pressure of work it was three days before Ashley could leave for Scotland, and while he was still home Meg persuaded him to take her to the maternity hospital to see Catriona. 'Miles said she needed rest,' he protested.

'I don't know what's wrong with Miles; he's in a most peculiar mood. All I know is that if I don't go Catriona will be livid. Besides, I want to see my first niece.'

187

Still complaining, Ashley capitulated but refused to visit with her. 'I'll be back at eight-fifteen, and don't blame me if you're not welcome,' he called as he drove off.

Catriona had a room to herself. She was sitting up looking exceptionally well. However, when she saw her sister her expression changed. She seemed to be trying to discourage the visit.

'Surprise!' called Meg, standing in the doorway.

'It certainly is. Didn't Miles tell you I was tired.'

'Yes.'

'I'd rather you didn't stay.'

'Surely I could just have a peep at Cindy! After all, she's my first niece and I've bought her a pink matinée jacket in honour of the occasion. Here, you unwrap it.'

Catriona left the parcel lying on her bed. 'I want to sleep,' she said stubbornly. 'Even Miles doesn't visit in the evenings.'

'Does he visit in the afternoons? I didn't think he could get away from work very easily.'

'Are you calling me a liar?'

Meg stared at her sister in astonishment. Ashley had been right, she shouldn't have come; yet Catriona looked so well, and according to Miles the birth had been straightforward enough. 'I'm sorry, Cat. I'll go.'

'Feeding time!' called a young nurse gaily, entering the room with a tiny baby hidden in a blanket. 'Oh good, you've got a visitor at last.'

'Are visitors allowed?' asked Meg, scarcely noticing the way Catriona snatched the baby and hid it in the crook of her arm.

'Of course.'

'I don't think my sister's feeling well enough to see many.'

'Nonsense. She goes home tomorrow,' said the nurse briskly, and then left, her shoes squeaking ferociously.

'They don't care how I feel,' muttered Catriona. 'I'll give you a ring when I get back, Meg.'

'Surely I can look at the baby now I'm here? Come on, Catriona, don't be so mean!' She pulled back the edge of the hospital blanket and stared down at a smaller version of Ophelia.

For a long time neither of the women spoke. Meg closed her

188

eyes and then took a second look but nothing had changed. The baby was still the same. She was white-haired, pale-skinned and quite definitely another child without a soul. Another of Ashley's children.

'I'm truly sorry,' said Catriona gently. 'I didn't want to hurt you like this. I've hoped all along that the baby wouldn't look like yours, that it would take after me. That's why I kept asking about Susan and Ryan. I wanted reassurance that you wouldn't have to know.'

'Did you have to have Ashley as well as Miles? Wasn't your husband enough for you?' cried Meg.

'No, he wasn't! He wouldn't let me have a baby. That was all I wanted, another baby, and he wouldn't allow it. Ashley only slept with me to make me pregnant. It wasn't love or anything like that, it was the same as artificial insemination.'

'Except that you did away with the unpleasant medical methods of ensuring conception and enjoyed the real thing while you waited to fall.'

'I'm sorry,' repeated her sister.

'How sorry?'

'What do you mean?'

'Are you sorry because it was so unpleasant, or because you've hurt me?'

'Because I've hurt you.'

'Then you enjoyed it?'

Catriona's eyes were full of remorse. 'Yes,' she whispered. 'I did. Not at first, but later on when I was used to him, it was ...'

'I don't want to hear any more. I never want to see you again; not you, your daughter or that pathetic husband of yours.'

'You certainly won't see Miles. He's left me.'

'Left?'

'He took one look at Cindy and that was it. I've lost him, Meg. He'll never come back.'

'Good, I'm glad. I'm glad he's gone because he was far too good for you. I hope you miss him, and I hope your precious Cindy brings you as much misery as Ashley's children bring me.'

'I don't understand.'

'You will, believe me you will.'

'Ashley's been to see us,' said Catriona quickly. 'He's been twice. He promised that he'd always be on hand to help with Cindy. I won't be alone, and I won't be unhappy either. She's a very good baby.'

'It's quite difficult to be thoroughly evil when you're only three days old. Just wait. Time's against you.'

'You're mad!' shouted Catriona as Meg walked away. 'Ashley said you were, and he's right. You're talking rubbish. If you don't pull yourself together he might get tired of you, and then where would you be?'

'In heaven,' retorted an enraged Meg, 'and blissfully happy.'

She didn't wait for Ashley to return but instead took a taxi straight home. She stormed in to the house, ordering the children out of the dining-room where they were still having their evening meal.

'*You bastard*!' she screamed at her husband. 'Wasn't it enough to have Roger Grantley impregnating numerous women at his bloody clinic? Did you have to make a fool of me with my own sister?'

'I warned you not to go.'

'You didn't say why!'

'She wanted a child, I wanted a child. It made sense for us to get together.'

'Yes, put like that it sounds very reasonable. It's stupid of me to make such a fuss, isn't it? Very narrow-minded. *I hate you*! I'll never trust you again. Haven't you got enough children yet? When are you going to stop?'

'I think . . .'

'Meg!' shouted Ryan from the top of the stairs. 'Come quickly. They're hurting Susan again.'

Quick as Meg was, Ashley managed to get to Susan's bedroom ahead of her. He was already venting his annoyance on Ryan, telling him crisply not to make such a noise, but when he finally entered his daughter's bedroom he fell silent.

Meg, only yards behind him, practically had to push her way past and then she too stood stock-still in disbelief. Olivia was kneeling on Susan's shoulders, pinning her to the bed, while Orlando was standing beside them, clutching Susan's pink

190

floral nightdress in his hands. Tim was bent over the naked body of his half-sister like specialist at a consultation, except that no specialist ever stood over a patient with a Stanely knife in his right hand. He held it beneath her chin, its sharp edge resting lightly against bare skin.

It was Olivia who saw her parents first. For a moment she glared at them both, but then she levered herself off Susan's shoulders, knocking against her twin's arm as she jumped off the bed.

'Don't!' exclaimed Orlando. 'I'm enjoying looking.'

'Give that knife to me, Tim,' said Ashley quietly. Tim twisted his head in disbelief.

'I thought you were out!'

'You were wrong. Give me that knife at once.'

'I haven't hurt her; it was only to make her keep still.'

'And you, Orlando,' continued Ashley, taking the knife from Tim's outstretched hand, 'give Susan back her nightdress.'

'Here you are!' said Orlando cheerfully, tossing it carelessly on the trembling figure still lying exposed on the bed.

'Now go to your rooms all of you.'

'Why?' demanded Tim belligerently. 'We were only playing.'

'Really? Were you enjoying yourself, Susan?' The girl turned her face into her pillow and began to cry. 'It appears not!' he continued icily. 'Games are meant to provide pleasure to all the participants.'

'We get extra pleasure to make up for Susan not enjoying herself,' retorted Tim, who still didn't look in the least ashamed.

'Where did you get this knife, Tim?'

'I found it in the loft.'

Orlando went pink and tried to hurry away to his room but Meg grabbed his arm. 'Do you know anything about the knife?'

'You're hurting me!'

'I'd like an answer.'

'I got it in Scotland.'

'Then what was it doing in the loft?'

'I hid it there, after.'

191

'After what?'

'Why, after I'd killed Beverley, of course.'

The only sound in the room came from Olivia who caught her breath in horror. Susan and Ryan were too busy clinging together to understand, and no one else could think of anything appropriate to say.

Meg felt strangely calm. She knew that she ought to be shouting and screaming, reacting in some way, but she couldn't. It was as though, deep down, she'd known all the time. Now she didn't have to keep wondering and questioning, feeling guilty at her own suspicion. All that was over. At last she knew.

'Get out of my sight, all of you,' said Ashley.

'Meg, they were being horrid to me,' whimpered Susan. 'They were rude, they kept...'

'It's over now,' murmured Meg soothingly. 'You've nothing to worry about any more. They won't touch you again.'

'Can Ryan stay with me?'

'If he doesn't mind. Will you stay, Ryan?'

The boy nodded obediently. 'I'd like to. Sometimes they come and frighten me. I'll be safer here.'

'I'm going to speak to Tim,' said Ashley.

'What's the point. You can't change him. You can't change any of them.'

'They need to be told that self-control is essential.'

'I doubt if they'd understand you. Your father never learnt any.'

Ashley looked puzzled. 'You're taking this remarkably calmly.'

'Only because I'd already guessed. Anyway, I don't think we've heard the worst. I think there have been other killings. Charles for a start; Tim's half-sister; the little girl at school; your mother.'

'My mother?'

'I don't believe she died by accident.'

'And you blame the children?'

'Who else is there to blame?'

Ashley shrugged.

'Not you? You didn't kill her, did you?'

'Would you prefer to believe the children did it?'

Yes, she thought. Yes, she would, because the children were young and couldn't help themselves while her husband ... It couldn't be him, that was unthinkable. How could she justify living with a murderer? Letting him make love to her, touching her with hands that had taken his own mother's life? No, it was impossible. 'Did you?' she repeated tentatively.

'No.'

She chose to believe him. 'What should we do about Orlando?'

'Nothing. He's far too young to be of interest to the police. They couldn't prosecute even if they wanted to.'

'And Tim?'

'I'm not sure. Actually we don't know Tim's done anything. You're assuming that because Orlando claims to have killed, Tim's done the same.'

'Claimed? Why would Orlando make it up?'

'For the effect of course! It's probably just a piece of boasting.'

'I don't think you believe that any more than I do.'

He raised his eyebrows. 'Worth a try don't you think?'

'It's so horrible,' shuddered Meg as they went downstairs. 'I just don't know how a child could be so callous. She was a lovely little girl, and delighted to be playing with the twins. Why did he kill her? And why isn't he sorry? What sort of child is he, Ashley?'

'My sort.'

She thought for a moment. 'How many children have you fathered?' she asked at last.

'I've no idea.'

'Try to the nearest dozen.'

He shrugged. 'About forty.'

'Forty children?'

'I can check it out with my friends if you don't believe me.'

'What friends?'

'The doctors at the clinics.'

'So there is more than one clinic using your sperm?'

'Of course. Don't worry, they do liaise with each other to try and keep the children geographically spread out.'

'I think that while you're checking up with them it might be a good idea if you suggested that they stopped using you as a donor from now on. Even you must realise that a breed of psychopaths isn't exactly what the world has been waiting for. Quite apart from causing a lot of misery among the unfortunate normal members of the population there's always the risk that they might start turning on each other. Think what a waste that would be!'

'My dear Meg, as usual you're exaggerating. I can sympathise with your distress — Orlando's confession was so incredibly guileless it even disturbed me. He doesn't seem to have any sense of self-preservation.'

'That's the only thing that gives me any comfort!'

He laughed. 'You're amazing. I'd have expected you to be running round in ever decreasing circles screaming your head off by now.'

Meg's legs suddenly felt weak and she sat down in the nearest chair. 'I *would* like to scream. I'd like to go running to the nearest newspaper and tell them everything. I want to challenge the B.M.A. about their incredible lack of controls where surrogate fathers are concerned. I feel that everyone ought to know not only what's going on but how much worse it will become. Yes, I'd like to make the biggest scene imaginable, including telling the world exactly what sort of people can become donors.'

'How interesting — then why aren't you doing anything?'

'Because three of these children are mine. My own children are psycopaths. Oh, I can blame you; I can blame the doctors; I can even blame Charles, but the truth is, as you pointed out, that I used the lack of rules to get what I wanted. I was as bad as the rest of you. They don't feel like my children, I don't love them as most mothers love their children, but I can't tell the world that they're insane. I simply can't do it.'

'Of course you can't, and that's not only because you took advantage of Dr Grantley, is it? It's because you're afraid that they get some of their characteristics from you. You're not too sure what you're really like any more. Since I met you, you've changed. Deep down you wonder what else lies hidden in your soul — this soul that you claim our children don't possess. It must be very uncomfortable for you as I expose your innermost secrets. First of all we've found a masochist beneath that mundane exterior; it's always possible that you could play the sadist too. We've never tried that, but we could. You might discover that we share equal blame for Orlando.'

'And Tim?' shouted Meg, angry because he had correctly pinpointed many of her fears. 'What about his mother? Was she warped in some way? Did she eat her fish raw from the village pond?'

'As far as I know she used the local fish and chip shop.'

'Then how do you explain Tim?'

'I'm not denying that he's mine. However, perhaps proximity to Orlando has increased his criminal tendencies.'

'You don't believe that,' she retorted.

'Whether I do or I don't it's what I shall say if you ever tell anyone about him.'

There was a short silence. 'Go to Scotland,' said Meg wearily. 'Go and find out everything you can about your family. After that perhaps you'll want to put an end to this yourself.'

'I might, but whatever happens in the future there are a lot of children like Tim and the twins out there. Nothing can change that.'

'If they bring back hanging the numbers will thin dramatically once they reach the age of criminal responsibility! I'm sleeping downstairs tonight. If you get lonely try sharing Catriona's hospital bed. I'm sure Cindy would be pleased to see you.'

When she awoke the next morning he'd already left but her sense of relief was quickly erased by the arrival of the twins. They walked slowly in to the kitchen and straight past her.

'I'd quite like a boiled egg for breakfast,' said Olivia to her twin.

'So would I, but I don't know what she'll cook. Who takes us to school today?'

'She does. Where's Daddy gone?'

'Your father's gone . . .'

'To Scotland,' interrupted Orlando. 'I know because I saw him there.'

'Stop ignoring me!' shouted Meg, but they turned their heads away.

'Susan's locked herself in the bathroom,' complained Tim as he came yawning in to the kitchen.

'She won't take long,' answered Meg.

'Did someone speak?' he asked the twins. They giggled.

'Yes, I did, and if you don't answer me, Tim, you won't get any breakfast.'

'I'll make myself some toast and marmalade,' he told Olivia cheerfully. She nodded.

'Stop it!' shouted Meg again. 'I will not put up with your rudeness.' Naturally they didn't reply. When she went upstairs to collect Ophelia she found that she was actually looking forward to the baby's welcoming smile. How ridiculous, she thought, to yearn for a friendly glance from a small child.

It made her realise how utterly bleak and friendless her life had become.

Chapter 12

Every morning when Meg entered the nursery, Ophelia would beam with pleasure and croon to her mother. Every morning until this one. This time Meg was greeted with a cold-eyed stare while her daugher remained silent.

'What's the matter with you this morning?' she laughed. Ophelia stared over her mother's shoulder. 'I'm doing boiled eggs, your favourite! Up you come.'

She had to carry the child downstairs, lying over her shoulder like a sack of potatoes. It was only when she saw the other children in the kitchen that she livened up and began waving her hands in the air.

'Thank goodness for that! I thought you'd forgotten how to move!' laughed Meg. All of the children looked away, except for Susan and Ryan who busied themselves with their mugs of tea. Placing Ophelia in her high chair, Meg began removing the eggs from the saucepan. 'Olivia, come and fetch yours, please.'

'She wants you to get your breakfast,' clarified Tim.

'Get mine too, Livvy, called Orlando.

Meg's hands were trembling but she fixed a determinedly cheerful smile on her face and handed the two eggs in their bright orange egg-cups to her waiting daughter. 'Thank you,' she prompted her. Olivia curled her top lip and returned to the table.

'Right, that does it!' exclaimed Meg. 'The egg is in the water if you want it, Tim. I'm going to give Ophelia hers.'

'She wants you to get your own egg,' Orlando told his brother. Tim sighed but obeyed.

'Here you are, Ophelia. I'll dip the soldiers in the yolk for you,' whispered Meg, wishing that her youngest child would brighten up. Her unusual silence couldn't have happened on a worse day. 'Open your mouth,' she urged.

Ophelia's eyes widened and her pupils shrank as she stared straight at Meg. 'Open your mouth, darling, otherwise you won't be able to eat.' Ophelia's mouth stayed firmly closed.

'Ophelia, what is the . . . Ouch!' Meg jumped as she felt a burning sensation in the middle of her forehead. Putting up a hand she was amazed to feel a tiny blister beneath the fingers, a blister situated right where she could feel the pain, right where Ophelia was looking.

'What on earth was that?' The twins smiled at each other while Ophelia drew in her breath and puffed out her cheeks. Her face turned red and her eyes almost disappeared as she screwed up her features in intense concentration.

'I hope you're not filling your nappy,' admonished Meg. As she spoke Ophelia's boiled egg rose out of the egg cup and hovered above the tray of the high chair. Meg screamed and jumped to her feet, the eggspoon still in her hand. The egg rose higher in the air, and then the yolk lifted from the spoon and spiralled upwards until it hit the ceiling.

Meg was crying now, stumbling away from her daughter whose whole chair was beginning to rock wildly. Susan and Ryan began to cry too, running to Meg's side for protection as slices of toast left the table and whizzed about their heads.

All the other children were laughing helplessly on a note Meg had never heard before. 'Stop it!' she cried at Tim, who was holding his sides with laughter.

'It isn't me!' he gasped. 'It's Ophelia!'

One look at Ophelia's face convinced Meg that he was speaking the truth. The toddler was still holding her breath, but her eyes were dancing with delight as she switched her gaze from one item of food to another until everything edible began to rise in the air. Quickly Meg snatched her daughter out of the seat and immediately the food fell to the ground. Ophelia's attention had been distracted and there was nothing left to keep it airborne. Crying with fear and fury, Meg shook the little girl.

'You're as bad as the rest of them!' she shouted. 'No wonder

198

you were so quiet. I suppose you're ostracising me too.'

'That's right,' said Tim gleefully. 'She's one of us, and we don't like you any more.'

'But how did she do it?' asked a bewildered Meg, indicating the food scattered round the kitchen.

'It's one of her special gifts. I can't do it, nor can the twins, but some of the others can. We'd better hurry now or we'll be late for school.'

'I'm not taking the twins,' said Meg determinedly. 'No doubt they're capable of flying there unaided, but even if they can't I'm staying here. I don't trust any of you, and I feel much safer indoors than out.'

Tim shrugged. The twins weren't his concern. It was up to them to get themselves to school. He left the house alone, leaving Olivia and Orlando kicking their feet aimlessly in the hall.

'I'm not walking all that way,' complained Olivia. 'It's P.E. today. We'll be too tired to enjoy it.'

Orlando thought for a moment. 'Get the pinking scissors,' he whispered. Olivia smiled.

When Meg went upstairs to fetch Susan and Ryan she found them sitting on Susan's bed, their eyes huge and terrified. Olivia was standing behind Susan and in her hand she held her mother's pinking scissors.

'Take us to school or I'll cut Susan's hair off!' she said quietly. Meg hesitated and Olivia dug the points into her half-sister's skull. Susan screamed, and Meg knew that once again — for the sake of Helena's children — she had to give in. She was alone in the house, Ashley might not be back for days and none of these pale-eyed children could be trusted.

'All right, Olivia. There's no need for the dramatics. Put the scissors down. I'll take you all to school.'

'And fetch us?'

'Yes.'

'Good. You shouldn't have favourites. Daddy doesn't have favourites.'

'Are you frightened of us?' Orlando asked as she fumbled to fit the key in the ignition.

'No, I'm shaking with temper.'

'We thought you were frightened.' She was, but to admit it would be dangerous.

Once they'd been dropped off she drove straight to the hospital, carrying Ophelia up to the maternity wing. Catriona was dressed, but it was obvious that she wasn't expecting her sister because she immediately clutched Cindy to her as though she thought Meg would harm the child.

'Don't worry, I don't want your precious daughter. Quite the contrary in fact. I've come to see if you'd like mine.'

'What do you mean?'

'Exactly what I say. Ophelia doesn't like me any more, she made that plain this morning. Perhaps she'd be happier with you.'

'Don't be silly, Meg. Ophelia's only a baby. I couldn't possibly . . .'

'No? What a pity. Still, it was worth a try. I hope you're not waiting for my husband?'

Catriona's blush showed that she was.

'Dear me. I'm afraid he's in Scotland. He's gone to do some research on his family tree. Would you like me to take you!'

'Meg, I . . .'

'I'm not annoyed any more. I can understand how it happened. You're in for some interesting times from now on. Let me tell you about our family breakfast this morning.' And she did, graphically.

'You're not well,' said Catriona quietly. 'Ashley said you'd become highly strung but I didn't realise you'd lost touch with reality. You should hear yourself! Tiny children can't manage levitation. It's adolescents who are said to cause crockery to fly about, or something like that, but never babies.'

'I didn't expect you to believe me, but I felt you had a right to be warned. Now, shall I run you both home?'

Catriona licked her lips nervously.

'I'm not going to hurt you,' Meg exploded. 'If that was my intention I'd wait until you were safely at home. Honestly, you're being paranoid! What do you think I'm going to do?'

'I don't know. What did you do to Charles?'

'*I* didn't kill Charles, the twins did! Catriona, these children are . . .'

'Is something the matter, Mrs Carson?' asked a passing nurse.

Catriona nodded. 'My husband can't manage to collect me.

Would it be all right if I went home by taxi?'

'You can't go on your own, it's against the rules.'

'Then I'll have to stay until my husband returns'.

'I'll take you,' reiterated Meg, moving towards her niece.

'Get away!' warned Catriona. 'Don't come near us, not now and not when we get home. You're sick, and I'll tell Ashley as much. He's been too lenient. You need locking up. I've never heard a mother talk about her children like you do.'

'Oh, drop dead,' retorted Meg, turning on her heel and walking away. She'd done her best. If Cindy ended up destroying Catriona's beautiful home it would serve her right for refusing to listen.

When the children got home that afternoon Meg shut herself away in the living-room. She toasted sandwiches for herself, Susan and Ryan but left the others to fend for themselves. If they chose to pretend she wasn't there then they could find out what her absence would really mean.

At eight o'clock Ashley rang. 'I'm hoping to be home by tomorrow night. There's one other doctor I have to see, then I'll set off.'

'The children miss you.'

'Really?'

'Yes, they're pretending I'm not here.'

Ashley sighed. 'Put Tim on the line.'

'No, I can cope. I'm pretending I'm not here as well. It's an excellent opportunity for them to learn self-sufficiency.'

'What about Ophelia?'

'Ophelia? She's the worst of the lot! Olivia's taking care of her. And don't worry about Sue and Ryan, they're with me.'

'I wouldn't worry about Susan and Ryan if there was a tornado heading their way. See you tomorrow.'

Meg slammed the phone down before he could hang up. Thanks to Ashley there was no one in whom she could confide. He had stopped her from making new friends because of the strong physical resemblance between the four children which was not easily explained away, and since he'd seduced Catriona she no longer had a sister to talk to. There was always Miles, but she didn't know where he had gone.

At nine o'clock she poured herself a large glass of wine and settled down with the paper and some magazines. Normally she wouldn't have seen it but because she was determined to stay out of sight until all the children were asleep she read every tiny paragraph in the paper. Tucked away at the bottom of page four was a paragraph headed, 'Killer Virus Strikes Again'. Thinking at first it was about AIDS, she read it more carefully when she found that it referred to a new strain of meningitis that was killing children within hours of the first symptoms presenting themselves.

Tristan Blakeman, age 10 years, of Middlesex became the sixth victim of the killer virus yesterday when he died in Middlesex General Hospital only three hours after admission. Although the sixth child to die he was the first in the Middlesex area. Doctors have so far been unable to find any link between the victims, whose ages range from twelve years to ten months.

Meg read a little more, discovering that the symptoms were mainly head pains and double vision, followed by trembling fits and internal bleeding. Shivering, she folded the paper up. The last thing she needed right now was tales of illness and death. She needed cheering up.

The next morning all the children except for Susan and Ryan had eaten breakfast and started to get ready for school before she even came down. They had also fed Ophelia and put her back in her cot. Helena's children were reluctant to go to school but Meg insisted that they did. It was natural for them to want to stay within reach of her but everyday life had to go on. Besides, with Ashley getting back that evening things would soon be back to what passed for normal in their house.

She was watching the six o'clock news when she heard his key in the door. The announcer was just informing the public that a baby boy had died in Penrith, Cornwall, from the new strain of meningitis, bringing the total number of victims to seven. A picture of the baby, complete with high, domed forehead and piercing blue eyes fringed by colourless lashes, flashed briefly on the screen. Meg caught her breath, but quickly pressed the red button on the remote control panel as her husband walked in.

'All right?' she asked politely, her heart hammering against her ribs.

'Not bad considering the driving I've done. Where are the children?'

'Upstairs.'

'Playing?'

Either playing or planning a mass execution, I've really no idea.'

'Don't start nagging straight away. I'm too exhausted.'

'And you don't suppose I am? Would you like to hear about our first breakfast without you?'

'Not particularly.' Meg told him just the same. 'I think your eyes were playing tricks,' he murmured. 'Probably Tim threw all the food when you were distracted by the others.'

'Like he made the fish vanish up his sleeve? Come on, Ashley, you don't have to pretend with me. Incidentally, Catriona was waiting for you to take her home yesterday.'

'Christ! I completely forgot.'

'She took a taxi.'

'I didn't think that was allowed.'

'In that case she's still there.' Ashley reached for the telephone but Meg put her hand over the receiver. 'First of all I want to know what you found out.'

'I can't leave her at the hospital.

'She isn't your wife, I am.'

'Cindy's my daughter.'

'Daddy!' screamed Olivia as she ran in to the room. 'You're home! We've been looking after ourselves while you've been gone. Mummy wouldn't cook for us, she'd have let us starve!'

'But you didn't?' smiled Ashley, putting an arm briefly round the small-boned figure.

'Nope, because Tim's a good cook.'

'Good for Tim! I'll be up to see you all later, when you're in bed and ready for sleep.' Olivia ran off to tell the others while Meg waited to see if he'd continue trying to see Catriona, but Olivia had diverted his attention.

'I think you're right,' he said at last, rubbing a hand wearily across his forehead. 'It's probably inadvisable for me to continue fathering children.'

It was what she wanted to hear, but now he'd said it she didn't believe him. 'What's changed your mind?' she asked suspiciously.

'I went back further than my father, back to my paternal grandfather.'

'And?'

'He died in an asylum.'

'Why was he there?'

'He'd committed a murder.'

'What kind of murder?'

'Rather an unpleasant kind. He'd ... Well, in the words of the prosecution he'd "slaughtered his step-sons like sheep".'

'You mean he cut their throats?'

'Yes.'

'What have you done?' she whispered. 'There are already forty children running around with your genes in them. Forty potential psycopaths and no one knows that they need to be watched! What are you going to do now that you've found out?'

'I've rung the clinics, told them that I want to withdraw from their programmes. They didn't query it. In fact, Roger Grantley sounded quite relieved. I think your visit put the wind up him.'

'Isn't there any way we can find out where these children are? Doesn't anyone keep track of them?'

'No.'

'I think it's disgraceful!'

'People would soon complain if they did. "Big Brother is Watching You", and all that kind of thing. Be fair, Meg. Would you have wanted people keeping tabs on the twins?'

'I suppose not. Once they were born I just wanted to forget that they'd come from frozen sperm. I wanted them to be the same as other children. Surely that's understandable?'

'Quite. Which is presumably why the law's so lax.'

'But I was wrong! Emotion shouldn't come before common sense. Women aren't in any position to judge this sort of thing for themselves. Giving birth is highly traumatic. Scientists should provide the protection discreetly, it's their responsibility.'

'We can argue the rights and wrongs of this forever more, it doesn't change anything.'

'If only you'd been more restrained. Why did you have to produce more children than any other donor? Wouldn't ten of these marvellous, emotionless, potential high-fliers have been enough for you? I would have thought that ten like that and two or three marriages would have provided enough for even a young Einstein. Let's face it, your children aren't that special. Unpleasant yes, but hardly potential Nobel prizewinners!'

'You're wrong!' he said scornfully. 'Completely and utterly wrong. My children *are* remarkable. They're way ahead of their time, can do things ordinary people wouldn't dream of. It was only right to father as many as possible. It was a duty I couldn't ignore.'

'Duty? How noble of you! What can they do that other people can't? Aside from killing, that is.'

'They can see into the future.' Meg stared at him in silence. 'You know that's true, Olivia's given the game away often enough. They also see people differently from the rest of us. To them everyone's got a kind of aura, a coloured mist that surrounds the body, and different colours indicate different personality traits.'

'Boy blue!' murmured Meg.

'That's right. Olivia didn't know his name, but she knew what he was going to look like because she'd already foreseen their meeting and noticed his aura. Blue — for intelligence and integrity.'

'Can you do this?'

'Not the colours, but I can pick out different types of people in a crowd. It's more of a sixth sense but it's useful. Once, when I was much younger, I could see into the future as well as the children can, but the more children I've fathered the less clear the future's grown. I suppose it's like everything else about us, it diminishes with age.'

'Is that all?'

'There are one or two other things. The flying food, for example. Ophelia's too young to know how to control it, but some of them can make physical objects move, and some of them can cause spontaneous combustion as well. Mind you, that's dangerous and best left until they're in their teens.'

Without thinking, Meg's hand moved to the burn on her forehead. 'Ophelia did this,' she told Ashley when his eyes followed her hand.

'The twins did it to you once, up in their bedroom. It was just before we were married.'

'But what good does it all do them?'

'I tell you about a miraculous advance in the psychic powers of human beings and you ask what good it does them? Where's your scientific curiosity? It opens up whole new worlds. If these children can do all this, then how much more will their own children achieve? Especially if they intermarry! It's the most exciting thing I've ever come across, and the fact that I'm able to help this progression come about more quickly is just fantastic.'

'Or would be.'

'What?'

'If they weren't flawed by their blood-lust.'

'Yes, I have to admit that is unfortunate!'

'So unfortunate that the entire experiment has to come to an end.'

Ashley flicked his eyes away and ran his fingers through his hair. 'All right, I admit I've got to stop now, but at least I've made a reasonable start.'

Meg shook her head. 'How can you be pleased when you know that they're all mad? They're not an advance on anything; they're warped, twisted deviants whose only satisfaction comes from blood, pain and humiliation. Hardly a brave new world!'

'They may not all be flawed. In experiments you expect mistakes. It's probably the mothers that make the difference.'

'Don't be stupid! My father wasn't a killer, and neither was my grandfather. You may well pass on sophisticated, advanced abilities to your children but you throw in a good number of primitive, regressive ones as well. Why do you think Helena's children are different?'

'I've no idea. It was the biggest disappointment of my life when they were born. I think she was too dull. I didn't think that I wanted a wife who was intelligent. I didn't want her asking questions or wondering why her children were different. As a result I chose someone who never did ask any questions, but who managed to produce two children of positively awe-inspiring dullness.'

'There's nothing wrong with Susan and Ryan.'

'Admittedly the world needs drones, but I've got better things to do than waste time fathering them myself.'

'Helena wasn't completely stupid. She was bright enough to be afraid of you.'

He gave a sharp laugh. 'Her fear was based entirely on sexual naïvety. She didn't care for what went on in the privacy of our marital bedroom! Fortunately I chose more wisely with you.'

'How did you know?' asked Meg curiosly.

'As I said, it's a kind of sixth sense. I could see it in your eyes.'

'And in Catriona's?'

'Does that really matter? If so you can relax; your sister's tastes and yours are not the same.'

'She still likes you.'

'I'd have been stupid to put her off when she wanted to bear me a child, but she'd bore me in a year.'

'I don't know why I mind,' said Meg in self-disgust. 'Any normal woman would be packing her bags by now.'

'I hate the use of the word "normal". We make our own normality.'

'That would certainly appear to be your philosophy! Ashley, do you promise me that the clinics won't be using you as a donor any more? That there won't be any more children like ours?'

'Of course,' he assured her, and smiled his most engaging smile.

'I want to believe you,' said Meg. 'I really do want to, but somehow . . .'

'*Daddy*!' cried Orlando, running in to the room and grabbing at his father's arm. 'Come upstairs now! Quick, Daddy!'

'What's the matter?'

'It's Tim,' cried Orlando, tears in his strange milky eyes. 'He's got a pain in his head.'

Meg remained in her chair and prayed that what she had just begun to hope really was true, and that nature was dealing with these experimental children herself.

Chapter 13

Tim was lying on the bed, his naturally pale face ashen. He was clutching his head with both hands as he moaned quietly to himself, and occasionally his teeth would clench with pain. He didn't notice his father enter the room but tossed restlessly. Ashley hadn't read about the new virus and knew nothing of Tristan's death, but he knew a seriously sick child when he saw one.

'Tell your mother to ring for the doctor,' he told Orlando tersely.

'I'm not talking to her.'

'This is urgent. Tell her it's an emergency. I want a doctor here straight away.' As he spoke, Tim's body began to shake uncontrollably. Then a tiny trickle of blood escaped from his left nostril and made its way down to his top lip. Gently Ashley wiped it away, but it was quickly replaced by another trickle, and then another, until it couldn't be restrained and flowed on to the sheets and pillowcases as Ashley desperately tried to staunch it.

'I got the new partner,' said Meg from the doorway. 'He's coming now.'

'Good.'

She took a few steps in to the room and couldn't prevent a gasp of horror at what she saw. Tim wasn't clenching his teeth any more, he was screaming aloud, and thrashing from side to side which aggravated the already heavy nosebleed. 'There's blood coming from his mouth,' she whispered.

'No, it's from his nose.'

'It's from his mouth.' She was right. As he screamed blood

208

flecked with foam oozed between his teeth, not dark blood but light and pink, almost innocent-looking. But it was far from innocent.

Meg was relieved when the doorbell rang. It was one thing to pray for the children's deaths, quite another to watch one of them in agony, screaming from the pain. She didn't want it to be like that.

The doctor was less than happy. 'What's the trouble?' he demanded, taking the stairs two at a time. 'A high temperature is it? There's nothing like a high temperature to get mothers fussing, which is ridiculous because it merely shows that the child's body is fighting the infection, as it should.'

Ignoring him, Meg pushed open Tim's door. The twins were still in there, watching the older boy with terror in their eyes. They had obviously tried to help him because there was blood on their hands, but even Ashley was having difficulty in keeping his son on the bed as Tim flung himself frantically around, muttering incoherently.

'Get those children out of here!' snapped the doctor, recognising that this was a genuine emergency. 'And ring for an ambulance.'

Outside the bedroom door the twins hesitated for a moment, their eyes fixed on Meg. 'What's wrong with him?' asked Orlando anxiously.

'I don't know,' she lied.

'Will he die?'

'I shouldn't think so, but he needs to go to hospital.'

'You want him to die!' shouted Olivia as her mother ran downstairs. 'You want us all to die!'

Yes, Meg admitted to herself, I do, but not like this. Why does it have to be like this?

By the time Tim was carried out on a stretcher he was unrecognisable. His features had shrunk, and despite all the doctor's efforts blood continued to seep from his mouth and nose. He scarcely looked human, and Meg turned away to hide her horror. Ashley didn't even glance at her, but hurried off to sit by his son's side during the drive to the hospital.

The house was strangely empty once they'd gone. It seemed to Meg that they all knew Tim wouldn't be coming back, although not a word was spoken aloud.

'You ought to get to bed,' she told the twins. 'Your father won't be home until the morning. He's bound to stay until they know more, and that will take time.'

Orlando nodded. 'Come on, Livvy,' he urged. 'I'm tired.'

Olivia stayed motionless in the hall, her eyes wide and vacant. 'Olivia, off to bed,' repeated Meg. Olivia didn't appear to hear. She continued to stare off into space.

'What is it, Livvy?' asked Orlando nervously.

This time she did respond. She turned to face her twin and she was trembling all over. 'He's going to die!' she told him in disbelief. 'Tim's going to die.'

Orlando grabbed her hand and pulled her upstairs. He didn't want to know. He didn't want it said. All he wanted was to sleep, and escape. Silently, Meg watched them go and wondered what else Olivia would soon be able to see.

At six in the morning Ashley rang. 'It's over,' he said abruptly. 'Tim's dead.'

'Couldn't they do anything?'

'Nothing at all. It's a new strain of meningitis. We've got to keep an eye on the others. If they develop even the slightest headache the hospital wants to know.'

'I'm very sorry,' said Meg gently.

'Really?'

'Yes. When will you be home?'

'Not yet. I want to talk to one or two of my colleagues at work.'

'Why?'

'I want to know if they've any new drugs that might be useful with this virus.'

'He's dead,' she reminded him. 'You can't help Tim now.'

'But suppose he isn't the last? Suppose the twins get it? I can't just stand by and let them die!'

'Surely drugs have to be approved by . . .'

'Bugger B.M.A. approval!' he shouted, slamming down the phone. Hearing a sound on the stairs Meg looked up to see the twins staring down at her.

'Was that Daddy?'

'Yes, Orlando. I'm afraid Tim died during the night.'

'I knew he would!' cried Olivia, her voice high-pitched with terror. 'I wish I couldn't see things. I don't want to know

210

what's going to happen, not when it's horrid. I don't want to see things! I don't! I don't!'

Meg tried to take the little girl in her arms but Olivia jerked away. 'Leave me alone. You don't care. You hate us all. I want my daddy.' And she began to cry. It was Orlando who put an arm round her and led her away, leaving their mother wondering how she was going to get through the next few days.

Only Susan and Ryan went to school, the twins flatly refusing to leave the house. Meg told Helena's children about Tim but they weren't affected. He had made their lives a misery and now he was gone forever. Who could blame them if they didn't feign grief.

It was mid-day before Ashley arrived home, and then he refused to discuss Tim's death at all. In the end everyone sat around in silence, waiting to see who would be next.

Days passed and still they waited. Meg's nerves were stretched to breaking point as she studied each child carefully. She kept reminding herself that their deaths were necessary. It would be best if they all died although it became increasingly difficult to believe this in the face of their fear, and the harrowing images of Tim's final hours that were fixed in her brain.

Three days after Tim's funeral they all began to relax. The twins started to play again, Ophelia began to smile and Ashley returned to work. Meg was sure that he still thought the virus was attacking children at random. Without the benefit of the newspaper information he had no reason to think otherwise. It was a fool's paradise that wasn't to last.

'Switch the news on,' he suggested on his first evening home from work.

'It's bound to be depressing,' said Meg, anxious to prevent him from making any connections with the news of the other deaths from meningitis.

'Bombs in the Far East don't keep me awake at night.'

She was doing the crossword when the announcement came, but she heard Ashley's muffled exclamation and lifted her head in time to see the photograph of the world's first test tube triplets that had been shown after their birth.

'The world's first test tube triplets today became the latest victims of a new strain of meningitis which is sweeping the country,' said Julia Sommerville gravely. 'The babies all died within minutes of each other in the Queen Elizabeth hospital where they were born. So far twenty children have died from the virus, but doctors have been unable to establish any links between the victims. The triplets were born after . . .'

Ashley pressed the red button and the picture vanished. 'It's *my* children!' he said in astonishment. 'It's *my* children who are dying. That's the connection.'

Meg shook her head. 'I don't think that's a very sensible conclusion, Ashley. They mentioned twenty children. How do you know they're all yours?'

'I don't, but I'm going to find out.' He jumped to his feet. 'Clive will know, he's keeping track of most of them for me.'

'Who's Clive?'

'A doctor at Barts. We trained together, until I dropped out.' But as Ashley began looking up his friend's telephone number, Olivia started to scream.

Running up the stairs, Meg was so certain that she'd find their daughter lying bleeding on her bed that she felt almost relieved when she saw her running round and round her bedroom, but it was a relief that quickly faded as she realised that Olivia was out of her mind. She was screaming for help in a high, hysterical voice; banging her head against walls and wardrobe doors; pounding on the windows with her bare fists, and kicking out at anyone who approached her. Even Ashley couldn't hold her, and they all watched with increasing fear.

'No!' shouted Olivia, banging her forehead against the mirror of her wardrobe door. 'No, I won't! I won't! Stop it, Daddy! Please, make it stop!' But when he tried to take her in his arms she fought to get free, still screaming her denials.

'What is it?' Meg asked a petrified Orlando. 'Does her head hurt?'

He bit on his bottom lip. 'No, she had a look at the future.'

'And?'

'Now she knows why she couldn't see who she was going to marry.'

'You mean . . . ?'

'She's seen her own death,' he whimpered, turning his face into his mother's skirts and seeming — for the very first time — like an ordinary five-year-old boy. 'She doesn't want to die, and nor do I, Mummy, I don't want to die!'

There was nothing that Meg could think of to say. She rested a hand lightly on his head and gently smoothed his hair. He looked up at her fearfully. 'Will I die? Is it true?'

'Orlando, I . . .'

Olivia came to an abrupt halt in front of her twin. She put out her hands and twisted his face round until he was facing her. 'Yes, you will!' she shouted. 'We *both* die, but I don't care about you. It's me I care about. I don't want to bleed and twitch. I don't want to!'

'Please, Meg, leave us alone,' asked Ashley quietly. Meg swallowed hard, then nodded and walked out. The three of them were best alone for she had no comfort to offer.

That night Ashley stayed in the twins' bedroom, but at seven in the morning he woke Meg and asked her to call the doctor for Olivia. This time Meg didn't go and look at the child, she couldn't face watching her suffer as Tim had suffered. Memories of his agony still haunted her, and she couldn't bear to witness her own daughter's.

She still thought that death was the best course — that Nature had picked up the potential threat to herself and was dealing with it in a highly efficient manner — but Meg found it surprisingly difficult to feel the anticipated relief.

Frightened and sick, the children seemed little different from their more normal contemporaries; their precocious maturity and self-induced isolation deserted them and they became ordinary. This sudden normality made their deaths almost intolerable.

By late afternoon Orlando too was ill. At first he simply went quiet, sitting in his father's chair with his eyes closed. Meg thought that he was trying to support his twin through her ordeal, but when he cried out and clutched his head she knew that he too was doomed. This time she didn't have to pretend anything. She sat beside him in the ambulance and cried while trying to calm him, promising that everything would be all right.

As they drew up in the emergency ambulance park, he opened his eyes. They were unclouded by pain and fear.

'Did you love me, Mummy?' he asked softly. Meg nodded. 'Good. I loved you, I really did. I wasn't really that special, you see, but I was bad. I did bad things and I'm sorry.'

'It doesn't matter,' she crooned, taking him in her arms and he closed his eyes, turned his face towards her and gave a gentle sigh. She didn't realise he was dead until the ambulance men took him away from her, and then she began to scream.

Thirty minutes later Ashley found her sitting in the Emergency Department trying to drink hot sweet tea despite her shaking hands. She glanced up at him. 'Is Olivia. . . !'

'Yes. they must have died within seconds of each other.'

'It was awful. Orlando told me . . .'

'Well, you've got what you wanted!' he said savagely. 'You said they weren't fit to live and now they're all dead except Ophelia. I'm surprised you're not dancing for joy.'

'Not like this!' she protested. 'I didn't want anything like this to happen to them.'

He took her roughly by the elbow and hurried her out to a waiting taxi. 'It isn't too late,' he muttered. 'According to the hospital there's a new drug that's just been released for the treatment of conventional meningitis and they're going to try that on the victims. The twins were too far gone, but it might save some of the others. Perhaps they can use it if Ophelia gets sick.'

Meg wondered how many were left.

'It's got to!' he continued fiercely. 'I can't believe they can all be wiped out. It's incredible. I mean, why my children?'

'I don't know,' she lied, keeping her theory to herself.

'I think I do. Their increased psychic powers must have diminished their physical powers. In other words, they don't have a normal child's resistance to infection. This virus is probably being shrugged off by your average child while mine — the elite among them — die like flies.'

That night the death of the twins made the national news but Ashley switched off before Meg could hear any details. However, next morning most of the papers carried the story of a 'tenuous link' that had been established between the victims. So far they had all been conceived either *in vitro* or by artificial insemination. The sensational papers made even more of it, one of the tabloids carrying the front page headline, 'Nature's Revenge!'

Throughout the tragedies Susan and Ryan continued their

normal routine and both tried very hard to keep out of their father's way. However, one evening they literally bumped into him as he came home from work. He looked grey and exhausted and glared at them both with hatred. 'Why couldn't it have been you?' he demanded harshly. 'If I had to lose some of my children, why not you two. You're no good to me, just useless Helena clones. It should have been you. You ought to be dead. I wish to God you were!' And he began slapping a terrified Ryan.

Alerted by the boy's screams Meg managed to grab hold of Ryan and pull him free. 'Get upstairs both of you,' she urged. 'I'll bring your tea up later. Just stay out of his way.' The two children ran off sobbing, leaving Ashley glaring furiously after them.

'They were all mine,' he said at last, the anger suddenly draining out of him. 'Clive's been checking and there's no possible doubt. All of my children are dying.'

'How many so far?' asked Meg.

'Thirty-six! I can't believe it. To think that thirty-six of my special children have been wiped out within a matter of weeks. It will take years to build the numbers up again.'

Meg looked away before he could see the shock in her eyes. She hadn't thought of him trying again, going back to the beginning. She had assumed that because he'd already stopped the clinics using him as a surrogate father then he wouldn't be able to continue, but supposing that she was wrong? Suppose that his friends did use him again, what would happen then? Could nature be trusted to react as swiftly the next time?

Catriona came to the twins' funeral. It was the first time Meg had seen her since the hospital visit and she was shocked by the change in her sister. Despite the obviously healthy baby lying sleeping in its carrycot on the pew, Catriona looked distraught. She was pale, her hair lank and she was painfully thin. All through the service she kept her eyes fixed on Ashley, for it was him that Catriona now wanted.

She wanted him to help her deal with her strange, ominously quiet daughter who never laughed, and she wanted him for herself. She needed him because he had taught her body the pleasure of pain and now she craved it for its own sake. She needed him not, as she had tried to tell herself before, for the sake of bearing a child, but for the ecstacy he could bring her.

She wondered whether Meg was equally addicted to her husband's perverted sexuality. Somehow she didn't think so; Meg was too quiet, too conventional to find pleasure in such things. No, probably Ashley would be equally anxious to resume their relationship. The deaths of his children she scarcely considered.

She was therefore disconcerted when Ashley and Meg didn't wait outside the crematorium, instead driving straight off in the black limousine that was becoming so horribly familiar to them both. But then she heard one of the mourners saying that their baby daughter had seemed unwell and she understood. Naturally Ashley hadn't been able to stop and speak to her, but he very soon would. Yes, she was sure of that.

Back at the house Ophelia's cries increased as she threw herself round the cot. Her eyes were dilated and she kept trying to beat her head against the bars. There was no point in calling an ambulance. This time Meg carried their tiny daughter in her arms as Ashley drove to the hospital. Neither adult spoke for there was nothing left for them to say.

'Let it be quick!' prayed Meg. 'She's only a baby. Take her quickly.'

Within minutes of their arrival Ophelia had been whisked away to a small isolation ward and then the paediatrician was there, bending over her, shining his torch into her eyes and watching as her nose began to bleed. Straightening up he reluctantly went outside to the waiting parents. 'I'm afraid there's no doubt it's the same virus, but we have got the new drug here and she isn't too far gone for us to try it. She's very young but it's the only hope I can offer you.'

'Give it to her,' said Ashley tonelessly. 'There's nothing to lose anymore.'

'If it's going to work it will work quickly. We'll know within the next couple of hours.'

Meg turned and walked away. She couldn't sit in the hot, friendless corridor and wait for two hours. She had to get away. Ashley chose to remain outside his daughter's room. The difference in their attitude was the result of their different hopes.

Meg went to Catriona's. She didn't feel any more kindly

disposed towards her sister but there was no one else to whom she could turn. Besides, although she refused to admit this to herself, she also wanted to see how Cindy looked. If events took their natural course then Cindy too must die.

'Meg, what are you doing here?' Catriona was astounded to see her.

'Ophelia's at the hospital. I couldn't stand hanging around waiting for news.'

'You poor thing!' sympathised Catriona, inwardly rejoicing at the thought that soon Ophelia too might be dead. After that he'd be certain to come to her and Cindy. 'You can't carry the infection, can you?' she added nervously.

'No.'

'Only all your children have caught it.'

'Not Susan and Ryan.'

'Well, no.'

'This isn't a normal virus, Catriona.'

'I know. There's been enough about it in the papers and on the news. At first they thought it was test tube babies, but Ophelia's conception was normal enough, so that's obviously wrong.'

'It's all of Ashley's special children.'

Catriona stared at her. 'Don't be stupid!'

'It is. All the children fathered through the fertility clinics and all the ones fathered by him in the normal way. Children who look like Ophelia — and Cindy.'

'You're lying! You're trying to frighten me just because you're annoyed. I'm not listening. Get out of here! Go on, get back to the hospital and join your husband because I don't suppose you'll have him for much longer.'

'Why on earth not?'

'Because it's me he loves!' gloated Catriona.

Meg picked up her handbag and moved towards the front door. 'Catriona, don't be silly. Haven't you understood anything about Ashley? He doesn't love anyone; he can't, he's an emotional cripple.'

'I don't care,' said Catriona defiantly. 'I love him.'

'I shan't give him up,' said Meg, as much to her own astonishment as to her sister's. 'You've got the baby you wanted, make the most of that while you can.'

By the time she returned to the hospital Ophelia was recovering. The new drug had worked. It was several days before Meg learnt that it had been developed and tested by Ashley's company and so — inadvertently — he had saved the future of his own children.

But there were so few of them left.

News of the drug's success was broadcast across the country and parents who in reality had nothing to fear breathed sighs of relief. Ophelia's recovery was carefully documented, and pictures of Meg taking her back home made the national press.

The publicity unsettled Ashley. Their neighbours, horrified by the triple tragedy of the family but delighted by the final miracle, took to calling on them and trying to become friendly. It was difficult to keep to themselves without seeming ungrateful and gradually, much to Ashley's horror, their privacy was eroded.

Then there was the problem of Catriona. As Cindy grew, her likeness to Ophelia was so striking that it became an embarrassment. There were people who had known Tim, people who remembered how alike he and the twins were and who knew that their only common factor had been Ashley. Now here was Ashley's sister-in-law boldly paying visits with what was undoubtedly another of his children in her arms. Naturally there was talk.

Miles too became a problem. He had spent some time brooding about his wife's behaviour, and although as anxious for divorce as she was he had no intention of letting her get away with a civilised mutual separation agreement. He wanted people to know what Ashley had done, and cited him as the third party. Catriona spent hours trying to get him to change his mind but he refused. This was his last chance for revenge for himself and for David and he intended to get it. Ashley heard of the impending divorce in silence, only the thinning of his lips betraying his fury.

He and Meg were also uneasy with each other. They still shared the same bedroom but that was all. Ashley rarely attempted to make love to his wife, but on the odd occasion when he did she turned away, terrified that she might accidentally conceive. He didn't mind, not for the present. He would

218

return to Meg once he'd made other, more important decisions.

The weeks turned to months and their lives settled into a new pattern of regular hours and polite, meaningless conversations. Susan and Ryan began to flourish. No longer teased and tormented at home, their confidence grew and their school reported excellent progress.

'Well done!' enthused Meg as she read their end-of-term reports.

'Daddy won't be pleased,' said Susan. 'He doesn't care about us. He'd rather have us dead and the twins back.'

'Yes,' agreed Meg, who thought it pointless to pretend otherwise. 'I know he would, but I wouldn't. I'm thoroughly enjoying myself these days!' The children hugged her, but they hid their reports before their father saw them. Rejection still hurt. If he didn't see then they could always pretend that he might have been pleased.

'I've been thinking,' remarked Ashley one evening. 'We ought to make a fresh start.'

Meg had been expecting this and was prepared. 'No more children,' she said firmly. 'You know what I think about all that. I hope that clinics haven't started using you again?'

'What kind of a fool do you take me for? Do you think I want to watch more of my children die? This time they found a cure, but what about next time? Who's to say it won't happen again in an even more unpleasant form. Viruses adapt very quickly. No, I wasn't thinking of having more children.'

'You mean you're willing to settle for Ophelia, Cindy, and the two or three others who survived?'

'Yes. You were right all along of course, they *were* flawed. My father has a lot to answer for. Probably they're better off dead. It would have been difficult for them to fit in.'

'Then what do you mean by a fresh start?'

'I want to move away. I'm tired of my job and tired of living here. I want a complete change.'

'It won't be easy finding a new job, will it? Your field's rather limited.'

'I've already been offered one.'

Meg stared at him. 'When? And why didn't you talk to me about it first?'

'I was offered it today. My interview was last month, and I didn't talk to you about it because it's my concern. I'll be working with a homoeopathic company, natural cures with no side effects.'

'You've always jeered at homoeopathic medicine.'

'Now that I've gone into it more thoroughly I think it's the science of the future. People are tired of antibiotics and steroids. They want something safe.'

'Herbs couldn't have cured meningitis.'

He looked steadily at her. 'If that's meant to make me change my mind, it won't. I admit that drugs saved Ophelia but I don't want to spend my entire life dealing with them. They're abused by the medical profession. No, this is definitely the path I want to follow.'

'And where is this new job?' asked Meg. She didn't believe him but couldn't think of any ulterior motive for such a change.

'Cornwall.'

'I don't want to move there! It's all coffee shops and tourists in the summer, and snow and solitude in the winter.'

'I didn't realise you'd lived there before,' teased Ashley.

'I haven't, but I've read about people who tried moving there and gave up. We wouldn't fit in.'

'I don't want us to fit in. I want us left alone.'

'There isn't any need for that now,' protested Meg. 'We've only got Susan, Ryan and Ophelia. Why shouldn't we socialise normally again?'

'We'll have Cindy too.'

'What!'

'Your sister is handing her over to us. She appreciates the necessity of letting Cindy and Ophelia grow up together.'

'But she desperately wanted a baby to make up for David. I can't believe that she'd just hand Cindy over like that.'

'She'll be well compensated.'

'You mean you're paying her to give her daughter up?'

'Who mentioned money?'

'Then how ... ?'

'This way, Miles will keep supporting her until they get a divorce in two years' time on the grounds that their marriage has broken down. Miles is quite happy to drop the adultery charge as long as Cindy isn't there to show the world that I put horns on his head.'

'Why should Catriona care if Miles does name you?'

'I've persuaded her to mind!'

'I don't believe a word you've said. I'm going to see her to find out what's really going on.'

'Please do, and when you realise that I've told you the truth perhaps you'll agree to give Cornwall a try? It will be a new start for us, Meg. The way we're going at the moment our marriage isn't going to last.'

She nodded in agreement, but her thoughts were already moving ahead to her visit to Catriona.

'I don't understand!' she exclaimed for the sixth time. 'You kept on and on about wanting a baby and now you're handing her over to me. You won't have anything left, Cat! No Miles and no baby. Why? Why are you willing to do it?'

Catriona stared out of her kitchen window and watched a pair of pigeons on the lawn. 'I'm more fond of my luxuries than I realised. Miles will agree to a decent divorce settlement if I get rid of Cindy. I'll keep this house, he'll pay all the bills and our marriage will end peacefully in two years time. Doesn't that make sense?'

'No! You don't care tuppence for this house, or who pays the bills. All you wanted was Cindy. How can you let Ashley take her away from you? Because that's what he's doing. He wants her, and he's determined to have her. He isn't considering you at all.'

Catriona turned and gave her sister a gentle smile. 'But he is. It's because he's considering me that it has to be done this way. It will all work out for the best in the end.'

'How can it? Cindy won't ever see you. She'll think I'm her mother. How can that be for the best?'

'Cindy doesn't need me.'

'Every child needs its mother.'

'Not Ashley's children.'

Meg felt chilled. It was true; Ashley's children didn't need their mothers. She wanted to continue talking but Catriona was already walking to the front door. 'I'm sorry but I'm busy. You'll have to go now. And don't worry about me, I'm

221

perfectly happy with the arrangement. Cornwall's a lovely place for children to grow up.'

Without another word, Meg left. For some secret reason Catriona had decided that she must part with her daughter, and it was obvious that nothing would change her mind. Now Meg had to face up to whether or not she was willing to bring up her niece. In all the discussions that had gone on it had apparently never crossed anyone's mind that she might not want her sister's child.

Twenty-four hours later, before she could raise the subject with Ashley, Catriona left her daughter on Meg's doorstep and took a taxi to the station where she purchased a one-way ticket to King's Cross. She also left a note asking Meg not to try and find her, but promising to make contact once the move to Cornwall had been accomplished.

'She's mad!' raged Meg to her husband. 'How can she be so irresponsible? Anyway, she can't contact us in Cornwall when even we don't know where we'll be living. It does cover a fairly large area!'

'She'll know,' promised Ashley. 'I'll put an announcement in the *Telegraph*.'

'Catriona doesn't read the *Telegraph*.'

'She does now.'

'You arranged this together, didn't you? In case I refused to take Cindy?'

'It was a double insurance,' he admitted. 'I sensed you were doubtful, and the waiting was wearing Catriona's nerves down.'

'How tragic! She bears a child by my husband and then comes over all weak and feeble because I'm not sure I want to bring the child up. I've a good mind to call the police.'

'And have Cindy taken into care?'

'Why not?'

'She's your flesh and blood.'

'*And yours*!' shouted Meg.

'Which is precisely why we're both well suited to ensuring her welfare. I knew you'd eventually see sense.'

'All right,' agreed Meg slowly. 'I'll come to Cornwall and I'll look after Cindy, but unless you start behaving properly towards Susan and Ryan I shan't have any hesitation in taking them away, leaving you there alone with Ophelia and Cindy.'

'I do believe you're threatening me,' he laughed.

'Yes, I am and it isn't an idle threat. What would you do then, I wonder?'

'Get Catriona in to replace you.'

And then she knew that Catriona had only removed herself temporarily from their lives. Somewhere her sister was waiting in the wings for a chance to step into her shoes. The separation was really because Catriona wanted Ashley. And if Ashley reciprocated this desire, then how safe was Meg? There were many ways of disposing of unwanted wives in the isolated coves and disused mines of Cornwall.

'It was a joke,' said Ashley.

'Was it?'

'How could Catriona ever take your place?'

'No, I suppose people might talk.'

'Yes,' he confirmed. 'And talk is something we most definitely don't want.'

Meg remembered Charles and knew that he was right. They both had things to hide. Just the same, before she left for Cornwall she changed her will in favour of Miles. If anything should happen to her, that alone might be enough to alert the police. Then, dismissing her fears as unfounded, she resolved to make their home in Poltreach a happy one. She had no choice. Life had to go on.

Chapter 14

As the years passed Meg admitted to herself that Ashley had been right. The move to Cornwall, although initially traumatic, proved beneficial to them all. Ashley was more content in his new job than she had ever seen him, and far more involved. He didn't discuss his work — that had never been his way — but at least it took his mind off his failed attempt to produce a super-race.

When Ophelia was three Meg thought she was pregnant again. She became so hysterical with terror than when it proved to be a false alarm Ashley agreed she could be sterilised. To Meg this was the final proof that he had accepted that any attempt to replace the dead children would be both doomed and dangerous.

Catriona didn't contact them after they moved. By the time Cindy was six she called Meg 'Mummy', and eventually Meg stopped talking about the child's real mother. Ophelia and Cindy were so alike and spent so much time together that it was easier to pretend they were full sisters.

They were both bright but Ophelia was so outstanding that occasionally the terms 'genius' and 'infant prodigy', were used to describe her. At eight she was doing the maths of girls nearly twice her age, while she could read a book and memorise every word in one sitting.

Surprisingly she was popular with her peers. Cindy was more aloof, with traces of the same disdain that had characterised the twins but Ophelia was happy and outgoing. She was also good at sport; in fact, sometimes Meg wondered if there was anything her daughter couldn't do.

Since Ophelia was well behaved and quiet it was possible for Meg — providing she kept her daughter's fringe long enough to cover the over-large forehead — to forget that she wasn't a normal child. Unlike the twins she never appeared to be judging Meg and finding her wanting. Cindy did, but she was overawed by her half-sister and this prevented her from behaving too outrageously.

On the evening of Cindy's eighth birthday, Meg mentioned to Ashley that she was tired of being a housewife. 'It isn't that I dislike the work,' she explained, 'but quite honestly, with the girls at school and you working such long hours, I get lonely.'

'I'm sorry,' he said flatly. 'What do you want me to do? Come home in the middle of the day for a quickie?'

Meg flushed. 'I didn't mean that. The truth is that it's time for me to go back to work.'

'Back to work? You sound like a slightly rusty brain surgeon! What work did you ever do except pound the keys of a typewriter? You won't find many typewriters around any more. Today it's all word processors and visual terminals.'

'We're not hard up, are we?'

Ashley raised his eyebrows. Meg had never been all that interested in what he earned; providing she could buy clothes when she wished and had plenty of housekeeping money she'd seemed content. 'No,' his voice was guarded, 'I wouldn't say we were exactly on the breadline.'

'I'd like to set up a little tea room of my own.'

'I remember you saying you didn't want to live in Cornwall because it was all tourists and tea rooms. Now you want to participate in the ever-increasing "tat" industry.'

'But my tea room won't be tat. So many places don't really cater for families. There aren't proper facilities for mothers with young babies; the tables are squashed together and the staff make it plain that any under-five who doesn't sit silent and motionless is a great inconvenience. That isn't how it ought to be. I'd make sure that I catered specifically for young parents with pre-school children.'

'What would you call this haven of bliss? "Tea for Tinies?" "Snacks for Snivellers"?'

'I'd thought of something like "Parents' Pantry".'

'Talk about finding your own level!'

'I do realise that I'm not as intelligent as your daughters, Ashley, but I was bright enough to give birth to one of them.'

'All I can say is you must have gone downhill pretty fast since we moved here.'

'Are you willing to put up the money to get me started?'

Ashley thought quickly. There were some things that he didn't want her to know about and if she was busy playing shop she was less likely to pry into his private affairs. Then there were the girls. So far they'd behaved impeccably but only because he kept warning them and held the example of Tim, Orlando and Olivia before them. Yes, on balance a small business would be excellent for them all, and he could certainly afford it.

'All right,' he conceded. 'Find yourself some premises and I'll go into it more thoroughly, but don't expect me to wait at tables!'

'I won't, although the girls might enjoy helping out during the school holidays.'

The venture was a tremendous success. Within two years it was showing a healthy profit and had been featured in one of the good food guides for families. Meg employed two local women to do the cooking and summer students to wait at the tables, which meant that she only needed two full-time teenagers who originally came to her through the Youth Training Scheme and stayed on. By the time Ophelia was ten, Meg had never been happier.

The following summer, trade was brisker than ever before. The restaurant now did morning snacks, simple lunches and cream teas. In the middle of August it wasn't unusual to find people queueing to get in.

Thursday 28th August started off quite normally. Ashley left the house before seven murmuring that he'd probably be working late again. Cindy complained about being woken up, while Ophelia sparkled with energy and high spirits as she chattered about the previous day and the lady who'd given her a piece of lucky lavender.

'She said it would bring me happiness. Will it?'

'I doubt it!'

'She gave me a charm as well, for my heart's desire!'

'And what is your heart's desire?'

226

For a fleeting moment Ophelia's eyes went blank and she gazed into space much as Olivia had done when trying to foresee the future, but before Meg had time to feel more than a fleeting unease her daughter's face was back to normal. 'I don't know!' she laughed. 'I'll have to think about it.'

'Don't be too ambitious. I don't suppose the charm is strong enough to turn you into a film star or a lady astronaut.'

'I wouldn't be an astronaut, space is old hat now.'

'Has anyone told the Americans and Russians?'

'I didn't mean *now* now; I meant the now when I'm grown up.'

'That isn't now. That's the future, not the present.'

'I know.'

'You're saying that space travel will be obsolete when you're grown up?'

'Yes. Can't you see that for yourself?'

'See it?' asked Meg, dangerously quietly.

Ophelia blushed. 'I meant work it out for yourself, not see with your eyes kind of seeing.'

'Did you really?' asked Meg thoughtfully, and all at once the day wasn't quite so wonderful.

As though trying to atone for the breakfast conversation, Ophelia was extra industrious in the restaurant. She helped slice the tomatoes and cucumbers, she filled sugar bowls, picked flowers for the table and even helped when some of the small children wandered in to the kitchen on their way to the junior toilets. Normally she didn't take much notice of toddlers but for once she made the effort to be as kind and friendly as all the regular staff were expected to be.

At six p.m. Meg turned the sign on the door to 'Closed' and sent the girls home. A local woman came at seven o'clock to do the cleaning but Meg always tried to tidy up before she arrived. As she straightened chairs and tables she was suddenly startled by a pounding on the front door. A frantic-looking woman was standing with her face pressed against the glass while a crying toddler pulled at her sleeve.

'What is it?' Meg asked, smiling as she opened the door. 'Has your daughter left a toy behind? It happens a lot every summer.' The woman brushed her aside and stared frantically round the room, while her husband came slowly in behind her.

'I'm sorry but we've only just left here and when we got to the car we realised that Toby wasn't with us,' he explained anxiously.

'Toby?'

'Our son!' screamed the woman. 'What have you done with him?'

'But . . .'

'He went to the toilets. I thought he'd gone ahead with Thomas while Thomas thought he was with little Kate and me. It was only when we met up at the car that we realised . . . Toby! Toby, darling, where are you? It's Mummy!'

'He isn't here,' said Meg gently. 'I couldn't possibly have missed him. He must have wandered off outside. How old is he?'

'Two next week. Toby, it's Mummy!'

Meg turned to the husband. 'I think you'd better let me call the police. He honestly isn't here and they're quite used to finding lost children in August.'

'He didn't come back from the loo,' volunteered the missing Toby's sister. 'Perhaps he got locked in.'

'He'll be terrified!' wailed the mother, dashing towards the Little Men's room. 'I told you to go with him, Thomas.'

'I couldn't go to the Little Mens room!' protested her husband. 'Besides, this place is meant to be safe for children.'

'It is safe,' affirmed Meg. 'We don't have any locks in the children's toilets.'

'He didn't go on his own,' continued Kate. 'He went with . . .' Screams interrupted the child's words. Terrible screams, almost inhuman in pitch and rising in volume until Meg's ears hurt. She and the husband immediately began running towards the Little Mens room too.

After one look inside, Meg back away, reaching instinctively for the telephone. Toby was lying on his back on the brightly coloured tiled floor with blood everywhere around him. His eyes were open, fixed on the ceiling with its paintings of well-known nursery rhyme figures, and his tiny arms and legs were tidily arranged so that if it weren't for the blood he could easily have been taking a quiet rest.

At home in their bedroom, Ophelia and Cindy were playing with the computer. When they heard the police siren they wandered over to the window and watched the car and the ambulance speed by.

'Did it feel good?' asked Cindy.

'Very good. I'm glad I got that charm. I wouldn't have dared to do it if the lady hadn't promised me my heart's desire.'

'Did he struggle?'

'Not much. It was a bit disappointing, but there was a lot of blood. I felt tingly inside when I watched it coming out. It was warm, too. I hadn't expected it to be warm.'

'Did you taste it?'

Ophelia shuddered. 'Do you think I'm mad or something? Why would I want to taste it?'

'I think I would have done.'

'How revolting! I suppose Mummy will be late home now. Shall we get our own tea? I could do sausages and beans.'

'Will Daddy be cross?'

Ophelia thought for a moment. 'Yes, he probably will, but as long as we keep it a secret he won't mind. And we will keep it a secret, won't we?'

'Yes,' said Cindy hurriedly. 'Of course we will.'

It was ten o'clock before Meg was allowed home. By that time the entire village knew of the murder, and Ashley looked unusually solicitous. 'You should have rung me up, Meg. I'd have come straight over to give you support.'

'I didn't want the children left alone.'

'They're not babies any more. What do the police think?'

'That it was the work of a local man. Someone who knew the layout of the place and was able to get to the boys toilet via the back entrance.'

'Was it a sexual attack?'

Meg bit her bottom lip. 'He'd been mutilated, Ashley. There was blood all down his legs and . . .'

'I'll get you some brandy.'

'I can't believe they're right. Surely one of us would have noticed if a man had come in through the back door? The kitchen's never empty.'

'If you were busy today it would probably have been easy for someone to slip past. Particularly if it was someone you were used to seeing; a delivery boy or someone like that.'

'He'd still have had to go right through the kitchen, out to the corridor and past the ladies toilets before reaching the boy's room. He took a dreadful risk.'

'Madmen do. It isn't your fault, Meg.'

'I feel responsible. I built up my business as a haven for harassed parents, somewhere where their children were welcome and safe. If it weren't for that those poor parents probably wouldn't have let their son go off on his own. He was only two.'

'It's criminal negligence to let a two-year-old wander off alone anywhere, haven or not.'

Meg frowned. 'His sister, who's nearly four, said he didn't go on his own. She said one of the waitresses took him, but they'd never have left him there unsupervised. Besides, the police have spoken to all the girls and none of them remember taking Toby.'

Ashley put out a hand and tilted his wife's chin. 'Don't take it so personally. It isn't your fault. I'll make you some soup and then we'll have an early night.'

'No!' exclaimed Meg, who knew what he meant by an early night.

'To sleep,' he laughed. 'Mind you, if . . .'

'No!'

'Look, children do get murdered in holiday resorts. That's the kind of world we live in. I know it's upsetting but . . .'

'If only you'd seen him you wouldn't be so calm. It was dreadful. He was lying, looking up at the stupid ceiling. He looked so peaceful as well, until you saw the blood, and his throat.'

'His throat?'

'Didn't I say? His throat had been cut too.'

'No,' murmured Ashley. 'You didn't tell me that.'

'I'd better go up to the girls while you heat me the soup.'

Ophelia and Cindy were already asleep. As usual Cindy had dropped off with a book in her hand and Meg carefully put it on the bookshelf. Finally she bent down to push Ophelia's sandals under the bed, and as she straightened up she caught sight of something red and white beneath her daughter's pillow.

Pulling it free she looked down at what she was holding. It was one of the large linen serviettes from the restuarant; one of the large, white serviettes. It was covered in blood.

She didn't know how long she knelt there, clutching the evidence tightly to her skirt as though in that way she could deny its existence, but eventually she rose slowly to her feet and walked quietly out of the room.

'Soup's done!' called Ashley cheerfully.

Meg crossed the room and held out the serviette.

'What's that?'

'I found it under Ophelia's pillow.'

'Has she had a nosebleed?'

'On one of the restaurant's serviettes?'

'They're not sacred, are they?'

'Don't try and pretend you don't know what this means.'

'I'm sorry but I haven't the faintest idea what you're talking about.'

'Of course you have. How long have you know that Ophelia was the same as all the others?'

Before he could answer the front door bell rang. Grabbing the serviette he pushed it inside the Aga. 'Go and open the door,' he ordered sharply. When Meg let the Inspector in the scene seemed horribly familiar.

'I'm pleased to say we've made an arrest,' he announced proudly.

'Already?'

'There aren't that many known child molesters in the village. Of course he denies it, but he admits he came to the restaurant today to deliver some paint you'd ordered. Of course he's educationally sub-normal, very low I.Q., so . . . '

'So he's a suitable scapegoat!' retorted Meg.

'Hardly a scapegoat, Mrs Webster. You wait, he'll be singing like a bird by tomorrow and with any luck he'll be put away for life. I can't pretend I'll be sorry either. This had been building up for a long time, but when you get these experts in court telling judges he isn't a danger to the public they listen to them. Not after this though!' He sounded extremely satisfied.

'I don't believe he did it,' said Meg loudly. 'My daughter . . . '

'In my opinion your daughter had rather a lucky escape today. From little Kate's description I'd say that it was young Ophelia who took Toby Patterson to the toilet. If she'd gone

231

inside with him she might have died as well, but naturally since it was a boys' toilet she didn't.'

'How do you know all this?'

'We've pieced it together from the various eye witnesses at the time. You must be very relieved.'

'We are,' said Ashley quickly. 'Unfortunately my wife feels that in some way she's to blame for the tragedy.'

'Only natural, but there isn't a thing you could have done. Between ourselves I don't understand any parents letting a child that young go off on their own, children's restaurant or not.'

'They probably thought he was safe with my daughter,' said Meg bitterly.

'She's very shaken up,' murmured Ashley. 'She'll come round in time.'

'Of course. I'm afraid the restaurant must remain shut for a couple of days, just until forensics have finished.'

'I shan't open it again,' said Meg firmly.

'Well, if there's nothing else you want to ask, I'll be on my way.'

'We're very grateful to you for letting us know so speedily. I suppose you . . .'

Meg closed her eyes as Ashley escorted the Inspector out. She didn't know what she could do. Nothing had changed. Here she was, ten years on from the twins' death, and once again a child of hers had killed, and this had been the most brutal killing of them all. Intelligent, attractive, popular Ophelia was as flawed as her predecessors.

There was one ray of hope. Apart from Cindy and Ophelia Ashley didn't have children to follow his daughters, therefore if the girls died then so did the line. But was she strong enough to carry out the obvious solution? she wondered. Could she murder both little girls? It would have been easier with the other children; Cindy and Ophelia had always seemed so normal. If it weren't for the serviette she would never have suspected the truth about them. She thought of them as a pair because they were too close for Ophelia to have done such a thing without her half-sister's knowledge. No, they were both flawed and they both must die.

A slight sound in the doorway alerted her to Ophelia's

presence. Her daughter's hair was swept back off her forehead and her eyes were cloudy; for the first time she looked exactly like an older version of Olivia. She drifted across to her mother and touched her lightly on the shoulder.

'Don't be unhappy. There's nothing you can do. I know, I've seen it all. By the time I die most people will be special, like me.'

'That can't be true. There aren't enough of you.'

'Oh, Mummy, there are! There are lots of us. Daddy's been growing us in test tubes and putting us inside women all the time we've lived here. He's got his own laboratory and his own doctor. Didn't you know?'

'He works for a herbal company.'

'He doesn't. He gets all his money from the women who want his children. They know they're getting something special, you see. Like those super-bright women in America who are allowed to be fertilised by geniuses. All mothers want their children to be special, and they'll pay a lot to make sure they are. Fancy you not knowing!' She laughed with amusement.

'And when most people *are* special, Ophelia, what then? Will you go round murdering each other to satisfy this perverted craving for blood?'

'Of course not! We'll always keep some ordinary people around, just for fun. Eventually, of course we'll go abroad. We'll start families all over the world. It will be wonderful! One day Daddy will be known as the second Adam. Aren't you proud to be one of his Eves?'

'I can think of better ways of being remembered.'

'You'll be famous in your own right too,' Ophelia consoled her. 'It won't just be because of Daddy. Does that make you happier?'

'It rather depends on what I'm going to do to merit the fame.'

Opehlia smiled a thin smile that didn't reach her eyes. 'I'll tell you,' she whispered. 'You're going to be one of the greatest murder mysteries of all time. There'll be books about you, and films too.'

Meg's heart began to race. Perhaps she was going to have the courage to do it. Ophelia had spoken confidently of her own future, but she could be wrong. 'Presumably it isn't a great mystery to you?' she queried lightly.

The strange eyes gleamed, the pupils contracted. 'Of course not!'

'Then tell me what happens.'

'You die, of course. You can't be a murder mystery if you don't die.'

'*I* die?'

'Yes.'

'Who does it?' she asked urgently. She hoped that it was Ashley, in retaliation for her killing Ophelia, because she wasn't certain that Ophelia was telling the truth about her father's work. She might simply be trying to divert her mother from thoughts of infanticide.

'You can't change anything,' continued her daughter.

'I'd still like to know. Is it your father?'

'Daddy? No, silly. It's me!'

Meg looked at her daughter's laughing face. 'You?'

Ophelia pushed back her fine silvery hair and rubbed at her high-domed forehead. 'Sorry, but you said you wanted to know.'

'I don't believe you. When will you do it? And why?'

'That's all I know. I can hear Daddy calling you. Goodnight!'

Meg felt sick, and when she tried to stand her legs refused to co-operate. She whimpered, and the sound brought her to her senses. She would not be terrorised by the threats of a ten-year-old. Ophelia was quite capable of lying to protect herself, but even if she were telling the truth no one had ascertained that it was impossible to change these strange children's prophecies. Perhaps, by revealing the future, Ophelia had made a terrible mistake. Yes, hopefully Ophelia had played directly into Meg's hands. If Meg killed her while she was still a child then she herself must be safe.

'Are you coming to bed?' asked Ashley. 'I've locked up.'

Meg straightened her shoulders and took several deep breaths until the trembling ceased. Providing that she was quick and careful there had to be a way, but she could not afford to fail. 'You do realise that they've arrested an innocent man,' she told Ashley as she climbed into bed.

234

'Rubbish!'

'Then why did you hide the serviette?'

'I didn't want to confuse the issue.'

'Ophelia killed that child. She led him away from his parents, took him to the toilet and then butchered him. She's mad, as mad as your father and grandfather. Why won't you admit it?'

'Because it isn't true.'

'How was work today?' she asked abruptly, and felt him go rigid with shock.

'Much the same as usual,' he said cautiously.

'What did you do?'

'The same as I've been doing for the past nine years! Really, Meg, it's a trifle late to start taking an intelligent interest in my career. Have you been reading *Cosmopolitan* again?'

'I merely wondered what sort of things you dealt with.'

'I'm an ambassador for the products. I wine and dine potential buyers and control the advertising campaigns.'

'Why do you work so late?'

'Because it's easier to do socialising after office hours. Look, why this amazing interest today of all days?'

Meg shrugged. 'I suppose I'm trying to take my mind off what's happened.'

'I can think of a much better way to take you mind off that!'

Later, when Ashley was asleep, she reflected on their life together. Sexually they were still amazingly well matched, and considering the years of sensual deprivation she'd endured with Charles she felt that she'd been lucky to have this opportunity of fulfilling herself. She'd long since ceased to feel guilty at the things they chose to do in the privacy of their bedroom.

However, apart from that, Ashley hadn't brought her anything but hurt and fear. The hurt was emotional. It had taken her a long time to accept that emotionally he was completely cold. Both he and Charles were men who — for entirely different reasons — were unable to express themselves with tender touches and physical closeness. Embraces and non-sexual kisses were still outside her experience, and she knew that normal people needed such affection.

Even her children hadn't provided an outlet for her natural

affection. Out of the entire family only Helena's children had been there when she wanted a child on her knee, or the comfort of a defenceless human being looking to her for strength and support. Yes, Susan and Ryan had at least shown her what normal children were like, but they were now gone forever. As soon as they were old enough to leave school both of them left home as well, returning to Scotland and childhood friends. They had cried when they said goodbue to Meg, but they hadn't made false promises of continued contact.

'I'm never coming back,' Ryan had told her fiercely. 'I hate him. I'd kill him if I could, that's how much I hate him. He's ruined my life so far, but now I'm free. I'm sorry but I shan't ever come back.'

Meg had understood, just as she'd understood Susan when she'd stood next to her on the crowded platform watching the train coming closer and closer. 'I'll write,' Susan had whispered, tears in her eyes. 'I'll write all the time, but I shan't visit. You do understand, don't you?'

'Yes, I do.'

'And if you ever want to leave him, please come to me. I'll always be able to put you up. You've been wonderful to both Ryan and me. We couldn't have survived without you.'

'Take care,' Meg instructed, tears blinding her as the train drew away.

Tonight, trying hard to be honest with herself, she had to admit that despite her intelligence and charm, Ophelia hadn't been any warmer than Ashley's other children. Not for her the unexpected cuddle or the swift affectionate kiss. She had kissed and cuddled, it was true, but always like a trained animal; someone trying hard to master a foreign custom. It hadn't come naturally to her. Cindy's shortcomings Meg had put down to Catriona's absence. If Cindy didn't want to be held then it was simple to tell herself that Cindy missed her mother, when the truth was that her mother's name meant nothing at all to Cindy and her emotional restraint was inborn.

Then there had been the twins. Ashley had given her the twins, and all the horror and grief that had been engendered by their short lives. And Tim, Ashley had been responsible for his arrival and subsequent behaviour.

Meg frowned. If she separated Ashley from his cold, twisted

236

offspring then could she honestly say that she had no regrets at their time together? She was tied to him by need, and a strange respect engendered by the understanding that he at least had acted as he believed right. He had been bound only by his own rules, not those of society. Sometimes such people became heros but Ashley would not because he was flawed.

Also, he couldn't be separated from his children for they were all that he thought about. He would never have married Meg but for the twins and the realisation that she could give him other such children. No, she might be bound to him but Ashley wasn't bound to her. Ashley used her. He probably quite liked her, he definitely desired her, but that was all he could feel.

It wasn't enough.

By the next morning she'd decided what to do and how to do it. All her previous confusion had cleared and her mind was sharp. At long last Meg was going to control her own destiny. She had finally broken free of Ashley's spell.

Chapter 15

There would never be a better time than this. Ashley was working late — Meg refused to consider what that work might involve — while Cindy was asleep upstairs suffering from a heavy cold. Only Meg and Ophelia were awake, the latter working in the dining-room doing revision for a maths exam the following day. She was working hard because she desperately wanted to do well, to prove to everyone how exceptionally gifted she was.

Meg was tempted to have a drink before she did it, but there was always the risk that it could slow down her reflexes, blunt her reactions, and she knew very well that her senses needed to be needle-sharp. She wouldn't even think about failure. Ophelia would never give her a second chance.

For weeks she'd been considering the method. Guns were out of the question; she didn't know where she could get one, and even if she did she wouldn't know how to use it.

She had also considered using a knife. The children had often used knives, they were presumably quick and reliable, but there was always a lot of blood and even the thought of pressing a sharp blade to the flesh of her daughter, feeling it slice through the layers of skin as though she were cutting a tomato in half, made her nauseous. No, she wasn't mentally equipped to handle a knife.

At first she'd thought that suffocation would be the easiest method. However, when Ophelia was in bed and therefore vulnerable there was always the presence of her cousin, and Meg had discounted the possibility of killing both girls at once.

No, this way, the way she had finally chosen, was virtually

foolproof. Ophelia would die relatively silently, and Meg could then go upstairs and deal with Cindy who would hopefully still be deeply asleep thanks to the double dose of cold cure Meg had given her that night. Yes, this was the best way, and afterwards she herself would bear witness to a crazed intruder and her desparate efforts to protect the children.

Meg entered the dining-room quietly. She carried a tray of glasses in her hands and when Ophelia glanced up and saw her mother she assumed that the glasses were to be replaced in the cabinet in the corner behind her. Meg moved towards the cabinet, glancing at her daughter's back. It was fortunate that she was such a small-boned child; it would make the task much easier. Placing the tray on the ground she undid the cabinet door.

'I'm trying to concentrate,' complained Ophelia, hunching herself further over her books.

'Sorry, won't be a minute.'

Ophelia sighed, putting a protective hand round her excercise books as though she thought that her mother might be trying to see her work. The movement amused Meg quite disproportionately, and nerves made her want to giggle. She bit her lip and the giggle faded.

Ophelia lowered her head to peer more closely at the text. Immediately Meg struck, grabbing her daughter from behind, both hands fastening round the long, slender neck. She squeezed with all of her strength but Ophelia didn't seem to be affected. She wasn't even fighting very hard. She was twisting round but without trying to kick or punch out at her mother, which was what Meg was braced for.

For endless seconds they remained locked together. Meg's breathing was loud and rasping as her daughter's wiry frame refused to buckle. It was taking far more energy than Meg had imagined.

Ophelia's eyes were almost white, the irises cloudy not with fear but with fury and a strange kind of satisfaction. She continued to wriggle, her hands scrabbling on the table, pushing aside the exercise book as the fingers fumbled across the shiny surface until at last they located what she had been hiding. With a superhuman effort the child's flailing fingers managed to get a purchase, and then she swung her arm in a fast semi-circle and heard her mother's gasp of pain as the blade of the knife plunged into her left side.

Immediately her grip on Ophelia slackened and now the child did begin to kick out. She kicked with all the force she could muster, and as she kicked she continued plunging the razor-sharp blade in and out of her mother's body.

Meg felt every blow. She felt herself beginning to weaken and saw her own blood dripping onto the carpet, yet still she squeezed her fingers tighter. The pain was intense but she didn't care. Nothing mattered anymore but success. If she was going to die it was imperative that Ophelia die too.

Ophelia was screeching now. Her face was twisted with hate, her top lip drawing back as she opened her mouth to spit at her mother. She couldn't believe Meg's powers of endurance. The Stanley knife had been plunged into the body dozens of times but it hadn't hindered her; despite Ophelia's efforts she herself was starting to loose consciousness.

With one last frantic effort she slashed out wildly, the knife catching her mother full in the face. Meg screamed in agony, staggering backwards, releasing her daughter as she lurched round the room, her nose no longer recognisable and her left cheek cut open to the bone.

Meg was still screaming when Cindy ran into the room, so loudly that she didn't hear her niece. She didn't realise that she and Ophelia were no longer alone. It wasn't until Cindy brought the heavy soup ladle from the restaurant crashing down on her head that she realised they had company, and by then it was much too late.

'Die! Die!' yelled Cindy, smashing the ladle down again and again and tingling all over with excitement as she heard the bones of the skull crunching beneath her blows.

'Stop it!' croaked Ophelia, swallowing hard to try and ease her throat. 'She's dead. You can stop now.'

Cindy smiled and put out a hand. Then she moved her fingers up to her mouth and licked daintily at them. 'Mmmm, lovely! I knew blood would taste nice.'

'Go and wash!' hissed Ophelia. 'Hurry up and then get back into bed. Remember, you didn't hear anything. Where are your gloves?' she added in horror.

Cindy gasped. 'I forgot to wear them.'

240

'Then wipe the soup ladle. You're so thick, Cindy. Thick and repulsive. Fancy tasting blood, ugh!'

'It's nicer than gravy.'

'Go and wash your hands quickly. Daddy will soon be home.'

'Let me have one more lick.'

'No! Go now or I'll make you burn.' And Ophelia fixed a penetrating glare on the younger girl.

'What about you? Aren't I meant to . . . ?'

Ophelia nodded. 'I suppose so, but not too hard. I don't want to die.' Slowly and carefully, Cindy picked up the ladle.

Twenty minutes later Ashley parked his car in the drive and wandered casually indoors. 'I'm back!' he called. No one responded. Not that he was surprised. These days Meg rarely spoke to him, and he knew that Cindy had a cold. He did wonder why Ophelia hadn't come running out, but assumed she was revising.

When another ten minutes passed and he still hadn't set eyes on anyone he felt a vague unease. Crossing the hall to the dining-room he opened the door. 'Ophelia? Are you . . . ? Ophelia!' As he ran to cradle the unconscious body of his eldest daughter he tripped over something he hadn't noticed before. Something soft and colourful that felt strange beneath his feet.

He could only recognise his wife by the clothes that she was wearing.

Naturally the results of that single night's work caused a lot of activity. The police spent months on the case. It was obvious that an intruder had broken in and killed Meg Webster, battering her daughter around the head at the same time, but there were many things that didn't make sense.

There were a multitude of bruises round Ophelia's throat that had been made by relatively small fingers, more the size of a woman's than a man's. Then there was lack of motive. Nothing had been stolen, even valuable silver ornaments in the hall had been left undisturbed.

There hadn't been any form of sexual assault. Meg Webster and her daughter were fully clothed and there was no evidence of any form of sexual abuse. This ruled out both a sex maniac and ordinary aggravated burglary. The longer the police continued their inquiries the less sense the entire tragedy made.

Ashley fell under suspicion; it is usually the husband or wife who heads the list of suspects and he was no exception. However, fortunately for Ashley he had a very good alibi. He'd been dining out with Dr Roger Grantley, an old friend from medical school, and there were countless witnesses who could testify that he had been in the Royal Angel Hotel from seven p.m. until ten-thirty. In other words, he couldn't have done it.

Not that all husbands murder their wives personally, and the police tried very hard to find evidence of a contract killing, although they didn't know why Ashley Webster would want his wife dead. She wasn't insured and they appeared to have had a good marriage, but appearances are often deceptive and her will — made out in favour of her brother-in-law — aroused their suspicions. However, no contract killer ever came to light.

'In any case,' said the Inspector to one of his Sergeants, 'I don't think he'd have wanted his daughter attacked. He dotes on her.'

'Perhaps she got in the way. Went to her mother's defence or something.'

'Possibly, but I don't really think that's what happened.'

'Then what did?'

'I wish to God I knew. We'll find out eventually, but so far we haven't got a clue.'

Months passed and they were no further forward. No one had seen anyone entering or leaving the house. No one had heard any screams or sounds of fighting. Of course there were always a lot of visitors to the village but peak holiday time was over now and most people were known by sight.

The one witness the police did have, the one person who could have shed light on the entire nightmare, was useless. When Ophelia finally came round in the children's ward it was discovered that she was suffering from total amnesia. Either as a result of the blow on her head or because of the acute trauma of the events, her mind blanked out everything that had occurred. Ophelia could tell them nothing. Six months later, after having treatment from a hypnotist who attempted to take her back to that terrible night, she was exactly the same. She remembered nothing.

The following spring Ashley Webster's sister-in-law, Catriona, came to help look after the two young girls. Eventually she fell pregnant and had a baby boy, a child with white hair and startling colourless eyes. The villagers noticed that at last Ashley Webster began to look as though life was worth living again, although the boy's mother became increasingly quiet and withdrawn the longer she remained in the village. It was assumed that she was finding it difficult living such a quiet life, but since she never spoke to anyone that assumption might have been quite wrong.

Shortly before the birth of their second son, Catriona married Ashley. Cindy and Ophelia were dressed in matching lilac outfits, while little Oswald wore a blue romper suit and displayed an astonishing number of teeth for his age. They made an attractive if somewhat unusual family group.

Then, six months before the birth of their third child, the couple put their house on the market and went away. No one knew where they'd gone, and when the house was finally sold the money stayed with Ashley's solicitor who was waiting to receive his client's instructions. He never heard from him again.

On the whole the Webster family's tragedy didn't do the village any harm. It was featured in many articles, which encouraged the visitors, and several years later the BBC re-enacted the entire drama using the correct location and paying very handsomely indeed for the privilege.

After all, said the residents as they carefully banked their money, it didn't hurt anyone. Mrs Webster was dead and past caring what happened, and the rest of the family couldn't have minded very much. Or if they did they kept silent.

No one realised that they might have more important things to hide than one small, domestic murder.

EPILOGUE

Extract from a review by M.P. Thomas, printed in the
Mail on Sunday

'Of all the books that have been written about "The Maths
Murder" as it is generally known, I found *"Maths and
Matricide"* by Oswald Kerr ludicrously far-fetched. Mr Kerr
would have us believe that Meg Webster and her daughter were
not both attacked by an unknown killer in the dining-room of
their Cornish home on that tragic October night twelve years
ago. Instead he suggests that Mrs Webster actually attempted
to murder her own daughter by strangulation, creeping up
behind the young Ophelia while the girl was studying for a
forthcoming Maths exam, but that Ophelia fought back,
stabbing her mother over forty times with a Stanley knife
fortuitously concealed beneath her text book.

Why Meg Webster should have wanted her daughter dead is
not mentioned, while Ophelia's concussion is dismissed as
"either excellent acting or the result of a blow on the head,
possible self-administered".

Possibly! But wait, Mr Kerr hasn't finished yet. He reminds
us that Ophelia's cousin, Cindy's presence in the house is
constantly overlooked. She too might have been involved in
the whole affair.

Well, I suppose she might. Perhaps she concussed Ophelia,
disposed of the Stanley knife, then went back to bed and slept
peacefully until her uncle arrived home and discovered the
body of his dead wife. Nine-year-old girls are diabolically
clever.

I have my own theory about "The Maths Murder" and I

think that it's equally original, and so presumably equally acceptable to some eagle-eyed publisher who thinks that there's still money to be made from this ancient tragedy.

I think the cat did it. It makes sense. After all, if your cat murdered a member of your family wouldn't it be enough to make you vanish off the face of the earth without leaving any trace behind you? And let's face it, that particular mystery is really far more interesting than the murder itself, unless you choose to believe the rumours of Ashley Webster having founded one of those quasi-religious sects in the wilds of America where everyone wears old-fashioned clothes and all children are reported to be fair-haired and disinterested in the outside world.

Surely there's someone out there who was involved? There has to be. And if they'll only come forward and establish their identity there's a lot of money to be made. Furthermore, we'll be spared books as laughably ridiculous as Mr Kerr's.

As a reviewer I'd be eternally grateful.'

Needless to say no one responded to Mr Thomas's appeal but they are out there, those strange, souless children of Ashley Webster. Out there waiting patiently for their time to come. And there is no one who can stop them. No one at all.